ADORA CROOKS

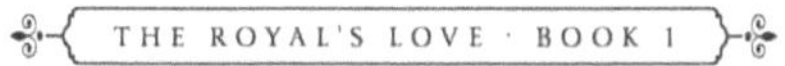

THE ROYAL'S PET

The Royal's Pet

Copyright © 2018 by Adora Crooks

Edited by One Love Editing

eBook Cover Design by Mayhem Cover Creations

Paperback Cover Design by Gabrielle Regina Book Covers

* * *

Subscribe to my newsletter for a free short story!

This is a spicy escape with larger than life characters, royal drama, and hot romance.

You can go to adoracrooksbooks.com/all-books-tropes for a full list of content warnings.

Happy reading!
XOXO,
Adora

CONTENTS

RORY

*A*dventurer's code, rule number one: never stop moving.

I shove a handful of crisps in my mouth and let the messy crumbs stick to my lips. I've parked myself in a colorful pub on Helmsway Palace Road called Bag O' Nails, which has rows and rows of liquors on the shelves behind the bar, coral-pink wallpaper, and a surprisingly bustling crowd for eight o'clock on a Thursday evening. Mostly tourists, fly-by-nighters, like me.

I try to smooth out the creases of my map of London on the bar in front of me, but I only end up smearing it with darkened grease stains. I can still make out the sprawling bus and train lines that run like veins through the city. A tabby cat lifts herself up from her bed of newspaper at the other end of the bar, stretches, and patters across the bar top, nails clicking on the polished wood. I scratch her head and let her sandpaper tongue lick the salt from my fingers. With my non-cat-occupied hand, I pop off the cap of my pen and circle bus routes.

I've gotten pretty good at reading maps. I've had to. I've

traveled all over the world: South Africa, Japan, Thailand, Nepal, Greece, and Beijing—you name it, I've probably been there. I've backpacked my way across the globe, skipping from continent to continent. My backpack is bulging—nearly the same size as me now, not that that's very hard. I'm a travel-size human. Even the soles of my sturdy Doc Martens are finally fraying with all the wear and tear.

For all my traveling, this is my first time in Europe. I've spent this past week digging my heels into Merry ol' England. It's nice here, *really*; I like the tea, the sights, and the fact that everyone speaks English. That's a plus for sure. These crisps—not chips, as I've been corrected, but *crisps*—loaded with vinegar, might nearly be enough to make me stay.

And yet… I can't stop. It's like an addiction, this need to keep moving. Even lingering in this small London pub is making me antsy. My blood is vibrating with the need to *go*. I'll finish my beer and pub hop a couple more times before crashing at my hostel.

As my brother, Oscar, says, *There is too much of this world to see and not enough time to do it in.*

My tabby friend gets bored of me and trots away, allowing me to focus on my map again. It's a five-minute walk from my hostel to the Tube, and I can take the blue line to King's Cross. There, I can catch the Eurostar to Paris. I haven't been to Paris, and even though it seems a bit like a tourist trap to me, it's just one of those places I feel like I *have* to see before I die. Oscar would like to see the Eiffel Tower, I think. On the other hand, if I cough up forty pounds, I can jet across to Ireland. There, I can think about replenishing my diminishing bank account, where it might be easier to pick up a part-time job, maybe something rural, helping on a farm in the Highlands and whatnot. I love animals; after all, who doesn't want to spend their time with a sheep—?

In the middle of my scribbling, I notice a man approach the bar in my periphery. He takes the barstool one spot down from me, leaving a polite distance between us. One thing I've learned about British guys in my short time here: they're not as gregariously affectionate as Americans. Instead, they tend to leave women a gulf of personal space, as though our feminine antics are something to be observed from afar, like a nature documentary. I'm still circling train times when I hear the low, gravelly voice growl, "Bitter, please."

That voice gets my blood humming. I can't help it; I steal a second, lingering glance. My bar-company is wearing dark jeans, slightly worn and frayed at the knees. His black T-shirt barely contains the muscled chest underneath it. Sizeable biceps stretch his sleeves. His raven hair is cut almost military short around his ears, and his entire physique screams *danger*. In a cotton tee and jeans, he's *all man*, and it's a painful reminder of my six-month chastity.

He has to be military, that's my guess. One of those razor-sharp men with as much good humor as a slot machine. It's really too bad my brain is flooding with thoughts of those strong arms pinning my wrists above my head.

Contain yourself, Rory. I tear my eyes away from the stranger and start filling in one of the O's on my schedule to distract myself. When I dare to lift my gaze again, the handsome stranger is looking right at me.

No. Not at *me*. He's fixed on my stuffed animal, a palm-sized otter holding a fabric clam between its two paws, which sits on the bar, leaning against my pint. Even my otter can't take its eyes away from him, it seems.

"Didn't you ever tell your muskrat it's rude to stare?" Hot-stranger frowns.

"Not a muskrat," I clarify. "An otter. Didn't they teach you animals at secret-agent school?"

He shakes his head and cradles his beer. "I'm not a secret agent."

"Then what are you? Double-oh? Her Majesty's Secret Service?"

"I'm a bodyguard at the palace."

"Knew it. Well, Mr. Bodyguard, I thought your kind was supposed to be smart."

"I let my gun do most of my talking."

Gun or *guns*? I'm doing a poor job of taking my eyes off those biceps. "I'm just saying, your guns are going to be useless when otters storm Helmsway Palace and you call for muskrat backup."

Not a smile from him. Not even a twitch of his lips. Tough crowd.

Unfortunately for him, I never back down from a challenge. I scoot over and steal the seat between us, inching closer to him. "So, bodyguard. Tell me more. Is it hard to stand outside the palace in a big hat and remain incredibly still? That would make me crazy. The being-still part, not the hat. That hats are pretty cool."

Bodyguard tilts his pint to his lips. "Wrong guard. I detail the royal family. The prince, actually."

He says it so damn casually, but my jaw nearly hits the floor. "The prince? As in future king of England, invisible man Prince Roland?"

"So they *do* talk about something other than pop stars in America."

I nibble a crisp and shrug. "He's rich, mysterious, and hot as hell. It's kind of what we're all about in America."

That was apparently the wrong thing to say. His thick eyebrows crawl together, and he lets out a disgruntled noise against the rim of his drink. "Right."

I bridge the gap between us with an offering of my hand.

"My name's Rory, by the way," I say. "Rory March.

Twenty-four. Hailing from Michigan. I'm a travel vlogger—you know, like a blogger, but with videos? I'm also a Gryffindor and an Aquarius."

Bodyguard sips the foam off his beer before he finally sets the glass down. "Ben Tolle." Ben. Of course, his name is something like Ben. Strong, solid, simple name. When he shakes my hand, his palm feels ice-cold from his pint glass. "Ben Tolle from East End. Ravenclaw. Taurus."

I retract my hand and roll my eyes dramatically. "Figures."

The corner of his mouth twitches in a near-smile. It's progress. He's warming up to me, at least.

"Do you like working at the palace?" I ask, resting my chin in my palm.

"It's a charmed life." He nods. "The pay is good. So are the benefits. They put you up in the help's quarters. There's never a dull moment. The company can be a bit melodramatic, but they're the British monarchs, so."

"What about the prince?"

"What about him?"

"Well? What's he like?"

Ben touches his upper lip with his tongue, and it sends a warm, tingling sensation through me. I decide that I like watching Ben think. I'm so starved for human conversation that I blurt out whatever is on my mind. He's frugal with his words, picking each one carefully as though he's been saving them up for a special occasion.

"He's gracious," Ben says. "Intelligent. Proud."

"Is it true that he hasn't left the palace since his father died?"

"Yes."

"That was… what. Nine, ten years ago?"

"Ten years exactly, as of tomorrow."

I whistle. "That's a long time to be stuck in your house."

Ben tilts his head. "It's a big palace."

"Still. What if he wants to see Monkey Hurricane?"

Ben stares at me for a long time. "What?"

"You know, Monkey Hurricane? The band?" I sing a couple lines from one of their latest releases. It's badly out of tune. "*Come run-away, run-away, we'll bang-a-rang the sun-away, sun-away.*"

I drum my hands against the bar. Finally, Ben laughs. "Somehow, I think Prince Roland will survive without *ever* hearing Monkey Hurricane."

I'm grinning broadly. "You should do that more."

"What?"

"Smile."

"Why?"

I shrug. "Your smile really turns me on."

Ben scoffs and tilts away from me. Still, I catch glimpse of the small upward turn of his lips.

* * *

THIS IS ALL WRONG.

I know that. Adventurer's code, rule number two: never go home with the hot, rugged stranger from the bar.

But the rule book should've had an asterisk for Ben Tolle.

With his strong grip on my arms, his warm, hard body against mine, and lips butterflying along my throat, I should be saying *no*, but my mind is swirling with *yes, yes, yes.*

I groan under the pale yellow streetlight as Ben pins me to the wall and vanquishes my self-control with his lips. It started out innocent enough; he asked me to keep him company while he "burned a fag" (yes, I was momentarily mortified and offended until I realize he was talking about a cigarette). It didn't take long however before his half-burned cigarette met the pavement and he cornered me into the shadows of the alley behind the pub. He kisses me, his tongue moving in purposeful swipes against mine, and nibbles my bottom lip. I'm a victim of my own lust-addled body, and desire flickers through my veins with every touch.

"Do I turn you on now, Rory?" he asks, his voice like a tiger's purr in my ear.

"Yes," I breathe.

Those dark eyes settle on mine. "Show me."

I'm hypnotized by his intense gaze. He tugs my jeans and pops the button out of its slit before his hand dives boldly under the zipper. I don't stop him, not even when he pushes my panties aside and his fingers find my sex. I'm sopping wet, and I bite my bottom lip to keep myself from moaning.

A cocky grin cuts over his mouth. "You *are* worked up. Spread your legs, love."

Love. The word is like honey, and it makes me shiver. I part my legs as far as my jeans will allow. He strums me like a guitar, his fingers curling and caressing as he makes me slick with my own arousal. I gasp when he zeroes in on my clit and flicks the bundle of nerves repeatedly, sending shock waves of pleasure through my blood. My thighs clasp around his wrist, and I grip the back of his neck for support. He boldly slips a finger inside of me, thumb still working my button. I'm writhing, rutting against his hand, and I hook my arms around his tall shoulders and pant against his chest.

It's wrong to let a palace bodyguard grope me in public—I'm aware of that. The pub is bustling behind us, and at any moment, someone could step outside and see us tangled up together. But I'm completely swept up by this rugged body-guard who dominates me so effortlessly.

I'm not normally this kind of girl. I know I wear combat boots and overdo it on the eyeliner, but I dream about a Prince Charming who opens doors and stands when I enter a room and whispers in my ear that he'd take down the stars in the sky for me. Ben is not that man. Ben is rough, calloused, and when my hips pivot against his hand, I can't be sure if that's his gun or his cock I feel pressing into me, because it's huge and hard as steel.

His free hand takes a handful of my hair and captures my aching lips in a messy kiss. I feel deliciously dirty, and I love every second of this.

"We need to go somewhere private," he informs me.

He removes his finger from inside of me and buttons my pants. He needs more than this—so do I. My sex feels achingly empty and buzzing with lust.

"My place… isn't far from here," I pant. "If you don't mind a little voyeurism."

"I don't follow."

"Well, it's a hostel."

"A hostel."

I nod. He looks like he's just bitten into a piece of tinfoil.

"We're not shagging in a fucking hostel." He latches his fingers around my wrist like a handcuff and tugs. "Come."

I stumble after him like a dog on a short leash, walking twice as fast to match his long strides. "Where are we going, exactly?"

"The palace, of course."

2

BEN

Helmsway Palace is hauntingly beautiful at night.

The neoclassical columns and half-lidded windows are underlit with spotlights. The memorial shines the brightest, however, the golden angel reaching up toward the night sky, her wingtips outstretched.

A tall black gate separates us from the palace. Rory stops and stares, her mouth hanging open. I shift her bag over my shoulder (it weighs nearly as much as her) and tighten my grip on her arm to pull her away.

"This way."

"But I thought you said—?" She points longingly at the palace, like a child whose parents won't let her inside the candy store.

"We're going through an underground entrance," I explain.

"Oh!" She lights up. "Like a secret passageway?"

"Exactly like that."

Rory is adorable. Painfully cute. I want to bruise that

smile with my kiss and consume her light. But I hold back. After all…

She's not mine. Not truly.

She belongs to *him*. To us.

This game of ours started four years ago. Prince Roland—twenty then, precocious, and a lady's man—had already had a taste of love in the palace. And still, his hunger wasn't satisfied.

"I think I'm going crazy," he'd told me one night. We'd been playing darts down in the rec room, a stone-encased underground space with a dartboard, pool table, and assortment of what the queen called "boy toys." Even with a belly of wine in him, the prince landed a bull's-eye. Every time. He'd mastered every game in the palace. He'd read every book in the library. Twice. And he'd fucked every viable maid, waitress, and pastry chef.

"If I have to hear *yes, Your Highness* one more time, I'm going to snap," Roland complained, chucking darts at the board. Bull's-eye, bull's-eye, bull's-eye.

The thought came to me so suddenly I wonder if it hadn't been sitting quietly in the back of my mind for a long time. "I may have a solution," I'd told him.

So the game was born. Roland couldn't leave the palace—he wouldn't hear the end of it from his mother. So I went instead. That night, I went to the pub and scooped up some pretty, pliable, sweet-tasting woman. I seduced her and snuck her back into the palace. I was fully aware that the action could cost me my job. If the queen caught me, she'd put my head on a pike. But for Roland, I would do anything.

We took her that night. Together. She squirmed and moaned underneath us. And then there was Roland. The prince with violet-vibrant eyes. I'd watched as he cradled the woman to him, cupped her face, and purred sweet nothings in her ear before he impaled her on his stiff staff. She was lust-stupid, her eyes half-lidded and lazy when I eased my own cock into her mouth. And how she whimpered, trembled, and begged for more and more…

At the end of the night, the three of us were blissfully spent, and Roland and I were hooked. Since then, I've continued sneaking women back into the palace. Sometimes we go months, neither of us mentioning it, before Roland clasps me on the shoulder and announces, "Ben, darts tonight. You and me."

Darts. That's our code. I used to live for those words. Now… I've become weary of the game. As much as it ignites my blood, it encourages an inch I can't scratch. I need *more.* It's Roland's fault. His magnetic eyes. His perfect body. His boyish, loud laugh.

It's his fault I feel… *like this.* Like my very blood is buzzing every time he's near me. And when we share a woman… he's so close and still so infuriatingly far. I've been thinking that maybe I want to end our *dart* game. I fear that one day I'll snap like a rubber band pulled too taut and let something slip in the middle of shagging some tourist.

But I can't tell him that. I can't let him know about the demons battering around in my chest. After all, how do you tell the man that you're supposed to protect that a simple touch on the shoulder from him sends your thoughts skittering in a million different directions?

So I keep silent. And pine. And do his bidding. And hate myself for it.

When Roland proposed playing our "game" tonight, I felt my heart drop and my cock stir. I should have just told him then. I should have told him that I like—

No, that I *love*—

No. Shut up, shut up, *shut up.*

I haven't mentioned to Rory that the prince will be joining us yet. I've usually brought it up by now. *Group sex* tends to be something of a hard limit for most women. But my tongue is stubbornly dormant as I press forward.

We walk beside the Thames to get to the palace. The black water sloshes below us and sends a quiet shiver through me. The river is dark and eerie this time of night.

"When we get inside," I inform her, "you'll have to sign a form that says you won't steal anything during your visit, and that what happens at the palace, stays here."

"So like an NDA?"

"Not *like*." No, not *like*. It *is*, pure and simple.

"So are there a lot of… uh… unmentionable things that go on around here?"

Rory asks a lot of questions. So I spout a couple of sordid facts clinically. "Our master of the household gambles, Queen Selena curses out the staff, and if you're lucky, you may see Princess Iris stealing liquor from the basement. You know. The usual."

Rory's jaw nearly hits the floor. "What about Prince Roland? What's his sin?"

I don't answer, but the corner of my mouth twitches in a near-smile. She'll find out herself… soon enough. "This way," I motion her, and we turn in to the palace.

3

ROLAND

*I*t's her.

I only catch a glimpse of her from the window. A short, slim figure hovering in the shadows near Ben. I'd recognize Ben's lanky silhouette anywhere. The ballroom has been mostly cleared for the event tomorrow, and the yawning cavern of tall hardwood ceilings and full-wall windows gives me a perfect view of the outside. I've lingered here in the dark for the better part of the last hour. Waiting. Pacing. When I see her, the book I've only been half reading tumbles from my hands. I press myself against the cool glass of the window.

As their figures cross in front of Helmsway Palace, I follow them. I flit from window to window, peeking through the curtains like a caged animal. I'm desperate to catch a hint of my woman tonight. Before she vanishes around the bend and out of my line of vision, she steps into a puddle of lamplight.

Red hair. There's a flash of it and then she's gone, but it's enough to make every vein in my body ache.

Ben knows I have a weakness for gingers. Then again,

Ben knows *a lot* about me. He knows how I like my tea. He knows how I like my women. He knows when I'm about to blow a casket. He knows exactly how to tame me.

That's what this redhead is. A sacrifice to the beast inside me.

I've been born and raised a Pennington. Second in line for the throne after my aunt. Every move is calculated. Every aspect of my life is controlled by the queen. I can't so much as leave my own house. I haven't, not in nearly ten years. Not since my father's jet suspiciously malfunctioned and dragged him to an untimely death. Paranoid that someone was gunning for royals, my queen mum locked me up in the palace. Yet as much as I try to play by the rules and do what's expected of me...

There's a nagging inside of me. A dark itch that needs to be scratched, or else I'm liable to rip the paintings from the walls and light the whole bloody palace on fire. I need human contact. I need flesh. I need the warmth of a woman —a *real* woman, not these painted-up dolls the palace provides as subservient entertainment. I need to feel her trapped between Ben and me. I need those soft, begging eyes fixed on me. I need her to moan for her prince.

These perverse ménages are the only things that get my blood moving anymore. I know it's wrong. Every time, I tell myself this will be the last time. I'll stop this indecency. This isn't how I've been raised. This monster inside of me is not the prim and proper prince my mother has trained me to be. I know that I'm inviting danger in every time I open the palace doors. I know I've been kept locked away for a reason. I know it's not fair to continue to tease myself with something I cannot have...

And yet I want it. Badly. And when Ben makes it so easy... I find it hard and harder to deny myself.

She'll be here soon. The thought makes me dizzy, and my blood roars with lust.

My shirt collar is too tight, and I unbutton the top button to give myself some breathing room. This waiting will make me crazy. My hands are trembling. I need to busy the idle things until I can get them on her warm, bare skin.

I leave the room and vanish down the hall. The night guards are posted along the walls, and every now and then one of them murmurs a bored *sir* to me. I approach my mum's room, and my feet stop at her doorway. The queen's bedroom door is pearly white, delicate filigree patterns carved into the wood. If she finds out what I'm up to tonight, I'm up a creek. She'll lock me in my room and throw away the key for sure.

Quietly, I knock on her door. "Mum?" I whisper.

My heart is lodged in my throat. I press my ear to the door.

Nothing. The queen is dead asleep. Relief fizzles through my blood.

The palace is mine tonight.

And so is my ginger angel.

4

RORY

I'm glad I had the foresight to use the bathroom at the pub, otherwise I would've peed myself with excitement.

Secret passageways? Underground tunnels? And now Helmsway Palace... all to myself? They haven't let civilians in here since they closed the gates ten years ago, but Ben strolls up like it's nothing. There's a dark service door underneath a bridge that goes over the Thames River. It's so embedded in the stone, with dark waterlines running down the sides, I wouldn't notice it if Ben didn't go straight toward it, tug out an ID card, and stick the card into a slot in the stone. The door clicks and swings open. I follow him, dazed and stupidly happy, as he leads me through an underground bunker and out into a second door.

A quick ID check and my signature at the door and I'm in.

Helmsway Palace is grand and intricate. The hallway arches upward in this beautiful, classic archway. My eyes lift to a fresco that stretches across the ceiling. A beautiful representation of heaven, with cherry-cheeked cherubs peeking out of the clouds and swanlike angels swooping around the crystal chandelier. I step back, my eyes following the painting, and nearly knock over a coat of arms.

"Sorry," I say and lift my palms. I've apologized to an inanimate object. It clatters noisily back into place.

Ben stops to turn to me. "Are you coming?"

I rock lightly on my heels and grin up at him. "This place is… impressive."

Ben's legs are ridiculously long, and he covers the space between us in a single step. "If you think the palace is impressive," he says, lifting my chin, "just wait to see what I have in store for you tonight."

I lean in to kiss him, but he pulls away at the last second, leaving my lips untouched and tingling with anticipation.

"This way." Ben leads me down the hallway—how many halls are there? Each one opens up to another room in a different color, this one purple, this one green. I want to stay and ask him a million questions, but I'm nearly running beside him just to keep up with him.

Finally, we stop in front of a door. The door is pearl white and trimmed in gold leaf. He pushes it open and holds the door for me. When I step inside, my feet come to a sharp stop.

Holy hell.

Now *this* is a bedroom. It's modern Gothic, like a set piece from the *Phantom of the Opera*, but if the Phantom was an English hipster. The wooden walls are paneled to match the rest of the palace, only instead of light, airy colors to match the aesthetic, these are gunmetal gray. The cabinets are dark, stained and polished wood, with a matching coffee table.

A gas fireplace, lit and ghostly, flickers quietly from its place carved into the wall. It's as though it were waiting for us. Even with the roaring fireplace, this room feels about ten degrees colder than the rest of the house, and it sends a shudder through me.

"This is your room?"

Ben closes the door behind him and shakes his head. "This is Prince Roland's room."

A stab of fear runs through me. Fear and… something else. *Excitement.* I'm in Prince Roland's bedroom! What I wouldn't give to see His Highness spread out on that bed, his golden blond mane glistening in the firelight. Does he sleep naked? Inquiring minds want to know. I want to stick my face in the pillows and just *smell* them. That's weird, right?

Weird.

It's weird that Ben took me *here*, of all places. I'm on pins and needles, and I twist to face him. "We shouldn't be here. What if he comes in and sees us—?"

"Sees us like this?" Ben crushes my mouth in his. That's what I've been aching for. His kiss is hungry, and it ignites a flame low in my belly. I get the feeling he's holding back; his kiss is delicate, but his whole posture is stiff. He cups the back of my head, and his fingers curl and tighten in my hair, making me gasp.

"You can pull my hair," I whisper. "I like it."

A small noise leaves his throat, like a sigh of relief, and it makes me wet. "Be careful what you wish for," he growls, his voice low and thick with lust.

Just then, he yanks my head back by the roots of my hair. "Ah!" I yelp. His lips are on my throat, ravenous, and the pain and pleasure sensations make me squirm. I'm soaking my panties; I can feel it.

He's been a gentleman and carried my bag, but now he drops it from his shoulders with a heavy thud. "Get on the bed," he orders.

He dominates me like it's nothing. The tight muscles in his shoulders and brow have relaxed, and his dark eyes shimmer with a new focus. It's as though it takes effort to rein in his controlling personality, but here, in the prince's bedroom, with me under his thumb—finally, he's in his element.

And I submit. I take pride in being an independent, strong woman, but get the right man to control me in the bedroom and I turn to putty.

The bed is plush, stacked with peach and olive throw pillows. It sinks when I sit on the edge. A circular light fixture hangs above me, as large as a ceiling fan, and lights twinkle from the stalagmite tips. It looks like a crown, looming and suspended over me.

Ben stands in front of me, reclaiming my attention. "Take off your shirt."

"You first," I tease.

He calls my bluff. He rips his shirt above his head and throws it to the ground.

I swallow.

Jesus. The man is stacked. His chest is strong, with a dusting of dark hair that trails tantalizingly down the center of his body. Those abs look perfect enough to trace with my tongue, and I lick my lips at the thought.

"Your turn," he reminds me.

Right. It's only fair, after all. I undo the buttons of my shirt and peel it off my arms. Then I reach behind, unclasp my bra, and let that fall as well.

Ben watches me, silently. Is he judging me? What does he think of my curves, my large breasts? Then I don't have to wonder when he grabs the enormous bulge in his pants and starts to fondle himself. *Jesus.* That shouldn't turn me on as much as it does, but it makes my thighs clench to watch him openly caress his erection. I want to peel open his pants and feel his fingers in my hair as he pushes me to my knees and parts my lips with the head of his cock. The thought nearly makes me orgasm then and there.

"Your jeans as well," he says huskily. "Now."

There's no room to wiggle out of that command, not by his tone. So I kick off my boots, my socks, and then unbutton my jeans. It takes a little maneuvering, but I shove them off my hips along with my underwear.

Now I'm completely bare in front of him. I'm sitting, naked, on the bed of the next king of England. I should be mortified, but instead I feel another jet of lust pool between my legs and puddle on the prince's blanket. *Whoops.*

"That answers it," Ben says suddenly and I'm so deep in my head that I nearly jump at the sound.

"Answers what?"

"You *are* a ginger."

Oh. He's commenting on the red thatch of hair between my legs. "Is that good?"

Those eyes, dark as well stones, meet mine. "You're fucking perfect."

Gulp. Before I can find the words to respond, Ben gets on his knees in front of me. He spreads my legs with his strong arms, bends his head, and—oh *God*. Those are his lips on my sex, his dirty kisses. His tongue spreads my slit, and he drinks from me, deeply. He laps at my nectar, that flexible muscle pushing *inside*. Before I know it, I'm gasping and my fingers thread through his black hair as I hump his face.

"Hands off. Palms on the bed," he commands. His mouth feels so damn good, I quickly retract my hands from his head and place them on the mattress instead to steady myself. Then he dives down again, but this time he's found my sensitive little nub. Sparks of pleasure zip all through my body as he swirls around it, sucking and gently nibbling the small bundle of nerves. My fingers twist the comforter. He presses one finger inside of me, and then another, all the way to the knuckle, and curls them.

That does me in. Before I know it, I'm careening against the edge. I shout as my orgasm floods through me, pulsing and throbbing around his fingers. He draws it out of me, coaxing every wave from me, until the smallest motion of his tongue makes me jerk and squeal.

When Ben sits up, his mouth and chin are glistening. He wipes both on his arm. "God," I pant, my legs still spread lewdly because I'm too blissed out to close them. "That was… incredible."

"Don't get too comfortable," Ben says as he catches my head in his hand. "I'm not done with you yet, love."

He claims my mouth in his, and I moan. I can taste myself on his lips. It's *dirty*, forcing me to taste myself like this, but I love it. I find myself lapping at his tongue, hungry for more. He shudders—it's small, almost imperceptible, but to put even a dent in this strong man's composure sends a thrill through me.

"Don't move," Ben says.

I obey, and he rises to his feet. Ben steps over to one of the rosewood cabinets and opens the top drawer.

"Are you supposed to be going through the prince's things?" I ask.

Ben doesn't answer. He procures two dark satin ties. He holds them out in his palms, as though in offering. "Put your hands behind your back."

I like where this is going already. I obey. Ben goes behind me. I can't see him, but I feel the mattress sink with his weight. The satin is soft as it slides around my wrists. I feel it loop around my wrists, then between them, and then it tightens. When I try to pull my arms apart, they won't budge.

I bite back a smile. This is exhilarating.

"Is that too tight?" he asks. He sounds oddly concerned, and I'm surprised he's asked at all.

I shake my head. "No."

The mattress springs back as Ben leaves it. He comes

back around in front of me and holds up the final tie. "Close your eyes."

I do. The tie goes around my eyes, blocking out the light. It's thick and I can't see a damn thing.

My world goes dark.

5

BEN

I'm good with knots.

Half hitch. Square knot. Clove hitch.

I grew up on the East End by the Limehouse Basin. You learned knots quickly on those docks. You learned a *lot* quickly in Limehouse.

Bowline. That's the one I used on Rory's wrists. It's a reliable knot. Used to hitch yachts to the dock. Won't slip. The knot I use to tie the wrap around her head is simpler. Easy. It takes me less than a second to complete it, and then I stand back to admire my work.

Here, like this, she's a picture.

I want her. Badly. I've been half-hard since the bar, but now that I have her naked pussy drooling on Prince Roland's bed, I could cut glass with my dick. My monster is throbbing in my pants, begging to be let out.

But I can't. Not yet.

She has to be presentable for her prince.

She's smiling—this innocent, adorable little smile that nearly makes me come undone on the spot. "Well, you've got me where you want me. What are you going to do to me?"

So much, I think.

I don't say it, however. Instead, I put my shirt back on. "Stay here."

"What?" Her smile drops when I walk toward the door. "Are you leaving me?"

"Only for a second. Stay."

"Wait—!"

I don't. I exit and close the door behind me. She'll be *fine.*

I adjust my pants around my hips and walk down the hall. I move to the door of my room and knock. No response. I press open the door—nothing. The room is empty.

My jaw tightens. Of course it is. He can't sit still to save his life.

Then I hear it. The trickling sounds of piano keys. Not any song—Concerto no. 4. I hate classical music. I know that one.

It's the prince's favorite.

I follow the sound into the sitting room. It's a wide-open room with filigree walls and pale love seats. A cage full of twittering yellow canaries hangs over the grand piano. The piano itself is bone white. Prince Roland's body is curled over the bench. His long fingers move dexterously over the ivory keys. His blond hair frames his face like a lion's mane.

I linger in the doorway. Silent. He looks nearly peaceful when he's like this. Focused. I cross my arms. I give him a moment.

"Highness."

His eyes lock with mine. Violet. Vibrant.

I shudder. I hate myself for it.

"She's ready," I inform him.

A boyish grin cuts across his mouth. For a moment, the pain is gone and there's nothing but bright youth in his expression, like a boy at Christmastime.

"Well, why didn't you say so?" He throws his limber legs

over the bench. He looks at me and knits his eyebrows, and I feel my shoulders tense. He's always been able to read me like a book. Then that smile returns; this time, it's a knowing one. "You had a taste of her, didn't you?"

I nod. Barely. "Yes."

"Verdict?" Prince Roland closes the distance between us. "Soft and sweet or spicy, like ginger?"

"Sweet," I tell him. Like wine, first summer's fruit, honeysuckle… the memory of her on my lips makes my dick twitch in my jeans.

The prince's grin widens. "Sounds delicious. I like her already. What would I do without you, Ben?"

I don't answer that. It's not a bodyguard's job to hypothesize.

"Lead the way, mate," Prince Roland tells me. There's that carnal look in his eyes again.

I do. Prince Roland gets what he wants. Every time.

6

RORY

*B*en is taking too long.

It's hard to tell how much time has passed—minutes? Hours?—but the fact that *any* time has passed means it's way too long. I'm naked, bound, blind as a bat, and in the prince's bed. If I get caught like this… well. That'll be an awkward trip to the embassy I'm not likely to forget.

My brain bounces through thoughts like a ball in a pinball machine. I hope Oscar the Otter is shoved to the bottom of my backpack. He's seen me though a lot of adventures; he doesn't need to see *this* one.

Then the door clicks open. The second I hear the noise, my spine goes stick straight.

"Don't panic. It's me."

Ben's voice. I sigh and my shoulders drop.

"Took you long enough. Did you stop for ice cream?"

"Yes," he says. "And I brought you back something sweet."

His mouth is on mine before I can respond. His lips crush me, his scruff grazes my cheek, and his tongue drinks me in greedily. In seconds flat, he has me exactly where he wants me once more, moaning and dripping for him.

"Down, girl," he growls. He barely has to press his finger-tips to my chest before I lose balance and topple onto my back. I feel his lips on my bare skin, taking their time now as he kisses my throat, my collarbone, down my breast. I pant for breath as my heart pounds in my chest. I want his lips everywhere. With my vision gone, my skin feels like it's on fire, all the nerves tingling at the very surface. I feel every swipe of his tongue, and I writhe under the friction of his hands. He sucks my breast into his mouth, tongue rolling over my perked nipple, and I feel the lust roll off me in waves.

His hands are everywhere. I'm a ladybug in a web, twisting and squirming, trapped under his caresses. Only this is a trap I don't want to be free from. His fingertips bring me to life, sending shivers through me. His hands are on my thighs, pinning them down; then they're deep in my hair, and then they're cupping my face.

Each touch makes me tremble, and all at once my body grows fire hot. He seems to be in a million places at once, touching me, caressing me, and I can barely catch my breath at his bold explorations. His hands grope me; he nibbles my nipple and kisses my neck…

Wait. How can his lips be at my breast *and* at my throat? It's then that I feel not one, but *two* mouths. There's more than two hands on me, too; I recognize that now. Just as the realization kicks into full gear, a velvety voice that definitely does *not* sound like Ben's low growl murmurs in my ear, "He's right. You're an angel…"

"Wait," I gasp. "Stop. *Stop.* Untie me. Now!"

All at once, the touches and kisses stop. My heart is hammering in my chest, but it's not lust that's kicked it into gear anymore. I've gone full *survivor* mode, fight or flight. This isn't what I signed up for. This isn't it at all.

I can't catch my breath. I'm nearly hyperventilating when

a pair of fingers gently pluck the tie behind me, unraveling it. As soon as I have use of my arms, I yank the blindfold from my face.

Light comes streaming in. I blink as my vision blurs and slowly comes back into focus, like twisting the body of a kaleidoscope.

There he is. The not-Ben. Wild, untamed blond hair. A nose straight enough to ski off. A strong chin highlighted by two plump, full lips. His beauty is practically celestial, and it sucks the breath straight out of my lungs.

That, and the fact that he's royalty.

"You," I whisper. "You're… Prince Roland."

"Of course I am." He smiles, and it's so fucking dazzling I could cry. "Who were you expecting?" Then, just like that, the realization sinks into his expression. Slowly, like an avalanche, his expression careens downward—his eyebrows slope first, then his smile falls, and the line of his mouth grows tight.

"Ah," he says, answering his own question. "You weren't expecting me at all."

I shake my head. I'm speechless.

Ben says nothing, either. He's perched on an elbow at the foot of the bed, watching Prince Roland as though he's a grenade that might tear us to pieces at any second.

Prince Roland turns on a smile then, and the change in his expression is so quick, it's almost eerie. "Will you excuse me for a moment?" he asks me.

Me. The prince of England is asking *me* for permission.

I don't know what to do. I just nod.

Prince Roland stands and his eyes fix on Ben. There are daggers in his gaze now. "Ben. I'd like to speak with you. Outside," he demands. "Now."

I can't read Ben's expression for the life of me. His eyes are cast down, and when they flicker toward my face, I'm totally lost by what I find in them. Is he guilty? Or proud of what he's done? Perhaps he's angry with me for ruining it all?

His eyes find the floor again before I can figure it out.

"Yes, sir," he says.

With that, the two men leave the room. And they leave me.

Bewildered and alone. Wondering—

What the heck just happened?

7

ROLAND

*T*his is all cocked up.

All I wanted was one night. One night when I didn't have to pretend. One night where I could put down the heavy weight of the crown and lose myself in her soft moans.

Ben Tolle—love him to pieces—has really buggered this up for me. And I'm furious with him. He's been my trusted bodyguard—no, my trusted *friend*—for over six years. He should know better by now.

The second the bedroom door clicks shut behind us, I lay in on him. "Have you lost your damn mind?" I hiss. "How could you not tell her that I would be there?"

A shrug from Ben. "She's American. They're usually up for anything."

His eyes are on the wall. That won't do. "Look at me, Ben," I instruct.

He does, those coal-hard eyes meeting mine. I want him to see the fury in my eyes. He needs to know just how badly he's messed up. I wish he were a dog so I could just rub his nose in it and be done with it. But he's not. I need to see repentance.

But I don't. He's a blank slate, emotionless. This isn't like him. He's not normally this bloody stupid.

"This is a betrayal," I tell him.

Something flickers in his eyes at that. "Forgive me, Your Highness."

"No. You'll have to earn that," I tell him plainly. "You're dismissed."

Ben sways on his feet, lingering briefly, and I can see that he wants to say something. Instead, he swallows it down, turns, and ducks down the hall in stubborn strides.

Well. That takes care of *one* of them.

Now I have to clean up the scared little girl in my bed.

I pinch the bridge of my nose and screw my eyes closed. I wanted a shag tonight. My blood is still screaming for her, my cock hard as a sword, aching to sink into her to the hilt. I can taste her skin on my lips, warm as fresh bread and soft as butter. And the way she moaned… well. That sent my good intentions straight to hell.

But now all that's dashed. Now, I have to do damage control.

I take in a couple deep breaths and take stock of myself. I smooth the creases in my forehead, relax my jaw, and drop my shoulders.

You're the future king, my mum would say. *So look like it.*

I know how to act, look, and smile like a king. I'd just hoped I wouldn't have to put on this performance tonight.

When I've got myself under control, I open the door to my bedroom and step through. The ginger is still sitting on the foot of my bed, but she's dressed now. Relief quietly washes through me. I'm not sure I would've been on my best behavior if she'd still been naked. I'm not sure I could have kept myself from finishing what I'd started.

It's hard enough to hold myself back as it is. She's nothing like the poised, jaded palace girls whose eyes always seem half-lidded, constantly bored. She's wide-eyed as a newborn doe seeing the world for the first time. Her innocence is intoxicating, and I curse myself inwardly when I feel my cock stir once more.

"Are you all right?" I ask, breaking the silence.

"I'm fine." She tucks a strand of hair behind her ear. I notice her hand is trembling. My heart breaks for her. I want to take her in my arms, stroke her hair back, and whisper in her ear that everything will be okay.

But I know better. The truth is—the only person in this palace she needs protection from is *me*.

"Can I get you a pot of tea?" I ask. "Water?" A thousand quid? A car? Whatever it takes to keep her from spreading this story around the press. "Where are you staying? I'll have a guard drive you home. A woman, perhaps."

She lifts her eyes. I didn't get a proper look at them before. They're jade green, and they shimmer like gems. I don't believe I've ever seen more hypnotizing eyes. "I'd like an explanation, please," she says politely, though her voice doesn't waver. Neither does her eye contact.

Good on her. Perhaps my kitten isn't quite as helpless as I assumed.

"Very well." I lower myself into a leather armchair across from the bed. I purposefully keep some breathing room between us; after all, I *did* nearly maul her only moments earlier. This will be hard to talk my way out of, so I start simple. "Do you know who I am?"

She nods, though she seems shier now. "You're the prince of England, Your Highness."

"Not *Your Highness*," I tell her sternly. "Never *Your Highness*. I prefer Roland." I smile. See? I can be pleasant. "I'm afraid I didn't catch your name…"

I didn't think it was possible, but her eyes get even wider. "Rory," she gets out.

"Rory. As you can imagine, my life is… complex. I am who the people want me to be. There is a lot of pressure, being in line for the crown."

Her eyes don't leave mine. She's listening intently.

I continue: "And I'm not complaining, truly… it's an honor. Most people would sell their grandma off to be a royal. But there are times when I want to… put down the crown for a little while."

"So… you bring strange girls to bed?"

"It sounds ridiculous when you say it like that." I smile. "But it helps, truthfully."

"You've done this before?"

"Yes."

She seems to think about that. "Why involve your bodyguard?"

I take in a breath. "I can't exactly… leave the palace. And the women who come here—countesses and royals—they don't interest me. Ben can come and go as he pleases."

"So Ben was grooming me… for you?"

"For us. To share you."

She lapses into silence at that, her eyes on the floor. Fear prickles my chest—I've lost her. She hasn't moved, but I feel her drifting away from me. Swiftly, I rise and sit down on the edge of the bed beside her. Here, my voice drops with my next confession. "What I do… it's wrong and naughty. But it's always perfectly consensual, and it's always done with my partner's knowledge. Do you understand?" My tone is urgent. I barely know this woman, but I *need* her to understand. "I'd thought Ben told you that I would join you."

Her eyes meet mine. "You didn't know."

"I should have. I'm the prince. I can't afford to be ignorant." I don't mean for my voice to get harsh, but it does. My boiling anger leaks, and Rory sees it.

"You aren't going to fire him, are you?"

That startles me. After what we put her through… she wants to *protect* him?

"Fire him?" I scoff. "I'm bringing back the bloody guillotine."

"Please don't," she says suddenly. "I mean… that's a joke, right? I hope it was a joke. Listen—" She twists to face me, and my shoulders stiffen. *Listen.* I'm not used to having a Normal tell me what to do. Normal—that's my mum's word. Normal, common-blood, *not one of us.* Rory sighs and says, "I mean, it's silly, really. We don't know each other. But the funny thing is, honestly, if he'd just said, 'Hey, want to come back to the palace and have a threesome with me and Prince Roland?' Then, *yeah*, I'd be all about that."

My heart suddenly starts to ricochet against my rib cage so loudly I'm afraid she can hear it. My mouth goes dry as possibilities swirl in my head. Rory is beautiful, bold, and kinky as hell…

She's perfect.

I'm nearly trembling with excitement. I need to contain myself. I put my hand on her thigh. She jumps at first, but she doesn't pull away. I haven't taken a woman without Ben… in a long time. But she's tempting me to break our unspoken pact. I need to keep this woman to me, if only for a little longer.

"Can I interest you in tea?" I ask.

She looks at me, and a smile broadens her mouth. "Yeah. Sure. I'd like that."

8

RORY

This is a dream.

This has to be a dream, right? Any second, I'll wake up back on the top bunk at the hostel, panties wet, swooning.

This doesn't happen to women like me. Women like me don't have tea with royalty after having the prince's lips all over her.

But here I am. Ragged jeans, combat boots and all, sitting on a chair that's probably worth my parents' mortgage and trying to figure out if I should actually lift my pinky when I take a sip or if that's just something people do in the movies.

Roland sits at his own chair across from me. We're in the sitting room, or entertainment room, or whatever he called it. Every room here seems to have a title, and I can barely fathom how they can find a different purpose for all of these rooms, but I know this one has a piano, paisley walls, a small rolling bar, and a twittering cage of canaries. The *bird* room, maybe.

Roland has pulled his shoulder-length hair back now so it's contained tightly behind him. This is more how I'm used to seeing him—or how he looks on TV and in the magazines anyway, when the paparazzi catches a stray glimpse of him through the window. He's composed, tucked away into a powder-blue button-up and nice slacks. The top button of his shirt is undone, which only gives him a *slightly* more casual look, but to me the hint of bare chest is enough to make me slippery between my legs again.

I can't help it. This man does strange things to me. I only take comfort in the fact that I'm not alone—he's literally the royal heartthrob to thousands. The caged, incredibly private Prince Roland has been the subject of many a woman's wet fantasy. Even I, who generally stays away from celebrity gossip, have stopped when I come across a Prince Roland headline.

Not that there's a lot to say about him. As far as anyone knows, Prince Roland never leaves the castle. He's never even been caught drinking tea at a café. Nothing. I remember that, once, some reporter leaked that all of Prince Roland's (rare) interviews were conducted at the palace with a green-screen backdrop. A rumor went around for a couple days that maybe the prince had some terrible medical condition that kept him from leaving the palace. And then Missy Gadot had a nip slip at her concert, and everyone forgot about it.

Looking at him now, he doesn't look sick. In fact, he looks quite strong. His sleeves are pulled up to his elbows, exposing his forearms, and I can see the pure muscle there and the ropey veins that lie just underneath the surface. He's lean, svelte, and his eyes are clear and unbearably intoxicating. I've noticed now that they seem to change color depending on the lighting. In the bedroom, they looked hot and violet. Here, under the crisp overhead light twinkling from the chandelier, his irises are cool, deep-blue pools.

We've been talking for an hour, maybe, just sitting here,

sipping tea, and chatting, and I still can't get look away from those eyes.

"That's very brave of you," he comments, though I've gotten lost in his gaze again and forgotten what we're talking about.

"What is?" I chirp.

"Traveling on your own," he explains. "It's hard enough to get on in a foreign place, but... I imagine it must be harder for a young woman. The state of this world being what it is. Especially one as attractive as you."

He winks at me when he says it. What kind of person actually *winks* these days? The prince of England, apparently. It's not the first time he's done something like this. I've noticed that he talks like a man who picked up all his vocabulary from books—earlier, he called my eyes verdant, over-pronouncing the *a*, as though he's never had an opportunity to use that word in a sentence. And now the winking. He clearly read enough Ian Fleming to think that that was just *how* people interacted with each other.

I can't blame him for being stilted. He probably hasn't had a decent conversation in... what. Ten years? That would make me animatronic, too.

Honestly, I think it's cute. Charming.

I shrug off a blush. "It's not that bad. And I'm not alone."

His eyebrows lift. "No?"

I've carried my backpack with us, and it takes only a little force to drag it over to my seat. I unbuckle the top and dig in until I find what I'm looking for. "Meet Oscar," I say and sit the stuffed otter upright on my knee.

A laugh explodes from Roland's chest. It's a delightful noise, and I find myself bubbling with pride for pulling it out for him. I can tell his laugh is genuine, not canned, since it creases the corners of his eyes, and all at once, he looks less like rigid royalty and more like an ecstatic boy who just saw Jack pop out of the box for the first time.

"All right," he says, grin still lingering on his lips. "You have to tell me the story behind that."

I press my thumbs into the otter's chest and spread his arms out. "My brother, Oscar, he's four years older than me. He's my best friend." I roll my words over on my tongue. This part is always hard to get out. "He was born with cystic fibrosis. It's terminal. Incurable. He's been sick my whole life, but... a couple years ago, it got really bad."

I toy with the otter, rubbing his ears. "I had just graduated college, so I took care of him for the better part of a year. Then, one morning, he turns me to and tells me that he doesn't want me to watch him die. He wants to watch me *live*. He always wanted to travel, so I bought a one-way ticket out of Michigan. I started a travel vlog... *March On! How to travel the world on a budget.* It picked up traction—people even send me donations sometimes, and they go straight to the Cystic Fibrosis Foundation."

I hand my otter over to Roland so he can look at it. "When I was little, I couldn't say Oscar. It just sounded like *otter*. It became a thing between us and... when I carry this little guy around with me, it feels like Oscar is right here with me. Like he's seeing all this, too."

I rarely let my precious otter leave my side, but he's safe in Roland's hands. He handles the otter gently, reverently, in his big hands. "Your brother sounds like a remarkable man," Roland says.

My chest swells with pride. "He is."

Roland's blue eyes pierce me through to my core. "I would love to tell him as much myself. How does your vlog work?"

My heart skips a beat, and my jaw nearly falls to the floor. "You... want to be on my vlog?"

"If that's okay. I have someone who handles all my social media… I must admit, I haven't the faintest idea how this works."

I breathe a laugh. He's so humble and charming it nearly sends me into a tailspin. I drag my fingers through my hair to pull myself together and then fish my phone out of my pocket. "Yeah… uh… it's really easy. Okay."

This is actually happening. Stay cool, Rory.

The prince of England sits patiently as my fingers swipe over my phone's screen until I get to the video recorder. "This goes live to my blog once it starts recording," I explain. "So just tell me when you're ready."

"How do I look?" He smiles.

Good enough to eat up, I want to tell him.

Instead, I say, "Perfect."

He taps his thigh. "Come here. I want you in the shot, too."

I mean, that's an offer I can't refuse. I perch on Roland's lap, and he winds an arm around my middle to keep me to him. Good luck, me, keeping my hands from trembling. I can feel the prince's breath on the back of my neck. I turn the camera's lens so I can see the both of us fitted into the screen.

"Ready?" I ask.

"Always."

I hit the red Record button at the bottom. Instantly, we're live.

"Hello, March On family!" I say. I couldn't fake a smile this big. "This is Rory March, checking in from the one and only Helmsway Palace. Tip top, Cheerio! Did I say that right —is that something you Brits say?"

Roland grimaces playfully and shakes his head.

"As you can see, I've got a *very* special guest with me… an incredible, can't-believe-he's-doing-this-with-me special guest…"

"Cheerio," Roland says and lifts a hand in a wave. "For the Yanks who don't know me… I'm Prince Roland Pennington. I have a message just for Oscar March. Rory told me your story, and you're an incredibly brave, strong man and a damned good brother. Don't worry—I'll take good care of your troublemaking little sister here for as long as she decides to bless the UK with her presence. I hope I get to see you in person one day, mate. Keep fighting the good fight." He points a finger at the screen. "And to everyone else watching, go make a donation to the Cystic Fibrosis Foundation if you can. I know I will."

"There you have it. From the mouth of royals." I salute my audience. "Rory March, March On!"

I hit the button at the bottom of my screen to stop recording and set the phone down on the side table.

"I think that went well," Roland says casually.

My face burns and I can feel the backs of my eyeballs prickle with unspent tears. I'm so overcome with gratitude that I can't speak, not right away.

Roland notices and asks, "Are you all right?"

When I turn to him, I can barely keep it together. "You're incredible," I tell him, and my voice trembles. I'm touched. Sincerely, genuinely touched.

Roland's expression turns serious. He cups the side of my face, and I don't realize that a tear has spilled until his thumb is there to catch it and brush it away. "I'm not," he says. "You, on the other hand. You're remarkable, Rory."

Softly, his lips meet mine. I gasp against them. They're so warm, so soft, and I can't help but melt into his kiss. I part my lips, and his tongue takes the invitation and licks the inside of my mouth, tasting every inch of me.

I need him. I need this. I'm too desperate to be delicate. Straddling him, I rip at his shirt, pulling the buttons away to reveal his strong chest underneath. My hands slip over his skin. He's burning up, feverish with passion. He pushes my shirt up over my breasts. I yank it off the rest of the way, and as I do, his lips connect with my swollen globe, his tongue swirling over the nipple.

I shudder under his hands. This is incredibly wrong. I came here with a different man, was moments away from an unsuspecting gang bang, and I'm shirtless in the middle of Helmsway Palace. I'm certain I've violated at least a couple dozen America-UK accords. But all I can think about is being violated by *him*. His touches and kisses are a painful mixture of delicate and hungry. I feel as though I'm a lamb caught in a wolf's gentle jaws. I sink into the heat of his contradictions, savoring every brush of his fingertips.

He unpins the button and zipper of my jeans. I step back, momentarily standing so I can take them off. The second I start to shimmy out of them, he says, "Wait."

I stop. He leans forward in his chair, and his long fingers take the hem of my pants. "Allow me."

I stand as still as I can as Roland inches my waistband down my hips. Every new inch of bare skin, he marks with a kiss, like a mountain climber leaving posts in the snow to remember where he's been. My breath hitches when he kisses the downy patch of ginger hair there. My eyes lock on his sea-blues as he extends his tongue and laps at my slit.

The noise that leaves my mouth is barely human—I sound more like a newborn kitten as I push my hips forward, aching.

The prince unbuckles his pants, and as he licks me, he takes his cock out. I see his arm moving, stroking himself, and that sends flames of desire through me. I sift my fingers through his hair and give it a small tug. "Wait," I plead.

"What are you doing?"

I get on my knees in front of him and grin. "Bowing to my prince."

It's almost unfair, really, for a royal to be this blessed. He has everything he could ever desire, *and* he's well endowed. With a beautiful, beautiful cock. How's a woman supposed to recover from a man like this? It occurs to me that I may never, but that doesn't stop me from replacing his hand with my own and taking the swollen head of his organ in my mouth. He sighs with relief and sinks back into his chair. His hand cups the back of my head and I feel his thumb pet the nape of my neck as he murmurs, "Good girl."

Another mewled noise from me. Where are these noises coming from? I can't seem to help it, just like I can't help the fact that I'm positively dripping by now. He's too much to fit in my mouth, and I keep a hand at the base of him while I swallow down as much of it as I can. I'm enjoying this, way more than I normally do. He's hot and salty in my mouth, and I love feeling his rigid length as I run my tongue over his velvety skin.

I keep my eyes on him; I want to drink in every reaction. His eyes go lidded, violet-hazy, and his breath picks up. I begin to stroke the hilt of him to where it meets my lips as I suck him forcefully. His nails dig into the back of my head and the arm of his chair. He moans and throbs in my mouth. It's incredible to see the prince lose control. I'm getting so wet watching him, tasting him, and I swear I can feel it drip down my thighs and onto the priceless carpet underneath me.

I don't care. I don't care about anything except this Adonis of a man throbbing in my mouth. "Ah… Rory," he says, and his voice is hoarse, urgent. "You're going to make me cum."

I whimper, needing it, and suck him harder. I flutter my tongue over his manhood, encouraging him to let go. When he comes, it's quiet—his grip gets incredibly tight in my hair, and I can see his jaw tense as he nearly grinds his teeth to keep himself from calling out. We are, after all, in the middle of the palace, the twin doors open, really *asking* for trouble, but Christ on a cracker if it isn't hot to watch him sweat through it. He inhales a sharp gasp and floods my mouth. I swallow him down, greedy for it, and continue to suck on him, coaxing. I taste him a little more with every pulse of his cock.

I drop him from my mouth, sit back on my haunches, and lick my lips.

The monster isn't satisfied. Not completely. His cock is fiercely red now, the veins bulging, and it bobs a little, as though hunting for the warmth of my mouth. The prince is lust-hazy, a sheen of sweat making his chest gleam, but the way he looks at me is completely feral.

God bless the queen and her son's unwavering stamina.

"Come here," he commands, and I can't oblige quickly enough.

I jump into his lap and crush those full lips against mine. Our kisses aren't sweet and delicate anymore—they're animal, messy, and desperate. I taste like him, he tastes like *me*, and good God why wasn't this in the tourist handbook, why didn't *anyone* tell me the prince of England was this kinky? Every orgasm, every wet dream, every fantasy—they all feel wasted up until now. I would've saved them all for *him*.

He reaches between us only to guide his manhood inside of me. He's huge and I brace myself for it, but I've never been wetter and he slides inside easily. He fills me, completely, and I gasp when he pistons his hips upward, until he's fully sheathed. I'm straddling him, gripping his chest, his shoulders, and his lips devour my throat and any bare skin they can reach. My mouth falls open, and I want to tell him to slow down, I want to savor this, but my body has other plans. I'm rutting against him like an animal, riding him ferociously. My nails dig into him; he grips handfuls of my skin. Every thrust of him hits a place inside of me that I feel hasn't existed until now, was maybe saved just for him, because it sends bursts of pleasure through me. We move as one, sliding and riding and gripping and faster and faster until—

My orgasm explodes! I shout and pure white euphoria burns behind my eyelids and sparkles through my blood. I hear his name in my ears, and it takes me a moment to realize that I'm the one repeating it, over and over, Roland, Roland, *Roland,* each utterance in time with the pulses of my body.

He groans between his teeth, jerks his hips upward, and spills over inside of me for a second time. My body is thirsty for his seed, and it clings and clutches at him, coaxing every last drop.

Finally, we're spent. Our bodies are slick with sweat, heat emanating from our skin, and it's all I can do to pant against him.

"Bloody Americans," he says as catches his breath. It's said reverently, in awe, and I can't help but laugh.

"If you thought *that* was good," I tell him, "wait until you taste our cornbread."

He cups my face and lifts it. My head feels heavy, exhausted, and his strong touch is nourishing. "I don't want to taste anything but you," he says, his voice low and heated, those eyes crystal blue once more. "Ever again."

I melt into his kiss, and finally, we take our time savoring each other.

9

BEN

*R*oland calls it my "lair."

It's not a lair. Lair suggests vampire, mad scientist, or psycho killer.

I'm none of those things.

I'm an ex-military royal guard with a minor interest in tech. We don't have lairs. We have state-of-the-art security systems and surveillance equipment to monitor the goings-on of Helmsway Palace. Tucked away in the back of the antiquated palace, through the kitchen, the imitation ice-cooler door, and down a curve of stone steps, sits a twenty-first-century, electric nightmare of wires and screens. The room is small, barely ten square meters, most of which are occupied by the sizable flat-screen monitors that checker the far wall and splay out on either side. There's nothing else but an L-shaped desk, two swivel chairs, and a bare bulb that hums noisily over my head. It used to bother me, that hum, but it's white noise to me now. The cold blue light of the monitors bounces off the backs of my hands as I survey the palace.

We've got cameras everywhere. Nearly everywhere anyway. The members of the royal family are allowed privacy in their own bedrooms, but that's about it. Hallways are mostly empty this time of night, save the guards at their stations. Queen Selena is asleep in her room. Her sister, Princess Iris, is helping herself to a nightcap in the queen's private cellar. The head of the household is playing cards with his cooks around a round table in the kitchen.

My eyes are glued to the yellow sitting room.

It starts out innocently enough, Rory and Roland sipping tea across from each other. Then she's in his lap, and they're fiddling around with something on her phone.

They kiss for two, maybe three minutes. She gets naked and so does he. I watch as Rory gets on her knees for him.

And it's…

Hot.

There. I said it. They're bloody hot together.

She's poised on the floor, the soles of her feet peeking out from under her round arse. Her head bobs up and down in his lap, her long hair curtaining over his legs. The prince sits back and cups the back of her head. The image isn't very well-defined, their edges fuzzy, but even with the hazy quality, I can still see the way his lips form a circle in a silent moan.

My cock has been restless all night, but that sight sends my blood surging south. I can't look away. I can't move. I can barely breathe. I can hear my heart pounding. It's not the only thing pounding. I'm throbbing and my erection rubs painfully against my zipper. I cup myself, but the warm friction of my palm only makes me need it more.

Wouldn't be the first time I've had a wank in here. Probably not the last. Doesn't mean I don't hate myself for it.

You're a coward. A deviant. A wanker.

Just go in there, push her deeper onto his cock, and claim his mouth with yours—

Fuck it. I can't wait anymore. I pop the button of my

jeans, slip my hand under my briefs, and pull out my cock. I can't stop the groan that pours out of me. The friction of my palm provides a morsel of sweet relief, and I'm desperate enough to take it. My erection is brick hard, my corpulent head blushing and leaking. My slick cock slides through my fingers.

My eyes are glued to the monitor. After a while, Rory gets off the floor and straddles him. They flow together in exquisite rhythm. I should be there. Right behind her. I want to kiss her throat. Pull her hair. Ease myself into her tight, round behind. I want to shag her at a pace that drives the prince crazy. I want to hear him moan under both of us.

Filthy fantasies rage through my skull. I'm jerking madly now. My balls boil, my toes curl in my dress shoes, and I can't contain my deep-throated moan as cum rockets from my cock. I shoot one load into my hand, then another, and it dribbles between my fingers and drips down my shirt.

I refocus my blurred vision. I've finished and so have they. They're curled up on the seat together like kittens, bathing each other with their lips and tongues.

Me? I'm the wanker in the surveillance closet who can't keep his fly shut. Relieved, but not satisfied. My thudding heart slows to normalcy. The immediate urge has subsided, but there's a deep, angry ache that vibrates through my whole being.

The sharp, painful pining for *him*.

How bloody pathetic.

I tuck my cock away. I have a blazer tossed over the back of the chair, so I put it on and pinch the button of my blazer shut to hide my mess. I can feel the wet spot on my shirt cling to my abdomen. *What the fuck is wrong with me?*

I'm accustomed to having a steel bolted lock on my impulses. Something about this ginger American has lit a match under my powder keg of carefully contained desires.

The metal door to the outside churns and squeaks open. My spine goes stiff, and I quickly pretend to be deep into my work.

"Should've known I'd find you here." There's the chipper voice of Tanner Worely, Helmsway's head of security. He's about thirty years my senior, his hair powder white, but he's got the eyes of a hawk and the cunning of a fox. He leans over my shoulder to look at the video feeds, and I jab my soiled hand underneath my thigh, discreetly trying to wipe my cum off on my trousers. I'm a bloody wreck.

"I see the prince has a guest," he states, his tone flat and unaffected as his eyes land on the sitting room. "What do we know about her?"

"I've done a full background check," I state quickly. "Rory March. An American from Michigan. Here on travel. Civilian. Clean record."

Tanner makes a low humming noise before he sits down on the chair across from me. I can feel his eyes on me, but I can't meet his gaze. I know he'll see straight through me.

"You know what bodyguards used to be called, Ben?" Tanner asks suddenly.

"No, sir."

"Knights," Tanner says. "Bizarre to think about, isn't it? It's a long history of honor, chivalry, and loyalty to live up to."

"I suppose so."

"Would you say that watching the prince lay his pretty companion over the monitors is more or less than honorable?" Tanner asks.

I see his point. I click my fingers over the keyboard, and the feed from the sitting room goes black.

"Good call," Tanner comments, as though it had been my idea all along. With that, Tanner stands once more and makes to leave.

My pocket vibrates. I fish my phone out. It's an alert from Roland's social media manager. His Twitter account is blowing up. I click around to a recently uploaded video. I hit Play and immediately my heart thumps against my rib cage.

A single word slips out my lips. "*Shit.*"

Tanner stalls at the door and turns toward me. "Everything all right?"

"Might not be my honor you have to worry about," I tell him and turn the phone so he can watch the video.

Tanner lets out a weary sigh. "Bollocks. Selena's going to have my head."

10

ROLAND

My mother has told me over and over how it will feel when I take the throne.

I'm next in line. The second she passes away, I'll ascend. The way she did when her father died, and so on and so forth. Our family has ruled England for over a century. We come from a strong line. A proud line.

When I become king, she claims, I'll feel reborn. It'll simply feel right.

I don't know about that. The crown has been nothing but a cloying shadow my whole life, its dark fingers wrapping around my ankles and holding me back.

But when I wake up after one wild, passionate evening with Rory, I think to myself, *So this must be what it feels like to be king.*

Rory left last night, with no other explanation than she simply *couldn't stay.* But her cheeky smile in our parting kiss shook me to the bone. My room seems somehow brighter this morning. I don't feel tired or sluggish, that near-debilitating weight in my limbs. Instead, the very blood in my veins feels fresh, reinvigorated. The taste of her lingers on my lips, and I swear I can still smell her own personal musk in my bed.

She's not the first conquest I've had in the palace. Not by a long shot. But she easily may have been the best. I haven't felt this good in as long as I can recall.

I throw off the heavy quilt and toss my legs over the side of the bed. The wood-paneled floor is icy, but it feels refreshing now instead of uncomfortable. I walk over to the bathroom, rinse the night off, and don fresh clothes. By time the maids knock on the door, I'm ready for them. There's three of them, all fluttering in a flock, and they pull at my hair and fuss over me.

The door is ajar, but Ben still knocks when he steps into it. "Sir," he says, announcing his presence. "Permission to enter?"

I don't even look at him. Instead, I turn to one of my maids. "Angelia, do you hear something?" I ask. "The water pipe must be roaring again."

"Must be, sir." It's Angelia's job to agree with everything I say, even when I'm being a petty bastard.

I can see Ben's form fidgeting in the corner of my eye. *Good.* Let him squirm. His lack of forethought nearly cost me my delicious sex kitten last night.

"Your Highness." Bloody hell, he doesn't give up, does he? "There is... something we should discuss before you see the queen. About last night."

"I've got it from here, thank you," I tell the maids. They scatter, and I swiftly exit my room with not so much as a look in Ben's direction.

I make my way down the hall. Damn Ben's long legs. He keeps pace with me effortlessly.

"I know I was... out of line last night," Ben says urgently. "And it won't happen again. But there really is something we need to—"

I brush Ben off, ignoring him completely, and push through the double doors to stride into the dining hall.

My mother—the reigning queen of England—sits at the head of the table. At forty-six, she shines brighter than any diamond in the palace. The press can say what they will about the Pennington reign—that our dynasty has been at times cold, aloof, and, back in the day, downright cruel—but what we've done, we've done in style. Queen Selena is every ounce a Pennington specimen, from her golden hair pinned back behind her head to the swanlike slope of her neck. Then, of course, there's the legendary strong Pennington jawline. For all her delicate femininity, her dramatic makeup and polished nails, there's no hiding the lioness's bone-crunching jaw.

Princess Iris sits beside her, spreading grape jelly over a scone. Even though they're twins, Iris has filled out where my mum's gone gaunt, and her skin seems warmer somehow, brighter. The spring to my mum's winter. She's always been a second mum to me, and when I step in, she gives me that cat-that-swallowed-the-canary smile.

I step behind the two and lean over to give them a customary peck on the cheek. "Good morning, Iris," I tell her.

"Isn't it, Prince Charming?" she smirks. She's hiding something behind that goading smile, and it's not yellow feathers.

When I go to kiss my mum, she swivels her chin just slightly out of my reach. "Sit," she commands.

Her tone is cold and hard. She's talking to me as queen now, not my mother. I obey and take my seat beside her.

"You are aware that tonight is the annual masquerade ball. The ball that I've worked very hard to pull together, mind you."

"I'm aware." A plate of over-easy eggs, sausage, and beans appears in front of me—magic—and I pick at it.

Once a year, the palace throws a charity ball to support the military. My father had started it years ago, and the queen took it upon herself to continue the tradition even after his private plane hit dirt and took him down with it.

The people loved my father, Duncan. Although he was only in-lawed into royalty by marrying my mother, he had such grace and charm that the press took to calling him "King Duncan," and the name stuck. They tolerated uptight Queen Selena and me, her royally spoiled son, but they loved my father. The yearly ball was a way of reminding them why they'd once adored the royal family… even if you had to be a member of the press, a noble, or incredibly, independently wealthy to afford the price of admission.

But—Queen Selena always stressed—it was a charity, after all.

The corners of my mother's mouth are tight and curved downward now like the lines of a scythe. "Then you can understand my confusion," she continues, "when I found *this* story making headlines instead."

She pushes her tablet over to me and taps the screen. For a moment, it's a still image of Rory and me. The pinwheel spins and the video starts playing.

The image rolls and yesterday's Roland gestures like a buffoon, praising her brother. I hate watching myself played back. No matter how sincere I am, it always seems practiced and forced. I see flaws all over my smile. It makes me cringe.

I focus on Rory instead. She's a natural and innately charming. I feel a grin twitch the corner of my mouth.

Rory March, March On! Rory signs off, smiles for the camera, and taps the screen with her finger.

"This is nothing," I tell her. "A request from a fan."

"Keep watching," my mother instructs.

"The ending is… positively *thrilling*," Iris cackles. My

mum shoots her a stern look, and the other woman shuts her mouth.

I watch.

The video doesn't stop there. Instead, the angle turns upward. There's a small clatter as Rory sets her phone down on the side table. This close, the arm of the chair cuts off the lower halves of our bodies. I can see Rory's face very clearly, however. She looks emotional. Touched.

My heart picks up against my chest. The video keeps going, and I feel the cold fingers of dread sliding up my skin.

Are you all right? I come into focus again on the screen.

You're incredible. There's the tremble in her voice that broke my heart.

I'm not, video-me tells her. *You, on the other hand. You're remarkable, Rory.*

We're kissing now. The memory of her lips sends a spark of pleasure shooting through my blood. I dig my nails into my palms to keep myself focused.

The video keeps rolling. And rolling. When Rory takes off her top, my mother mercifully taps her manicured nail over the screen. We remain like that, frozen, tangled in one another.

"It goes on like that," she says, "for forty-seven minutes."

"This was an accident," I explain quickly.

"Was it?" My mother sighs. "She used you, darling. To get notoriety for her… whatever it was."

"No. She's not like that. If I could address the people myself," I say, "I could explain my side—"

My mother's eyes go hawk-like. She turns away from me and briskly barks, "Mr. Tolle."

Ben, who has no doubt been hiding in the doorway, now steps through it. I can see the vibrancy in his eyes—he wants to step to my aid—but instead he lingers a respectable distance away, shackled by loyalty to the crown. "Yes, Your Highness?"

"How did the *Normal* get in?"

"I invited her in, ma'am, but—"

"Thank you. You're fired."

That is like a sucker punch to the chest. Ben's eyes go wide, but he holds his tongue. What can he do? Nothing. Me, on the other hand… I can't lose him. He's the one person who keeps me sane in this place. The only friend I have to lean on.

I jump to his defense immediately. "Mum—it was my decision. I requested that Ben bring her into the palace."

My mother's hand snaps across my face. Fast as a mongoose. My fork clatters to the ground. The servants, instead of running to pick it up, go statue-still. There is nothing more frightening than a lioness losing her temper.

Even I don't dare to budge now. I stare ahead, tense my jaw, and wait for the stinging pain to leave my cheek. The only sound comes from Iris, who is still scraping jelly off her plate and onto her scone.

"After everything I've done to protect you," my mum hisses. "You throw it away. On a girl."

"I never asked you to protect me." I don't mean the words to come out, and I certainly don't mean for my tone to be so knife-sharp and bitter.

The queen rises from her chair and walks over to Ben. She hands over the iPad. "Mr. Tolle, you are officially rehired. See what you can find on this girl. Shake some skeletons out of her closet and spread it out for the world to see. I want her disgraced. Understand?"

"Yes, ma'am."

A cold sweat prickles the back of my neck. This is all my fault. I told Ben to fetch her. I can't let Rory go down like this, especially not to cover my own sordid nature. "I was thinking we'd invite her to the ball," I blurt out suddenly. "As my girlfriend."

My mother spins to me, and her eyes go wide. I've never spoken out against her before, not like this, and she's looking at me as though I've raised Nessy from the lake. "Have you lost your mind?"

But I've got my armor now. I'm pragmatic. *Problem solving.* I stand, plant my palms on the table, and explain calmly, "Tell me, Mother, what's a better headline: Strange Woman Breaks into Palace and Tricks Gullible Prince into Filming Sex Tape? Or Media Capitalizes on an Intimate Moment Between Prince and his Loving Girlfriend? One story calls into question our entire bloody security system. The other paints a target on the press, and God knows everyone hates them already."

My mother stares at me. She knows I'm right—she has to know. But she doesn't like it.

"Your girlfriend?" she says as though the word is grit between her teeth.

"Yes, Mum," I reply. "My girlfriend."

Finally, she turns away from me and faces Ben again. "Find the girl. Invite her tonight. Make sure to stress that her presence is nonnegotiable."

"Yes, ma'am."

"You're dismissed."

Ben leaves but not before casting me a glance. We've been around each other long enough to speak without saying a word, and I know his eyes are asking, *Are you sure this is what you want?*

I nod, just a small tilt of my chin. He understands and leaves.

Nothing is as cold as the look the queen of England gives me when she faces me again. Her voice drops low so only I can hear her. "If this girlfriend of yours calls into question the Pennington reputation again, even the American Embassy won't be able to keep her safe. Do I make myself clear?"

She's being dramatic. I know that. We're the royal bloody family—we've earned the right to our histrionics. Still, I don't doubt that she could make Rory's life a living hell, so I submit.

"Yes, Mum. Crystal clear."

"Good." There's a sudden shift in her expression then—she looks weary, suddenly, as if the argument took all the remaining strength she had left. Her eyes soften and all at once she's switched from queen of England to simply my mum. "I'm only trying to keep you safe, Roland. I lost your father. I can't lose you, too."

With that, she leaves through the double doors. Her dress trails behind her, making her look like a ghostly apparition, and her bodyguard peels out from the shadows to follow her.

A chill has fallen over the room. Even the chandelier above me looks like it's carrying icicles. Princess Iris breaks the mood with an elaborate stretch and a wide-mouthed yawn, as though physically shaking off the moment.

"Oh, ducky. Your mother means well." She takes my mum's chair to be closer to me. Her fingers rake through my hair, and she pulls at it lightly. "Your hair's getting so long," she muses. "It's positively unmanageable. Have Angelia trim it down before tonight."

"I like it long."

She rolls her eyes. "And I like world peace and ponies." She plucks my mum's untouched scone from her plate and picks at it. "Even royals don't get everything they want."

11

RORY

I wake up in the top bunk of Free People Hostel.

Hostels get a bad rap, but I've grown to love them. There's a sense of community here that you can't find in a Four Seasons. Sure, I've learned the hard way to sleep with my valuables under my pillow, but for the most part, the people I've met at my hostels have been the best short-term travel companions a lonely traveler could ask for.

Free People has proven to be one of the best hostels I've stayed at. Free Wi-Fi, clean showers, and a short walking distance to some great pubs and cafés… it's more than I'm used to. My co-ed dorm fits six, and the beds are in constant rotation, mostly with college-age students. I claimed top bunk after my last bunkmate moved on, and now I have a sweet, quiet girl, Nadia, underneath me. Nadia is still asleep, and so are a couple others, but the rest of the beds are empty, everyone eager to start a new day of sightseeing.

I savor a couple more moments underneath my cotton blanket, feeling as spoiled as a fluffy cat with a diamond-studded collar.

And then memories drift in of the opulent Helmsway

Palace, the spotless furniture and the throw pillows lined with rabbit fur. It all feels like a dream. That couldn't have possibly happened—not to *me*. But then I shift in bed, bending my knee, and feel a sudden pang between my legs. I'm *sore* there, a delicious, stretched sensation from the way the prince's cock impaled me, again and again, and all at once I know: *not a dream.*

Last night was very, very real, and my body aches with the memory of Prince Roland.

Slowly, so as not to rustle my blanket, I slip my fingers underneath my panties to check the damage. The brush of my fingers sends a jolt of memory—Roland's fingers playing my sex, his mouth on my breast, his hands on my hips. My nether lips are puffy, swollen, and I'm sopping wet all over again.

I can't help myself. My fingers start moving of their own accord, drawing tiny circles underneath my needy nub. I came… how many times last night? Twice? Three times? I lost count, but my normally docile sex drive is suddenly insatiable. Roland isn't the only one I'm fantasizing about, either. Ben slips into my daydream like a shadow. I remember the scratch of his teeth against my throat, and I shudder all over.

How did I let these two men turn me into such a horny mess? I bite my lip hard to swallow back a moan.

There's a cough from the bunk across from me. *Shit!* I quickly cease all movement and hold my breath. I'm no longer the only one awake. My fingers are stilled, curled at my most sensitive parts, and my body is pulsing with the desire to finish what I started.

That's not going to happen. There's a lot more rustling in the bunks, a voice in a language I don't speak, and a second person wakes up. Everyone's getting up and I don't want to get caught wet-handed. I discreetly slip my hand out from my panties, roll over in bed, and grab for my phone.

Distraction. That sounds good right now. My phone died at some point at the palace last night, but it's recharged now, plugged into the wall outlet by my cot. I flick through to my emails and try to ignore the needy buzzing between my legs. I want to send Oscar an email and tell him all about last night. I can already see him rolling his eyes. I want to hear his dry, sardonic humor. I know how he'd react, too—the older brother, forever chastising me for my bad behavior, all the while doing a poor job of hiding his proud smile. *You're a train wreck, Rory,* he'd tell me, lovingly. The thought is enough to make me start grinning.

As soon as I open my email, however, it refuses to let me send anything. I get a warning message explaining that I've used up all my cellular data for the month. How can that be? I'm usually so good at budgeting. I'll have to call my provider and maybe work out of internet cafés for the time being.

I sigh, drop my phone, and get up. I have torn jeans folded at the edge of my bed so I don't have to run around a bunch of strangers in my underwear, and I shimmy them on underneath my blanket.

Otter-Oscar sleeps beside me, and I pluck him out of bed before I lower myself down the stepladder and to the ground. Nora is still sleeping soundly, her face mushed against her computer, so I try to do everything quietly so as not to disturb her. I unlock my locker and pull out my clothes and toiletries. I take these to the communal bathroom, wash up, and get changed. I crack all my bones in the process—Prince Roland did a number on me. Muscles that I didn't know existed are sore.

No. I can't let my mind drift there again. I have a limited number of clean panties, and I don't want to have to change out of another pair before the day has even begun.

Besides. It's a bad idea to linger too long on the idea of the prince. I know what last night was—a hot fling. Even royalty need to get their rocks off every now and then. I get it, I do. In the words of the famous Roman orator: I came, I saw, and I came again. Prince Roland probably doesn't even remember my name, but you know what?

I had sex with the future king of England.

And oh God—

So worth it!

But there was more to Roland than mind-blowingly good sex. He was kind, thoughtful, and generous in unexpected ways. Then there were his eyes. Sometimes violet with desire, sometimes crystal blue, and other times as cloudy and gray as the London sky. Even surrounded by the gilded palace, with literally the world at his feet, there was something sad lingering in the prince's eyes. Something I couldn't put my finger on.

But things don't make a person happy. With nothing to my name but a backpack and a stuffed animal, I know that as well as anyone. There's a quiet, nagging part of me that wants to make the prince happy. I want to hug him or send him a toy otter of his own, even though I know both thoughts are impossibly silly.

There's free coffee in the rec room. I'm low on money, so I make two to-go cups before slinging my bag over my shoulders and heading out. Brekson—the guy behind the counter with tattoos and huge ear gauges—gives me a nod on my way out. I set one of the cups of coffee in front of him.

"You're a peach, Rory," he tells me.

"I resent that," I say and point to my red hair. "I'm clearly a carrot."

He chuckles and sips his coffee. I like to make nice with the watchmen—after all, he did let me stumble to bed in the wee hours of the morning.

"There's a bloke waiting on you in the lobby," Brekson informs me.

I blink. "For me?" I parrot stupidly.

He nods and points through the double doors. Through the tinted circular window, I see a figure sitting on the bench.

My heart bangs against my rib cage. What if it's Roland? I'm not the kind of girl to hope against hope, but maybe, just maybe, Prince Roland will wrap his arms around me, pull me into a kiss, smile against my lips, and tell that he can't bear to be away from me...

The pounding of my pulse could scare a flock of birds, it's that loud. I push through the doors and try not to drop my cup of coffee.

Ben Tolle stands when he sees me. His face is a mask and his tone as crisp as the London chill. "Rory," he says. "Let's chat."

12

———

BEN

My mug has a stain on it.

A rosy, faint lipstick mark right on the rim. I try to keep my lip from curling with displeasure, and I resist the urge to take it to the sink and start scrubbing. Instead, I leave my fingers curled around the handle and let the tea steam on, untouched.

We're in some kind of communal living space, surrounded by lumpy, mismatched sofas, a projection screen, a pool table, and a "kitchen," which consists of a sink, a cup holder, and a filter for hot water. The whole place smells like mold and unwashed bodies. It brings back something familiar, a wave of memories from the docks. I shake it off and refocus.

Rory sits across from me. She's clutching my phone, eyes wide, as the scandalous video rolls on in front of her. She either doesn't realize or doesn't care that moans are pouring out of the thing. I have to forcibly focus my attention on anything but those sounds to keep myself from getting hard in the common room.

I keep my eyes on her face. Rory looks like a deer in head-lights. There's a terrible, sadistic part of me that enjoys her discomfort.

"Oh my God," she groans. "This can't be happening."

She turns off the video (thank God) and drops her head on the table. Red hair splays out like bloodstains. My palm twitches with the urge to run my fingers through it.

"Was it a media ploy?"

She lifts her head from the table. Her eyes blink blearily and refocus. "You think I did this?"

"You tell me."

"No! I would never… this is humiliating. Not to mention, the prince… oh my God. I have to take this off my site. Now."

Her fingers start flying over my phone.

"It won't matter," I tell her. "The video has already been ripped and reposted on hundreds of other sites. It's out now."

She drops the phone as though it's burned her palms. Slowly, her emerald eyes rise to me. "Does he hate me?"

The question catches me off guard. Her neck is on the line… and she's asking about Roland? I'm not prepared for the pinch of guilt in my chest. "The prince?"

"Yes. I need to apologize to him, somehow… I know he probably won't want to see me, but if I can pass a message through you, maybe—"

"You can tell him yourself." I cut her prattling short, swipe my phone from the table, and pocket it. "Tonight. He's invited you to the royal masquerade ball."

She looks like a beached fish, her mouth opening and closing speechlessly before she spits out the words, "But that's… isn't that a royals-only thing?"

"Yes. You're the first Normal that's been allowed inside in ten years. So look nice and be on your best behavior."

"Normal?" she chirps. I quietly detest myself for using royal talk.

"It's what the royals call civilians," I explain.

"Charming." She crinkles her nose at the hubris. I can't blame her. I hate it, too. "Anyway, tell *His Highness* I appreciate the invitation, but I can't go."

I blink. I've just offered her Willy Wonka's golden ticket… and she's declining it? I grind my back molars. "What do you mean, you can't go?" I ask. Even I can hear my patience waning. I sound like an overworked nanny.

"I mean… I shouldn't even have stayed here that long. I'm on my way to catch a bus to the airport. I'm going to Edinburgh and maybe heading to Ireland from there—I'm not sure—kind of see how it goes, you know? Anyway, then I'm gone and I'm out of your hair and… you don't have to worry about any of this."

Her speech speeds up as she speaks, her words tripping on their way out of her mouth.

"You're going," I tell her. *Fuck* the nanny. I've gone into full-dad mode now. *You're going to do what I say. End of discussion.*

She whines and opens her mouth to complain, but I cut her off.

"You're *going*," I repeat, "because the prince of England expects you to be there. Maybe you can run from this, but he can't. You can do him that kindness."

Rory's expression twists in contemplation. She knows I'm right. She's going to say yes. I can see it written all over her expression. Her bleeding heart. She strikes me as the type of woman who picks worms off the sidewalk and plops them into the grass to keep them from frying in the hot sun. She's not going to leave Roland hanging.

"I don't… exactly have anything to wear," she gets out. The last feeble protest of someone who has already made up their mind.

She's not lying. Her jeans are ripped at the knees, her

shirt baggy, and there are mud stains on her Converses. I doubt she has a matching pair of socks, let alone a palace-ready dress.

"A representative from the palace will come by tonight to drop off a dress and pick you up."

I stand. So does she. Rory's fingers wrap around my wrist to keep me there. The touch of her fingertips sends a jolt of warmth through me. "Ben." There are those eyes, wide and forest green. "Will you be there?"

Most everyone knows better than to put their hands on me. Everyone except Rory. She's as naïve as a blind kitten, looking to me for protection. She sticks her hand in the mouth of a starved wolf and trusts me not to bite her.

But how I want to. I want to suck a welt into her snow-white throat, bend her over the rickety table, and make her ours. The spoiled prince took her without me. I want to even the playing field. My need is throbbingly fierce now, and for a moment it nearly blinds me.

I take a breath. Force my heartbeat to simmer down.

"I'm the prince's bodyguard," I tell her. "I have to be."

There's that smile, soft and warm on her plump lips. "Good. Maybe you can keep an eye on both of us. The last thing I want to do is embarrass him… you know. Again."

"You'll be fine." My voice sounds quiet, gentle, and utterly foreign in my ears. It doesn't sound me like me. It sounds… domesticated.

It's placated her, at least. "Thank you, Ben."

"Don't mention it."

Really. Don't.

I rip myself away from her touch. I turn my back on her and push out the double doors. The cool London air chills the sweat on my neck. My heart is hammering by the time I reach the town car and let myself in. Wordlessly, the driver takes me back to the palace.

I swipe my fingers through my hair. My hand is shaking. Like a little girl with a bloody crush.

Get it together, Ben.

13

ROLAND

Helmsway Palace is alive.

The ballroom has been cleared in preparation for the masquerade tonight. Everything has been dusted, polished, and cleaned. Sunlight hits the chandeliers, and they glimmer, it seems, for the first time all year. The ballroom is suffocated by royal reds and highlighted with bands of gold. There are buffet tables along the walls, filled with plates containing whole salmon, saddles of mutton, plump woodcocks, plovers, and trays of deviled herring and cream cheese. The bar is stocked with the king's reserve, and staff in simple ruby and gold masks waltz around handing out small glasses of champagne, which will be swapped out with port at the end of the night. Bodyguards are posted every couple of yards, and I wonder if there's less security in a prison yard.

The doors have barely opened and already the place is bustling.

I linger at the fringes of the party. My years of solitude have made me introverted. Furthermore, I can keep a close eye on the doorway from here. Every time the doors open for a new guest, they're always backlit with a flash of camera light as reporters cram up against the gates to get a glimpse of the palace's elite guest list. I know what they're really hoping for, though, is a shot of the secluded prince himself.

Every time the doors open, my hopes go up, and every time they're dashed when I see another masked face without an explosion of ginger hair behind it. I wear my father's signet ring—a gold reminder of him with the image of a reared lion pressed into the soft metal—and I twist it back and forth impatiently.

"Presenting the duchess of York!" the presenter announces at the top of the steps. A blonde in a dress layered like a wedding cake pulls back her Renaissance mask to reveal a pinched face underneath. Another champagne socialist. She finds me with hawk-like precision and winks at me.

If I have to keep this smile on any longer, my face will surely crack. "Rory isn't coming," I mutter between clenched teeth.

"She is." Ben, my shadow, lingers behind me. Like the other guards, he's dressed in his familiar black-and-white uniform so he's not mistaken for a partygoer. Not that anyone *could* mistake that perpetual frown. "I made sure of it myself."

"Angelia, do you hear that buzzing?" I ask the waitress next to me. "Very strange."

"Most strange indeed, Your Highness. Champagne?"

"I'll need it."

I take the flute and down it. The bubbles pop and fizzle on my tongue. Ben curses under his breath, so low he must think I can't hear it.

With every second that ticks by without Rory, my mood only grows darker. I feel like a bloody jester. My face is pasty with powders and foundation, half of it covered in a white mask ornamented with glimmering gold and silver lace. My hair is so slick that a pence could float on top of it, and I'm stuffed in these tight black pants that leave little to the imagination. My shirt overcompensates with frills and poufy sleeves. I cringed when I first saw it, but my mum positively fawned over it, and I knew I had to pick and choose my battles with her today. At any minute, she could revoke Rory's invitation, and as the minutes fly by without hide nor hair of my girl, I'm beginning to fear that that's exactly what happened.

I'm picking irritably at the lace at my sleeves when the presenter's bored voice booms out again. "Presenting Miss Rory March, ah…" The old geezer never stumbles over his words, but he seems to be struggling with it now as he reads off a slip of paper. "Lady of Detroit, Michigan."

I see her and my heart stops. Her auburn hair cascades in rivulets down her shoulders. Her dress is the same color of her lips, carnation pink. It's strapless and hugs the swells of her feminine form before falling to the floor in a bounty of sheer lace. She's wearing a simple, black mask around her eyes, and it frames her face with bold, dark raven feathers. For all her delicate beauty, her smile is still crooked, still wild, still *Rory*, and I find myself transfixed by it.

I'm frozen in my spot. I can't move. I can barely breathe. I hardly notice the tremor that ripples through the crowd as our guests murmur amongst themselves. Perhaps they're wondering who she is. Worse—perhaps they already know.

I don't care what they think. I can't take my eyes off her.

My God. She's beautiful. An angel straight out of one of Raphael's frescoes.

When she spots me, her eyes light up. She glides down the steps and makes her way over to me. Immediately, she gives me a grin, lowers her eyes, and lifts her dress in a curtsy. "Your Highness. Thank you for the invite. This is…" She laughs. "It's *insane!*" She waves to my bodyguard behind me. "Hi, Ben!"

"Lady Michigan," Ben replies. "What the hell is on your feet?"

"Oh, yeah." She kicks out a foot to reveal her black combat boots underneath. "I didn't want to trip coming down those steps, so… the heels were a no-go. Sorry. Does it look too weird?"

I didn't think my heart could get any bigger, but it does. It swells so much I'm certain the engorged organ is crushing the very breath from my lungs. "It's very you," I tell her. "It's perfect."

I take her in my arms then and cover her mouth with mine. I don't think twice about it. I want her and I claim her with my lips, my hands, and my tongue. She yields with a soft mewl, and her body molds against mine. She gives herself to me effortlessly, and her willing submission makes my blood grow hot.

I break our kiss to murmur in the shell of her ear. "I want to take you. Right here. In front of everyone."

She shudders like a baby bird in my arms. She can't hide it. She wants it, too. But she puts her hands on my chest to give us some distance and says, "Technically, you've already taken me for the world to see. So. Let's do something we *haven't* done." She winks and offers her hand. "Dance with me?"

I take her soft hand in mine. "It'd be an honor."

14

RORY

I can feel eyes on me wherever we go. Some guests shoot me looks and whisper about me in the open, and I know they must have seen the video. Others glare at me for hoarding the prince's attention. I even catch some confused, squinted expressions flashed my way, as though to say, *What is the* Normal *doing here?*

Roland pulls me onto the dance floor, and not for the first time tonight, I think, *Thank God for sensible shoes.* In heels, I would've probably twisted my ankle by now, and I don't need to give them another reason to stare.

The dance floor is sectioned off with a large patch of polished wood. Roland sweeps me against him and draws me close, an arm around my back, his other hand still in mine. We're not alone on the dance floor; a couple of others have decided to sway to the melodic music, but they give us a wide berth when we approach. I'd thought the music was coming from the speakers, but when I look over Roland's shoulder, I spot a full band: a grand piano, a couple of violins, flutes, and even a huge arching harp.

"I should warn you, I'm not much of a ballroom dancer," I

preface. "Get them to play Backstreet Boys and we're golden, but..."

"Follow my lead," Roland assures me. "Look at me. Not your feet."

"Okay." *Twist my arm.* I can't stop staring at him. His luxurious mane of hair is tied back with a black ribbon, and his brows are primed to make the wild man look more groomed. He smells clean, like mint leaves, lavender, and sandalwood, and I'm tempted to bury my face in the opening of his airy shirt where his chest is left bare and inhale him. My fingers itch with the desire to take off the mask covering half of his face so I can see him in all his glory.

Roland guides us back and forth with incredibly lithe, graceful movements, and I surprise myself by keeping up with him. He notices, too, and smiles proudly. "You're a natural," he says.

"Or I'm just good at doing what I'm told."

A hint of fire in his eyes, a violet flash. "That too."

The harpist begins to pluck thin dreamy notes from her strings, and I fall into a trance. I can't help but take in this place. The chandeliers are huge, like glaciers hanging from the ceiling. The people around us look like old-school marionettes with their extravagant dresses and suits and their wild, bizarre masks. I feel like I've fallen through a wormhole into a different time, a different dimension. Surely, something this grandiose can't exist in the same world where every other sock I own has a hole in it.

"What are you thinking?" Roland asks, suddenly breaking the silence between us.

"Honestly? I wish I was livestreaming this. Oscar would love to see this." I crinkle my nose when I hear the words come out of my mouth. "Sorry, that was... incredibly not romantic."

"Don't apologize. You love your brother."

"Very much."

"Don't you think he'd want you to be right here, enjoying yourself, instead of worrying about him? That's the point of all this, isn't it? You're living your life to the fullest in honor of him."

I nod. "You're right. I know you are. It's just... hard to turn it off."

"Luckily for you, you have an incredibly charming, handsome prince standing right in front of you. And he can't take his eyes off you." How can someone be so arrogant and so sincere at the same time? I laugh and I want to call him out on it, but when my eyes meet his—well. He's right. I fall right into them. Those sparkling blue pools are staring right at me, and suddenly, it's hard to think about anything else but him.

"Better?" he asks.

I wind my arms around his neck and draw him in closer. "Better," I agree.

I only get to enjoy the strong grip of his arms for a few seconds longer before the song dwindles to its end. The dancers break apart to clap. Everyone but us. Roland tucks me in closer and kisses me. His lips break open my petals, and I'm dizzy for him. I sigh into his mouth and melt against his sturdy chest.

"Enjoying ourselves, are we?" The crisp female voice sends jolts of alarm through my body, and I break apart from Roland. When I turn to face the onlooker, my mouth goes cotton dry.

Holy Christ on a cracker.

It's the queen of England, flanked by a pair of guards. The queen is dressed to the nines in this gorgeous black-and-white gown that's tight around her slim waist and then fans out at her hips. Her hair, like Roland's, is long, blonde, and lush, but hers is contained in braids that wrap around the back of her head like a ribbon and tumble down her shoulders. For a mask, she has nothing but a small eye piece that matches her dress, and she holds it on a long stick between her fingers. After all, what would the queen of England have to hide from?

Roland swivels to a stop. "Mum." He winds his arm around the small of my back. "This is my girlfriend."

"Girlfriend?" The word leaves my mouth more of a squeak than anything, and I stare at Roland. I'm his girlfriend now? I like it, but… a little forewarning would have been nice, maybe. He just smiles at me, but it's a hard smile that says *go with it.* Then I remember that I'm in front of the *queen of England*, and I manage to jut my hand out. "Yes. That's me. Hi."

"Rory, is it?" The queen ignores my attempt at a shake, and her ice-hard eyes meet mine.

I don't know what to do. Nothing in life has prepared me to come face-to-face with the queen of England after getting caught with my tongue down her son's throat. I'm sure I'm as red as my hair, and I pull myself together enough to drop my eyes in a curtsy. "It's a pleasure to meet you, Your Highness."

Now that introductions have been made, the queen ignores me completely. She turns to her son and says, "Roland, may we have a word?"

Her tone is tight and leaves no room for debate. She's calm and collected, as cool as an ice sculpture, but there's a tightness to her lips that gives me the impression that she's capable of unleashing the fires of hell when angry. When Roland looks at me, I can see the apology in his eyes. He looks utterly mortified, but I'm not an idiot. I know better than to get mixed up in family drama, especially when it's the royal family of England. I take a step back. "I'm going to check out the buffet table," I tell him.

"I'll find you." He brushes his lips once more against mine. Leave it to Roland never to miss a second to claim me. I'm stiff now, though, anxious, and I can barely meet his kiss. My heart is going rabbit fast in my chest. His hand is firm, secure at the small of my back. Selfishly, I want to beg him not to let go of me.

But he does. The guards close ranks around the prince and queen, and I'm cut out of the circle.

I flounder like a fish cut from the line and let the crowd swallow me. I suddenly feel incredibly out of place, surrounded by nobles with lifted chins and thousand-dollar smiles. I'm an imposter in this world, woefully out of my league. They have rules. Traditions. Propriety. I have a semi-popular blog and a stuffed animal. I ate a bowl of dry granola in the common room this morning for breakfast. In my pajamas. Without milk, because milk was one pound and the granola was complimentary.

I can't even *fathom* the way these people live.

I twist my way off the dance floor, through the crowd, and sneak out of the ballroom. My feet flop aimlessly on the ground, and the sound echoes down the tall halls. I need to find a bathroom to hole myself away for a second. I haven't been this antisocial since high school prom. I want to find a plate of cookies and shove them in my mouth one by one until the confidence of a sugar high kicks in.

A woman exits the bathroom looking more swan than woman—white dress, flowing snowy feathers, and a tall headpiece curling up from her head. She lets the door swing closed behind her, and I reopen it to head inside… but then I stall.

Around the corner, the adjacent hallway has been cordoned off with velvet rope. No doubt the palace's way of keeping all the partygoers from wandering too far.

I wait until I hear the click-click of swan-woman's heels vanish back into the party.

You shouldn't be straying from the crowd, a voice in the back of my head warns me.

But the adventurer in me won't be quelled. I have to explore.

I let go of the bathroom door and duck underneath the velvet rope. My dress swishes across the floor, and so I bunch it up as I walk to keep from giving myself away.

It feels like I'm walking through a museum. As I walk down the hall, I pass the kings and queens that have reigned throughout the years. Beautiful, giant paintings hang above me, larger than life. My history is fuzzy; I can't name half of them, but I admire their strong scowls and the proud lift of their chins.

Oscar would love this. He'd be able to name every one of them, the years they reigned, and when and why they died.

There is one portrait I recognize immediately, and I come to a stop in front of it. The title card reads Prince Consort Duncan Hughes. Roland is a near-perfect match of his mother, but there are bits and pieces of his father that he retains. His strong stature. Those deep, intense eyes. The smile. Mostly the smile. All of the other portraits are frowning and solemn, but Duncan stands there, holding a staff, and there is this small Mona Lisa smile on his mouth. As though hc knows some grand secret no one else does. It's charming and warm, and I can't help but like him.

Roland has his likability. *Roland will make a great king.* The thought pops into my head suddenly, and pride swells my chest.

Duncan's eyes seem to be staring at the door behind me.

Well, if you insist, Your Highness...

I continue my adventure and push quietly through the wooden door across from me. The room I enter is completely swathed in crimson red. Red carpet, red walls, red ceiling, red furniture… *red.* Like someone went Carrie on this room. Red with gold trimmings, gold chandeliers, gold fringe, gold lining the twin chairs at the head of the room. Then I realize… they're not *any* chairs. They're thrones, perched on a platform, where the king and queen can sit proudly above everyone else.

I'm immediately hit with a feeling of awe. I'm standing in the middle of history. Royal leaders were crowned in this room. Out of respect, I take my mask off my head and set it down on the counter beside me. It scrapes a line of dust across the cherry wood. No one's been in this room for a long time.

"You shouldn't be in here," a voice states.

I nearly jump out of my bones. I see her then. She's wearing a ruby-red dress with a matching mask perched above her head and blends almost seamlessly into the color scheme. It's Selena's twin—she has to be. She has the same flowing blonde hair, the same beautiful and strong bone structure in her face. She's lounging across one of the chaises, her bare feet up on the furniture, and pulling from a long cigarette. The smoke twists and curls in the air above her.

"I'm so sorry," I stammer. "I was… I thought this was the bathroom. I'll… go."

"Hold on." I feel her stare, penetrating. "You're Roland's girl, aren't you?"

Roland's girl. The implication that I'm his property gives me that shuddery feeling, like I've just bitten deep into a sheet of tinfoil. "Roland and I are… a thing," I say. The words sound worse when they leave my mouth. I should've stuck with *Roland's girl.* Now I just sound like a wishy-washy teen. I adjust, remember his introduction to the queen. "I'm his girlfriend."

Yes. Girlfriend. That sounds better the more I say it. It's growing on me.

"The one in the video." She draws a fox's smile. "I like your style, ducky."

"Thanks." It's a weird thing to be praised for. This whole situation is weird. I feel like I've caught her in an intimate moment, enjoying a cigarette in the throne room. On second thought—is *she* even supposed to be here?

Benefits of being the queen's sister, I guess.

Feeling a little bolder, I step forward, out of the doorway. "You're the queen's sister. Princess Iris, right?"

She waves her non-cigarette hand. "Call me Iris."

Thank God, because I have no idea how to properly address a noble.

"Are you enjoying the party, Rory?" She doesn't sit up, just rolls her head lazily to face me.

I nod like a child at the kids' table. "Yes. It's incredibly… grand."

Grand. I don't think I've used that word in a sentence… ever. It makes Iris laugh, a purring, throaty sound. "Yes. My sister certainly has a taste for opulence." She takes a pull from her cigarette, and for a moment, the smoke clouds her face. "Do you have any sisters, Rory?"

I shake my head. "I have a brother. Older."

"I see. Let me guess… he's the golden boy?"

I shift from one foot to the other. "Sort of. He's been sick my whole life, so… he got a lot of the attention when we were little. Not that I mind." I add the last sentence quickly. I've spent a lot of my life apologizing for my brother. I don't want to sound ungrateful. He *needed* the extra attention. I'd give anything to make him better.

"Funny, isn't it?" Iris says. "How much of our lives is decided for us at birth. Selena and I are exactly four minutes apart. Four minutes. If I had just shouldered my way through the womb, that crown would be on my head. But no. Selena has always been the more bullheaded of the two of us."

Her eyes drift toward the thrones. The edge in her voice sends a chill through me. She flicks the edge of her cigarette and lets the black ash embed itself in the carpet fibers. I find myself wishing I hadn't left the party. "It is bizarre," I agree, lamely.

Her eyes fix on me again. "Come closer," she says. "I won't bite."

I don't want to. But I do. I step forward until I'm standing across from her.

Iris sits up. She cups my face in her hand. Her skin is incredibly soft, but her fingers are bony and they latch around my jaw. "You're such a pretty girl," she says. "Roland is a sweet boy... I love that man like a son. But he has his mother's arrogance. Don't live in his shadow, understand?"

"Yes, Princess," I say. My bones have gone rigid.

Her lips curl into a sneer. I've said something wrong. Was it the princess comment? She drops her hand from my face. "We should rejoin the party, shouldn't we?" she says.

By *we*, I can tell she means *me*. She's over me.

Fine by me. I'm eager to leave. I skitter backward. "Have a good night," I try.

But she's already ignoring me again. Curled up on the chaise, cigarette to her lips. I leave her there, staring at the throne with half-lidded eyes.

15

BEN

I'm a shadow on the fringes of the party. No one sees me, no one notices me. I maintain a clear vantage point to the prince. The last time the palace had this many people in it, we lost Sir Duncan. I need to make sure we don't lose another royal tonight. Everyone at this party has been vetted, down to the bakers making miniature quiches in the kitchen. I keep my eyes peeled all the same. I recognize a lot of familiar faces, mostly noble houses. The royal staff is here as well.

I watch when Roland takes Rory in his arms. They sway together. Smiling. Staring into each other's eyes.

They're having fun. Relaxing. That's not in my blood.

Then the music stops. I hear a snicker of laughter to my left.

"Check it out. Royal disaster is hitting the dance floor."

There's a duke and his lackeys standing beside me, their eyes on Roland and Rory.

"Have you seen the video? Polished his knob like a pro."

They chuckle. My blood pressure rises.

"Prince and the Slut. Think Disney wrote that one."

They holler with laughter. All right. Maybe I'm allowed a little fun.

As the duke passes by, I jut my foot out just enough. It's all it takes. Gravity does the rest for me. He lurches forward, loses his balance, and tumbles straight into the buffet table. As he hits the floor, a full tray of shrimp comes crawling after him. His friends grab him and fuss over each other as the staff quickly sweeps the whole thing under the rug.

I watch on, enjoying the fruits of my small but satisfying victory when my eyes catch a man in the corner. He's wearing the red-and-gold uniform of the event staff, but when everyone else rushes to clean up the duke's embarrassing spill, he shies away from the scene. He's stocky and tall with wide shoulders. I don't recognize him. I follow him with my eyes. His face is half-covered with a masquerade mask, but I can see a small pink scar poking out from the mask and curving underneath his chin.

"Ben!"

I jump in my spot. Rory has materialized in front of me. I recognize her voice in the nick of time. She has no idea how narrowly she missed getting twisted up in a headlock.

"What?"

Her irises bounce back and forth. She looks frantic. "Where does a girl go when she needs to escape an awkward situation? Maybe you have one of those secret tunnels lying around? Oh! Or a bookcase that leads into a secret room?"

I look over her head and find the prince. He's trapped in a conversation with the queen and looks like he wants to sink into the floor.

"You met the queen," I state.

"I wouldn't say we *met*. Meeting requires two people interacting. We exchanged words around each other. And then I found Princess Iris. She's... interesting. Are these for anyone?"

Rory reaches out to pluck a champagne flute from one of the walking trays. She puts it to her lips and tilts her head all the way back, downing it.

I can't leave her like this. I chance a final glance toward the prince. He's with the queen. He'll be fine.

"Come." I take Rory by the wrist. I drag her through the sea of people until we hit the terrace. Rory tries to grab another champagne flute along the way, but I take it from her and set it down on another table. It's like escorting a child with sticky fingers.

"You can't get drunk," I tell her. "On your best behavior. Remember?"

"I'm not getting drunk," she sighs. "I'm just trying to take the edge off."

It's dusk now. The pale sun sets over the perfect manicured royal garden with its topiaries and gas lanterns.

There's a couple lingering on the terrace when we get there, but they spot Rory, murmur to each other, and then leave quickly, their eyes avoiding us. Rory is the party pariah. Between the video, her low-class slouch, and her American accent, she never stood a chance in this crowd. Anger burns in my chest for her.

If Rory notices, she doesn't seem to care. She goes to the edge and leans her elbows on the stone rail. I take the spot beside her and pull a pack of cigarettes out of my blazer pocket. I offer her one, but she declines with the shake of her head. "I don't smoke."

"Suit yourself." I light up. I need this small creature comfort. We watch the garden in silence for a moment. There are goose bumps on her bare shoulders. I want to offer her my blazer, but the words stick like gum on my molars.

"We used to be friends," Rory says out of the blue and turns to me, her brows knit. "What happened?"

"We were never *friends*," I correct. "I seduced you for the prince. That was it. And now he won't talk to me. So thank you for that."

"Hold up, buddy," Rory says and lifts a palm. "You're the one who blindfolded me right before a threesome. Do you want to talk about that?"

"Not particularly."

I take a drag and blow the smoke away from her.

Rory sighs. "Listen… whatever you and Roland have going on… that's between you two. As far as I'm concerned? You and me… we're golden."

"Right." I take another drag. This time I hold the smoke in my lungs until it hurts.

I can feel her eyes on me. They're inquisitive. "Speaking of you and Roland. What's that about?"

My chest clenches up. I keep a straight face. "What about it?"

"You've worked for him for a long time, right?"

I nod. "Six years."

"So you know each other pretty well."

"You could say that."

"Did the two of you ever…?" Her voice trails off suggestively.

I stare her down, daring her to finish that thought. "Ever?"

"You know." She shrugs. "I don't know. You seem to have… a special relationship. Did things ever get… intimate?"

"No." The word comes out more forcefully than I would like. I pad my rising temper with: "There's always a woman involved. It's not like that."

"Not like what? Like… you're not gay?"

"I'm bi."

Why am I telling her these things? I need to shut up. I need to keep my mouth closed. But Rory is stubborn. She gestures dubiously. "You mean to tell me that you two have slept with the same woman… at the same time… and you've never bumped uglies?"

A red heat climbs up my throat. I pray my dark stubble and the dimming sunlight hides it, and I turn away from her. Like an idiot parrot, I repeat, "It's not like that."

She's watching me. I can feel the heat of her eyes. "Maybe not for him," she says softly after a moment. She looks out over at the garden, and she lets out a breathy laugh. "*Oh.* I get it now."

I eye her warily. "What?"

"Last night, when you brought me to the palace… you *wanted* to scare me away."

She's getting dangerously close to the truth, and I square my shoulders. "What are you talking about?"

"That's it, isn't it? You blindfolded me and conveniently forgot to tell me about Roland… because you wanted me to freak out and leave." Her eyes meet mine, and she blurts out, like she's bloody Sherlock Holmes, "You're in love with him."

She may as well have stabbed me through with an ice pick. My feet root in the ground, and my molars grind. "You don't know what you're talking about."

My stubborn denial gives me away. "It's *true,*" she gasps. "Does he know?"

I can't speak. Literally. My words seppuku themselves on my tongue.

All at once, her expression grows somber. Those big eyes are wide and sad and pitying. "Oh, Ben," she says. "I'm sorry. If I knew—"

"That's enough." This is painful. I would rather be dragged over hot coals, eat the barrel of my gun, or be buried alive than continue this conversation. I smash my smoke on the stone railing, and it spits out sparks and embers. "We should go back inside. I'm sure the prince is looking for—"

"Roland!" Rory raises her voice, a gracious signal to cut the conversation short.

The prince is backlit by the light from the palace, and it creates a halo around his golden hair. The heat from inside has made him unkempt, frizzy, and his cheeks are flushed with rosy splotches. He's wearing that unbearable grin he always wears, as though he knows some incredible secret.

My heart is thudding in my chest, and I try to force it to slow down.

"I thought you'd run off," Roland says as he approaches Rory. "I was going to start hunting for a glass slipper."

Rory deepens her lean against the railing and half shrugs. "Ben was keeping me company."

Roland glances around as though he's looking for the invisible man. His eyes intentionally never hit me, and his forehead scrunches in faux confusion. "Strange, I don't see anyone else here."

One of these days, I'm going to punch the prince of England.

I'm going to ball my fists into that stupid, gaudy shirt, shove him hard against the wall, and—

No. No! Fuck!

My thoughts race around my head and trip over themselves. Rory has me all worked up. I need to extract myself from the situation immediately.

Wordlessly, I leave the two of them and slip inside. I wish I weren't on duty. Maybe Rory had the right idea. I'm tempted to down ten of those champagne flutes.

I need my heart to stop pounding. As usual, it doesn't listen to me.

16

ROLAND

I can't keep my hands off Rory.

She's everything I shouldn't want. A common-born Normal. Punk. *Ginger.* But there's something about her that makes me insatiable. The second Ben skulks away, I press her against the ledge and swallow her mouth in a kiss. Her lips taste like cherry. She makes a small, muffled noise of surprise before her body goes limp and pliable against mine. Every time I feel that switch in her—from rigid and tense to soft and submissive—my dick gets diamond hard.

"Stay with me tonight," I murmur at her lips. "The worst part of today was waking up without you."

She grins. "All my… stuff is at the hostel…"

"I'll have someone collect your things." I trail kisses under her ear and along her neck. She tilts her chin upward to give me more access and sighs deeply. I warn her, "I'm not letting you out of my sight."

I feel her throat vibrate on my lips when she laughs. When I draw my hand under her dress, however, her thighs close tightly to keep me out.

"People can see us," she whispers.

"You're right. We should move somewhere more private. My room, perhaps."

She bites her lip, and her eyes dance with mischief. "Shouldn't we stay for the rest of the party?"

"Sod the party. I hate these things anyway. They're a bunch of stuffy wankers. They've got their heads so far up their arses they can't remember what sunshine feels like."

There's a shift in her expression, and her eyes look almost sad suddenly. Her small hands rest against my chest. "Are you okay?"

I frown. "Yes. Why?"

"You're just…" She waves her hand as though trying to pluck the word from thin air. "Frantic. It must be weird to be around all of those people after being alone for so long."

"I'm not alone. I have Ben."

That sounded better in my head, but when the words fall from my lips, it sounds pathetic. Truthfully, Ben has been my only *real* companion over the past ten years. He's been my brother when I had no one. I can deflect with charming smiles and hot kisses, but even I know how sad that sounds.

Rory, mercifully, doesn't push the subject. Instead, she hooks a finger around the horrid lace on my lapel and toys with it. "Speaking of Ben… I was thinking. What if we invite him back to your room?"

I blink. "You mean dead-to-me Ben Tolle? That Ben?"

She rolls her eyes. "You don't mean that. Besides, you two have slept with the same women before, right?"

"Yes. We have."

"So… it would turn me on. A lot." Those doe eyes lift from my shirt and meet mine. "Please?"

I realize then and there that it's physically impossible to say no to her. More than that, I don't want to. I love this side of her—my bold and brash girl who isn't afraid to ask for what she wants. "Smart *and* kinky." I grin. "I like it."

"I'm one of a kind," she jokes.

I, however, am not joking, not in the slightest when I tell her, "You absolutely are."

Even in the low light coming from the palace, I can see her cheeks flame up with a blush. If I get any harder, I'm going to burst out of the confining prison of my pants.

"I'll text him," I say. I dig my phone out. Ben's number is at the top of my recent calls. I shoot him the text: *Your presence is required. My room. Stat.*

I hit Send and tuck my phone away. "Done. He'll meet us there."

With that, I step to the edge of the terrace. A lantern flickers above us. There's a small switch next to the lantern, impossible to spot if you weren't looking for it. I flip it upward and the secret door clicks as it unlocks. I use the neck of the lantern as a door handle, and the stone splits down the crevices, revealing a hidden entranceway.

Behind me, I hear Rory gasp. When I turn to her, her eyes look like they might pop out of her head. "Is that…?"

"A getaway door? Of course. Useful for assassinations and the like. It's a little tight," I warn her. "You'll have to duck."

I slip inside and take Rory's hand to help her down the initial steep drop. She bunches her dress up and steps into the spiral stone staircase.

"Okay." Rory's laugh echoes as she follows me inside. "I'm *officially* wet."

17

RORY

I don't know what makes me hotter: Roland's deep, lust-fueled kisses or the palace's secret passageways and hidden doorways.

What can I say? I'm a slut for history and espionage.

It's dark in the spiral staircase with only a string of emergency electric lights to lead the way. The stairs are steep and clunky as though they were built a long, long time ago, and I follow Roland down. It ends abruptly in front of a sturdy door with a latch handle. Roland yanks the latch back—it groans with disuse—and pushes it open.

We step into a brightly lit room. It's cozy in here, something about it inviting and homey, and then I realize why—we've entered the palace library. Instinctively, I feel right at home among the stacks and stacks of books. Roland pushes the door closed behind him.

It's a bookcase. *Of course.* I'm fangirl screaming on the inside. I love this.

"Which book is the secret lever?" I cling to his arm. No use hiding my fangirlishness now; he'll find out sooner or later anyway.

Luckily, Roland looks amused rather than turned off. "The one book least likely to get picked up."

He points to a copy of *The Da Vinci Code.*

I laugh and shove him. "You're lying! You snob. I loved that series. Read it cover to cover."

"I am lying," he smirks. "But now I know you have terrible taste."

"I must." I grin and grip his chin. "I'm crazy about an arrogant asshole."

"You're mental," he says, an impish look sparkling in his eyes.

"Insane," I agree and link my hand in his. I lean back against a bookshelf and urge him closer. He takes my cues and flattens my body between his and the bookshelf before closing his mouth over mine.

I like him like this—boyish, playful, teasing. My brother and I always showed affection by taunting each other, and I've grown a thick skin over the years. It's nice to have a man who doesn't treat me like I'm delicate, breakable, or skittish. I push, he pushes back, and right now he's pushed me against the bookcase and the heat between us is almost unbearable. I want to rip his clothes off. I want to feel the warmth of his bare skin against mine. I want, I want, I *want.*

We're making out like teenagers in the library when I hear it. Footsteps click loudly down the hallway. A voice follows soon after, muffled at first, but I recognize it when the person gets closer—Princess Iris.

Roland hears her, too, because he holds his finger to my lips to gesture me to stay quiet.

"Yes, he was just there, you bloody oaf," the princess is saying to someone. "How could you possibly lose the prince at his own ball?"

Oh God. They're *looking* for us.

Another deep voice mutters a response that I can't make

out, and the princess scoffs. "You're as useless as a pig's arse, you know that?"

My heart is pounding so loudly, I'm afraid it'll alert the princess to our hiding place. I've done my share of petty crimes—trespassing empty lots, loitering, using my expired college ID to get student discounts, and the good old running the thermometer under hot water to get the day off from school. But escaping a royal masquerade ball and sneaking around the palace with the prince himself... this is definitely next level.

It's scary and exciting all at once.

Roland isn't helping the situation. His finger still on my lips, he pushes it in and invades my mouth. I let him, sucking it softly, digit by digit. My eyes stay on his; those deep violet irises do something dangerous to my inhibitions. His other hand reaches under my dress.

I gasp before I can stop myself. He's teasing me, petting my swollen sex through my underwear. I'm soaking wet, I can feel it, and I'm positive I've drenched straight through. I know this because he presses a finger against the soaked fabric and hits the bull's-eye immediately against my aching core.

My vision blurs with want. I groan and bite his finger to keep myself from begging him. I grind against his crooked finger, so badly wanting it inside of me. Instead, his knuckle nuzzles against the soft fabric, tormenting my needy entrance.

I'm panting lewdly, his finger stuck between my teeth like a horse's bit. Roland looks positively entranced as he watches me unravel under his touches. I feel so hot underneath this dress suddenly, my pebble-hard nipples chafing on my bra.

The footsteps are coming closer. Soon enough, the princess and her companion will pass, but until then, I'm trembling. Roland's finger slips under my panties then, and I feel him between my legs. I whimper—I can't help it.

Roland's lips graze my ear. "Quiet," he murmurs. His breath beats on my neck and makes my skin tingle. I'm trying so, so hard to be quiet, but he's caressing me, pushing my wet arousal around my slit. The tip of his finger hits that sensitive bundle, and I jerk like I've been shot through with electricity. Roland pins me in place with his body, and his lips attack my throat. His hard cock presses against my hip, and I want it inside me so badly I could cry. With a single flick of his finger on my swollen little nub, he has me right where he wants me. I'm shivering with pleasure as he flicks it over and over, unrelentingly, and everything in me feels tight all at once, from my cunt to my lungs to my trembling heart.

Suddenly, Roland crushes his lips against mine. I break. My orgasm comes crashing at the very tip of his finger. I moan, inhibitions gone out the window, the sound muffled only by his mouth. I'm throbbing, grinding, thrashing, battling the intensity of my pleasure with my desire to keep quiet. Roland doesn't stop until I'm flushed, and twitching painfully.

"God, you're so good at that," I whimper.

"Good." Roland's mouth stretches out in a cocky grin. "Because I'm only getting started with you."

The noises outside have stopped. Princess Iris has gone, and we're alone again. Only then does Roland remove his touch, readjust my panties, and finish me off with a sweet kiss. I'm buzzing, still hot and bothered. My clit, the needy thing, is now ultrasensitive after his ministrations, and even the soft kiss of my cotton panties is painful now.

Roland licks me off his finger, and it sends another stab of lust through me. "You're delicious," he says.

"You make me breathless," I tell him.

He takes my hand in his. The warmth of his palm is

comforting, and it feels ridiculously natural to hold his hand. "Come on," he says. "While we have the chance."

I stumble behind Roland as he pulls me out of the library and we sneak down the hall. I'm practically limping, my legs wobbly and barely operable, but somehow we make it to his room.

I forgot how dark it was in here, but now the gunmetal gray of his room feels soothing, like putting a cold washcloth on a migraine.

"Take off my dress," I beg and turn my back to him, pulling my hair up so he can get at the zipper. Roland slides the zipper down, and I shove it off my hips, kicking the heavy thing to the floor. My boots come off, my bra, my panties, and I make a messy pile of clothes on the floor.

Next, I attack his shirt, trying to get all the buttons off. "I need your skin on mine," I tell him. The cold nips at my already peaked nipples.

"Couldn't agree more," he says. He express-lines the buttons and rips his shirt down the middle completely. Buttons fly, his flouncy shirt becomes a pile of rags on the ground, and dear God, that chest.

He sweeps me up in his arms, and there's nowhere I want to be more than right here, wrapped up in him. His bare skin is soft, his muscles hard, and his body is hot as a furnace. I run my hands up and down his form, tracing his slim waist, finding the hook of his hips.

I intend on screwing him until I can't see straight, but when our lips touch, I fall into a different kind of swoon. The fire between us has shifted from all-consuming heat to a low, delicious burn. My back hits his fluffy mattress, and Roland falls on top of me, his lips never leaving mine.

"I love kissing you," he confesses, and the genuine, gentle tone of his voice makes my heart beat faster.

"I love it, too," I whisper.

We roll around in his bed, kissing and tasting one another. I could lie here all night with him, lip-locked, but the moment is interrupted when the lights in his room flicker once and then cut abruptly. The room is doused with darkness, and I let out a surprised squeak.

Something is wrong. Roland sits up, and I prop myself up as well. "What was that?" I whisper.

"Stay here," Roland says. The urgency in his voice makes my bones go cold, and I freeze in my spot, even though there's a part of me screaming, *Don't leave me! When people split up, bad things happen! I've seen horror movies, I know how this works!*

Roland goes to the door, and I hear the handle squeak when it twists but then—nothing. The door doesn't budge. He pushes at it, trying to force it open.

It's no use. We're trapped.

"Well," Roland says jovially, "that can't be good."

BEN

The ball is in full tilt when the electricity goes out.

The air leaves the room in one collective gasp. The musicians skip a beat, and the song dies. The dancers go still. The whole room has gone dim, lit only by the candelabras stationed along the walls. It looks like a haunted Halloween house.

The hair on the back of my neck stands on end. *Roland.* I swiftly push through the people until I get to the balcony. No sign of Roland or Rory out here. I duck back inside and scan the crowd, hunting for an edge of her red hair or his billowing white shirt—

Nothing. My one job was to keep an eye on him. Keep him safe. And I've lost him. I've lost the prince. All because I couldn't keep my shit together around him.

I turn and run smack into my boss. Tanner composes himself quickly and neatly touches my chest with two fingers to halt me.

"Where's the prince?" he asks immediately. His voice is curt, all business. We're all on alert now.

I swallow and shake my head. "I looked away for a moment and… he slipped me…"

Tanner's jawline tenses.

Queen Selena comes between us. "What the bloody hell is going on?" she hisses.

"We're getting to the bottom of it now, ma'am," Tanner says quickly. "Someone's cut the power."

"I can *see* that." Even in the dark, her eyes flash with Pennington rage.

"We'll need to evacuate you and your son and interview everyone that's here."

"Interrogate my guests? On the one day I get to dedicate to my husband? You'll do no such thing." The queen sighs. "It seems I have to do everything myself."

"Ma'am—"

But if there's one thing I've learned about the Pennington family, it's that they're stubborn and impossible to control. The queen slips through the bustling crowd and makes her way to the bandstand. Queen Selena lifts a microphone before she seems to remember that the electricity has been cut and tosses the thing to the side. The queen of England doesn't need a microphone to get everyone's attention. She lifts the hem of her dress and steps up onto the stage where the band remains still and quiet.

"Good evening, everyone!" She smiles out to the crowd. Immediately, all eyes are on her. The woman is the textbook definition of poise and grace. "I hope everyone's enjoying the mood lighting." A rumble of relieved laughter from the audience. The queen is in charge; the sheep are no longer anxious. "I want to thank you all for coming… it warms my heart to see this ball lit up—so to speak. Duncan loved gatherings like this. Any excuse to bring everyone together. It's only appropriate that, ten years after his tragic passing, we come together to do exactly what he would've wanted: dance. Now, everyone, I implore you to remove your masks and take a moment to appreciate the one with you. Life is too short. You never know when a bright flame may be extinguished."

Even as she speaks, her voice doesn't shake and she never once loses composure. The woman is magnetic. Now, a smile brightens her face. "Now… enjoy the rest of the party. And dance!"

There's applause all around. Finally—*finally*—the band starts back up again. The queen gracefully leaves the stage. Smile still intact, she comes over to us and addresses Tanner once more. "Find out what's going on, but keep it *quiet*. I will not have Duncan's memory blemished with a stampede of people fleeing the palace."

With that, she leaves us. Her dress ripples behind her. The queen is an earthquake, and she leaves shock waves with each step.

"God bless the queen," Tanner murmurs. His eyes flicker back to me, and he adds, "I'll figure out who's behind this. Go find the prince, for goodness' sake."

"Yes, sir."

I dip out of the ballroom. A blast of frigid air kisses my sweat-dampened skin. The hallway is cast in a blue, low light. It's strange to see the palace dark like this, and the whole thing sends a shiver through me. I feel for my gun. It hangs solidly at my hip. If this is a coup, the prince is in trouble. I need to find him. Immediately.

I lift my cell to call Roland and see that I've missed a text from him.

[TXT: Roland] *Your presence is required. My room. Stat.*

.   .   .

RELIEF FILTERS THROUGH MY BLOODSTREAM. Mystery solved. I put my phone up and move swiftly down the darkened halls to the prince's bedroom.

99

19

ROLAND

My fireplace is gaslit. Even with the power down, all I have to do is stick a lighter to it and it whooshes to life. The orange and yellow flames crackle over the ceramic replica logs.

"That should do it." I get to my feet and glance back at Rory. "Better?"

She pokes her hands out of the insides of her robe to give me a thumbs-up. Well. My robe. It's crimson red, velvet soft, and it has my initials, *R.P.*, stitched into the chest pocket. It swallows her. I lent it to her thinking it would make her more comfortable, but now she looks like a wilted rose.

I ease down on the edge of the bed beside her and move my hand to the small of her back. Her fiery hair droops down the sides of her round face, and the fireplace light gives her skin a honeyed glow. I want to hold her close. Wrap my arms around her. Protect her. "Are you all right?" I ask gently.

"Oh, yeah, totally." She cocks a half grin, but I can tell she's putting it on. "I've always dreamed that one day I'd be locked up in a dark palace while there's potentially an armed killer running around the premises."

I exhale a breath of a laugh. "It's funny. For years, my mother implanted this boogeyman image in my brain. According to her, there's always an assassin right around the corner, waiting to strike as soon as I part the curtains a little too wide."

Those moon eyes meet mine. "How does it feel to have your worst fears realized?"

"Oddly refreshing."

The corner of her mouth turns up, and her head tilts quizzically. Before she can ask any further questions, however, my bedroom door cracks open. Rory hastily tightens the robe over her chest.

Ben's raven-dark hair peeks around the door.

"Took you long enough, mate," I tell him.

Ben shoots me a sharp look. He squeezes through the small gap in the door as though he's stepping behind enemy lines.

Rory and I shout simultaneously: "Ben, don't—!"

But we don't get the words out before the door clicks shut behind him. Rory sighs and murmurs, "—shut the door."

"What?" Ben intones, incredibly confused.

I point to the door. "It locks behind you. No doubt, one of my mother's infinitely paranoid safety measures."

Ben tries the door—of course he does; he's a tactile person, and he has to touch it for himself—but naturally it doesn't budge under even his strong arms. I see the line of his lips thin in frustration.

"Your mother put in an automatic safety latch—"

"I gathered that," I interrupt him. "Now how do we get out of it?"

Ben lifts his phone and taps his fingers over the screen. "I'll phone Tanner."

I curl a leg up. "Put it on speaker."

Ben steps over and barely perches himself on the edge of the mattress. He makes no comment about my lack of shirt or Rory's obvious nakedness under my robe. Instead, he stares ahead with blank eyes until the ringing stops.

"Yes?" Tanner, curt, to the point.

"I found Roland," Ben says into the bottom of his phone. "He was in his room. The safety protocol engaged, and we're locked in."

"Probably the safest place for him to be right now, then. Hang tight until we get this all sorted. Are you two alone?"

"Rory's here."

"Does the girl check out?"

My jaw clenches. I know it's his job to question everyone and everything, but I feel a vicious urge rearing up to defend my girlfriend. "Yes," I say, barely curbing my anger. "Rory is the last person you have to worry about. How's my mum?"

"She's well guarded," Tanner assures me. My blood still fizzles and pops with worry. I'm trapped in this room, safely, and my mother is… still outside. Still vulnerable. If this is, in fact, a coup and they're after anyone… they're going after my mum first.

"Don't let her leave your sight," I order. "Not for a second."

"Yes, Your Highness. Keep your phone close, Tolle. We'll come collect you once we're clear up here."

"Yes, sir. Copy."

Ben ends the call and tucks his phone back in his trousers.

"What now?" Rory asks. Her timid voice breaks the solid pond of silence.

"Who's up for a game of Connect Four?" I joke. Humor has always been my favorite crutch.

Ben, however, is not playing. He stands quickly, as though

he's been bitten by a snake, and paces across toward the fireplace, away from us. "Tanner told us to wait," he says, his voice a flat monotone. "So we wait."

I know Ben. I know when he's brooding. It's incredibly unlike him. Sure, we're in the middle of a potentially dangerous situation—but that's the point. Ben loves this sort of thing. High stakes. Adrenaline. It sharpens him. I swear, he throws me to the ground every time so much as a bird hits the window.

So moping, huffing… no. That's not like Ben.

I broach the subject amicably. "What's up your arse now?"

Ben snaps, "Just because you're talking to me now doesn't change the fact that you've been a right prick all day."

The words leave him in a flurry, as though he's been waiting all day to let them out. Perhaps he has a point. I did ignore him all day, and now that we're in trouble, all sins are pardoned. I only find myself reaching for him when I need him, like a boy who refuses to be weaned off a comfort blanket.

"You're right," I tell him and flash him a cheeky grin. "C'mon, mate. Let's kiss and make up."

Ben turns away from me at that. The shadows in the room darken his expression, but I can hear his bitter growl. He's not amused.

I roll my eyes. "Fine, kiss *Rory*, then." I motion to her. My sweet, scrumptious, sacrificial lamb. "I know you want her."

Who wouldn't want her? Those lips are plump enough to break even in the dark. When her eyes meet mine, they go wide. But she can't hide the way her thighs squeeze together, just so. My kitten wants to be licked.

"This is hardly the time," Ben grumbles.

"What the hell else are we going to do?" I lift a hand and drop it on the mattress. "C'mon, Ben…"

20

RORY

"… Have a taste of my girl."

My heart is pounding. I shouldn't like being on display like this, sold to the highest bidder. But I do. I'd give it to either of these hunks for free, but they have a grudge, an axe to bury, and I wouldn't mind if they buried it in me.

Ben stalks over and stops in front of me. I'm magnetized, my blood thrumming. He takes the knot on my robe in his hand, but then his arm goes still.

Those dark eyes meet mine. "Rory." It's a word—just my name—but the way he says it, the questioning look in his expression, I know what this is. He's asking me for permission. He won't take me without my consent… prince's orders or not.

My heart flutters and I wet my lips. "Please," I beg. My throat is dry with lust, and my voice cracks. "I want it."

The knot comes undone and the ribbon slithers off my waist. My robe parts freely at the middle now. I'm exposed, but I don't try to cover myself. Especially not when Ben is looking at me *like that,* taking me in with those deep pools.

"Well?" Roland says impatiently. "What do you think?"

As though he's taught his pet a new trick. Sit. Stay. Spread your legs.

Ben's eyes find mine. "She's beautiful."

I bite my lip. He unpins my pink flesh from my teeth with his thumb and kisses me. I part for him immediately, both my lips and my legs.

Ben peels back and lowers himself to his knees in front of me. My pussy throbs in response. He's trained me like Pavlov's dog. I remember just how well he can use his tongue.

Sure enough, when he rolls my panties from my thighs and presses his tongue flat against my sex, I swear I see heaven. I whimper and arch into his mouth as he licks me. The rough facial hair on his jaw prickles my thighs. His hands brace on my knees, holding them apart.

Roland finds a place behind me. He slips the robe off my arms, and his lips trail wet kisses down my neck and shoulders. I'm trapped between two beautiful, dominating men, hungry to spoil me with their mouths and hands and *everything*. Last time, I got scared and shoved them off. This time, I melt into their touches and sigh, savoring every second.

Too soon, Ben lifts his head from between my legs. He wipes his arm across his mouth, but even that doesn't catch all of my arousal. Some of it glistens off his scruff, and I swallow hard. *Holy hell.* I'm sopping wet.

In one swift movement, Ben rips off his blazer and the white shirt underneath it. "Flip over," he tells me.

Gone is the awkward bodyguard from the ball. The man who looked uncomfortable in his own skin. Here, in charge, Ben is in his element.

I do as he says and roll over. My movements are sluggish and clumsy, my legs like rubber underneath me. I get on my hands and knees on the bed.

I'm practically in Roland's lap now. He cups my face and sifts his fingers through my hair. His eyes scrutinize me. "Are you okay, love?" he asks, checking in.

I let out a small noise, half a laugh, half a whimper. "More than okay," I purr.

He grins. "Good." I feel Ben stall behind me. Those strong, calloused hands grip my hips and then cup over my round ass. "Our pet has a nice bum, doesn't she?" Roland says, looking over my shoulder.

"Yes, sir," Ben responds.

I can tell from his tone that the *sir* is reflexive—less a pecking order here, more an unbreakable habit.

"Spank her," Roland tells him.

Before I can register what's about to happen, Ben's palm smacks my ass. I gasp. I've never been spanked before. Hell, I've never been in the middle of two ravenous men before. Yet it all feels so natural somehow. I feel red-hot heat crawl up my neck and explode on my cheeks.

Roland laughs and it's this beautiful airy sound that brushes against my ear and sends shivers through my whole body. "I think she liked that, mate." He uses his grip on my hair like a handle, pulling my neck back so I can look at him. "You did, didn't you, kitten?"

"Yes," I croak. I'm dumb with lust. I can barely speak.

Roland's eyes dance as they focus on Ben. "Do it again."

He smacks my ass again. Ben's hand is like a goddamn plank of wood. He does it again and again. At first, my behind stings with sharp pain, but then the pain turns into tingling, and the tingles to a low burn. I moan as another heavy swing hits my bottom, only this time I rock back into his palm when he tries to pull it away.

I'm dripping down my thighs. I can feel it. I *need* someone inside of me.

As if he knows, Ben pushes a finger inside of me. I gasp

loudly and push back against his finger. I feel him insert a second finger, and then they curve, stroking my inner walls.

"You enjoy the way Ben fingers you, love?" Roland coaxes. He strokes my hair back, which feels both soothing and possessive all at once.

"Yes," I whimper.

Roland's other hand travels over my chest, and he catches my hard nipple between his fingers. I yelp as he rolls it and tugs. His ministrations on my breasts make me throb around Ben's fingers. It *clicks* now. Roland and Ben—they're damn good on their own, but together? They're in sync, a perfectly tuned instrument. They move like one until I'm a doughy, pliable sex kitten. My endorphins are shooting off like crazy, sending sparks of pleasure through me. They've got me at their mercy, and I would do anything they wanted.

With Ben's fingers deep inside of me, Roland petting my hair, caressing my tits… it's overwhelming. I cry out and suddenly my body clamps down on Ben's fingers. I'm in the throes of an orgasm before I even knew I was close, and Ben and Roland are coaxing it from me, kissing my bare skin, touching me. Every inch of me feels loved. I melt into their adoring hands as I shudder with every throb.

"Good girl," Roland keeps saying, over and over.

Two men. Two rock-hard cocks. And they can't stop pleasing *me*. I've never had anything like this before. Ever.

I'm still pulsing when Ben growls, "Tell me what you need."

"I need you inside of me," I gasp. Then I draw my fingers down Roland's chest, his stomach, and paw at his belt. "And you."

"Greedy little pet." Roland grins. "Be careful what you wish for, love."

With that, Roland gets up and stands behind me, beside Ben. I hear the click of their belts, the hiss of their zippers.

"What do you say?" Roland challenges. "Last one to blow gets to cum down her throat."

"You're on," Ben growls.

I shouldn't be this turned on by the way they're competing over me, but… I am.

When I look up, I can see that there's a long, full-length mirror propped on the wall across from me. I almost don't recognize myself at first. It looks like there's some sex-crazed wild woman in the prince's bed. My red hair is frizzy and insane—literally insane, like I've stepped off the set of a Tim Burton movie. My lips are swollen, my face is flushed, eyes lidded and makeup smeared.

My eyes focus on the men standing behind me. Ben reaches into the cupboard beside Roland's bed, pulls out two condoms, and tosses one to Roland. They're naked, completely, and I wonder not for the first time tonight how I managed to steal two Adonises.

Ben wraps up his manhood before I feel the thick head of him against my narrow channel. He rubs it up and down my soaked slit, lubing himself on my arousal, and then presses it inside of me. I moan loudly and lean back to pull him in deeper.

Oh God. He feels so, so good. He's thick and fills me completely. He doesn't need any more foreplay, and neither do I. He starts to pound into me, and I can hear his hips slap mine. It's exactly what I need, and I grip and twist the blankets.

And then it stops. Ben pulls out of me. I whine at the empty sensation.

"I wonder," Roland says. "Can you guess which of us inside of you?"

I'm not empty for long—Roland fills me. I shudder at the sensation. He's not as thick as Ben, but he hits me deeper, and I decide it's completely unfair that they both have perfect cocks.

"You love the way I shag you, don't you?" Roland says as he rolls his hips.

"I love it," I whimper. I do. I really, really do. My pleasure builds and burns to a near peak.

His cock leaves me, and I feel myself stretch again to fit the other meaty organ.

"Ben," I gasp. "Ben, Ben, *Ben*."

Ben is on me again, in me, pounding me. They go back and forth like this again and again until I lose all track of who's inside me. I shout Roland's name, and then Ben's name, and then it's just a mantra: *Roland-Ben, Roland-Ben!*

All I know is that I love the way they feel. I love being a victim to their desires. I love the ebb and flow of their bodies against mine. These men know how to fuck, and they know how to work together to make me squirm. Roland calls me a good girl over and over and makes me tell him how much I enjoy it. Ben grunts, growls, and kisses my back. Before I know it, I'm tight, shivering, sweat soaked, and I'm reaching my edge again. I've lost count of how many times I've cum.

"Wait," I say suddenly and reach back to press my palm against a chest. Whose chest, I'm not sure.

"Are you okay?" That's Ben, all worry on top of me.

"Yes… I'm good. I just want to look at you."

Ben pulls out of me, flips me to my back, and then presses himself inside of me again. "Better?" he asks.

I wrap my thighs around his hips. "Yes."

Both of my men look as lust-drunk as I feel, their bodies hot and shimmering with sweat. I hook my ankles behind Ben, holding him deep inside of me, and I shift up, propping myself on my elbows.

Roland waits, his cock hard as steel and pointing skyward. I reach out and take it in my hand. He groans, forever the vocal one. His skin is velvety smooth and pulled tight over his swollen erection.

This is what I crave. Both men aching. We're all in that intense, sex-wild moment where anything is permitted. It's now or never.

I wet my lips, flicker my eyes between the two of them, and make a single request that I know will change things forever. "Kiss each other."

2 1

BEN

I must have heard her wrong.

I'm balls-deep in Rory, throbbing, and savoring each breathy whimper. Surely, she didn't say what I *thought* she said.

Roland lets out a low chuckle beside me. She's jerking him off, slowly, and I'm trying not to focus too hard on *that.* "What?" he asks. Clearly, he must have heard her wrong, too.

"Kiss each other," she repeats. It's clear, that's *definitely* what she wants. Those doe eyes look so damn *innocent,* and she bites her lip. "Please? It would... really turn me on."

My eyes connect briefly with Roland's violet blues. *Bad idea.* I stare at Rory instead. I'm panting. I can't look hopeful. I can't look *anything.*

Then Roland—careless, conceited, and consequence-free Roland—says, "Sod it." With that, he lifts his head and catches my mouth in his own.

My bones practically turn to stone. I'm tense and stiff as a brick. For a second, I feel paralyzed. His lips are cloud soft and full on mine. And he's not pulling away.

Me? I can barely breathe, let alone kiss him back.

Do it! my subconscious screams at me. *Quit being such a coward!*

I know why Rory suggested this now. I know she's trying to help. But this isn't helping. This feels like a blow to the chest. There's a moment there when I think about bolting. I can still shove Roland away, run off, and hide in my lair, my cave, where things are safe and orderly and emotions are best kept repressed. But then—

I go for it.

I grab Prince Roland's silky mane of hair, and I yank the other man close. I part his lips with my tongue and drink him in deeply. A small, surprised noise escapes Roland, but he doesn't pull away. Instead, he leans into it. He swipes his tongue against mine and invades my mouth. I've dreamed of this moment. I imagined it would be hot. But I didn't think it would be like *this*. A dam breaks inside of me, and untethered passion comes spilling out.

I can't get enough of my prince.

I'm hungry and ferocious. Rory's pussy clutches me in butterflying pulses. Shit. She's getting off on this.

Shit. *I'm* getting off on this. My gasp breaks the kiss. "Oh *fuck!*" I pull out of Rory and rip off the condom just in time to shoot all over her stomach and thighs.

Fuck is right. Not only have I lost our bet, but I'd hoped I could savor the prince's lips a little longer. Now, the spell is broken in pearly white drops spilling down Rory's curves.

I pant for breath. Roland smirks.

"Looks like that sweet mouth is mine." Roland winks in that cheeky way of his. "Next time, mate."

If he calls me *mate* one more time…

No. No *if*. I'm not letting the brat prince get away with this.

Seven years of military training make it easy to grab Roland's arms and twist them behind his back. He lets out a surprised yelp. He wriggles, but his wrists are stuck fast in my grip. His back is to my front, and I growl in his ear, "What did I tell you about calling me *mate?*"

Roland chokes on a laugh. But I can hear the nervousness in his chuckle. His mouth has gotten him into trouble and, finally, he has to pay the toll. "What's got your knickers in a twist?" he complains.

When I look over his shoulder, I see Rory has gone still and wide-eyed. She's probably trying to figure out whether we're going to shag or kill each other.

Honestly? I'm not sure myself, until I say, "You want to suck your prince's prick, don't you?"

Her cheeks are flushed. She nods eagerly. "Yes."

"On your knees, then."

Rory lowers to her knees in front of Roland and opens her mouth, ready. Those sweet eyes will be the death of me. I adjust both of Roland's wrists into one of my hands. With my free hand, I roll Roland's condom off his cock. His beautiful cock. It's hard as polished marble under my fingers, and I find it difficult not to linger there, especially when I hear him draw in a sharp breath. I flick the condom to the floor and then cup the back of Rory's head. I guide her lips over his cock so she sucks him down.

Roland's head falls back. He moans. "God, yes. Just like that, love…"

I bunch Rory's ginger hair in my fist and use my grip to direct her pace. I feel her neck tense when I've pushed her down too far. I'm quick to learn her limits, and I find a pace suitable for the both of us. Soon, she's sucking, slurping him like a woman starved. Little mewling noises leave her every now and then, and before I know it, I'm hard again, the stubborn organ bumping on Roland's ass.

Roland's eyes pinch shut, and his mouth falls open. His breath comes in short, rapid pants. I've seen this before in him. When he finally shuts the fuck up and gets quiet—*there*. He's close. I know it. I just never thought I'd be the one to get him there.

Roland groans and shakily confirms what I already know. "I'm going to blow."

"Beg," I growl in the spoiled prince's ear.

"Bugger off," he hisses.

That won't do. Someone has to train the brat. I tug Rory's hair back. His angry cock pops out of her mouth and twitches in the empty air. She licks her lips.

That does it. *"Please,"* the prince gasps, his voice thick and strained. Goddamn. That sound sends shivers through me. I reward him. I push Rory down so she deep-throats his cock. Then I fasten my teeth on his neck and bite.

Prince Roland howls as he cums down her throat. His body jerks, muscles contracting and twitching, and he moans and lets out a string of swears as I make sure she sucks every drop from him. Not that she needs much encouraging—Rory is positively thirsty for it.

Finally, the prince goes limp in my arms and pants for breath. "Bloody hell," he breathes.

Rory stands and kisses him. Then she leans over his shoulder and kisses me. I taste her peach lips and his sweet salt on her tongue.

For the first time that night—no, for the first time in a long time—I don't feel anxious, pent up, or self-loathing. Instead, a bizarre, cooling peace falls between the three of us.

Just then the lights flicker on overhead. The room bursts into a bright, clean light. Like that, our dark, wicked little ménage is over. It's back to reality for us.

Almost immediately, there's a knock on the door. Rory's eyes fly open wide. "Shit," she squeals.

"Loo," Roland whispers to her, motioning to his wash closet. She scampers out of bed, snatches up her dress, and hides in the bathroom. Meanwhile, Roland and I hastily throw on our trousers and button up our shirts. Nothing to do about Roland's wild sex hair or the stench of sweat.

"Sir?" Tanner's voice comes muffled through the other side of the door. My heart drops. What would he think if he saw me now? *Not very knightly of you, Tolle.*

Roland gives me a once-over. I nod. "Come in!" Roland shouts as he finishes up the last button on his shirt.

Tanner cracks the door open and peeks in. "Electricity is back on," he announces and then taps the door. "We got the lock reset."

"We noticed." Roland points up. "How's it out there?"

"Party's over. Your mum is retiring in the sitting room. All's clear."

"Good."

I have a bad poker face. I feel a red heat crawl up the side of my neck under Tanner's scrutiny, and I'm trying to keep cool. Tanner's eyes move to Roland, then me, then back to Roland. "Everything's all right here?" the older man asks.

"Fine," I say, perhaps too forcibly.

"Right." It's clean, crisp, Tanner's way of saying *I don't want to know.* "Carry on," he says and closes the door behind him.

As soon as the door clicks closed, Rory stumbles out of the wash closet. She's not so much wearing her dress as she is holding it to the front of her body like a shield.

All at once, the three of us burst into laughter. We're a ragtag sight, and it's impossible not to see the comedy in it. I laugh until my lungs hurt. It's a good release. As good as my orgasm earlier. I don't remember the last time I've laughed like this.

"I'm knackered," the prince says to no one in particular once he's caught his breath. "Let's go to bed."

"Should I… leave?" Rory asks. My heart goes out to her. Like me, she always anticipates the worst.

"You should stay," I inform her. "Just to be safe."

"And," Roland says, hooking an arm around her and scooping her tight against him, "there's no one to kiss you good morning at the hostel."

A smile breaks over Rory's lips. "Mmm, you two make a hard case," she says.

Roland kisses her. Then I kiss her. Then I kiss Roland. We're lazy and high off endorphins when we pile into the prince's bed.

* * *

MY INTERNAL ALARM clock wakes me up before either Rory or Roland. I blink unmoving and stare up at the circular light fixture that looms over our heads. I haven't had a nightmare, nor can I recall hearing anything strange in the night, but when I wake up, my heart is quietly pounding in my chest. A single thought cleaves through the fog of sleep.

I don't belong here.

It's the jolt of panic that wakes me up night after night in the palace. No matter how long I've been here or how much I've done for the royal family, nothing will erase that nagging doubt. The dirty, scrappy little punk from Limehouse has no place in Helmsway Palace.

But then I tilt my head and see the two of them sleeping soundly beside me. Rory is nestled in the middle like a small kitten, and Roland clutches her. I watch their chests rise and fall in deep sleep, and, slowly my anxiety turns into a dull tingle and then evaporates completely.

I replace my morning terror mantra with another thought: *I'm exactly where I should be.*

Rory's body is soft and warm. Her hair smells like autumn

leaves. It's soothing, but now that I'm awake, I can't go back to sleep.

I can't bear to wake them. Quietly, I get up. I pick my clothes off of the floor and slip them on. I sit at the foot of the bed to lace up my shoes.

"Ben."

I glance over my shoulder. The prince is awake. He looks insane, his hair sex-wild, his eyes sleepy, blinking heavily. I resist the sudden urge to pet his hair back and kiss his pillowy, warm lips.

"Yes?"

"You're leaving." It's said plainly, no judgment, just mild confusion.

"I'll be back," I reassure him. "I have to check in with Tanner."

"Good. Right-o." Another couple of tired blinks. "Ben, you'd tell me if I crossed any lines last night, wouldn't you?"

For a second, my throat contracts and I can't get any words out. Roland is the one covered in teeth marks and an embarrassingly vicious welt on his throat. I'm the one who restrained him, bit him, and claimed him like a wolf in heat. Yet he's the one checking in on *me*?

I recover with a curt nod. "Yes, sir." After a second, I add, "And, no. You didn't cross any lines."

His sky-blue eyes brighten at that. "Good." And that's it. Band-Aid ripped. He yawns and flops back in bed. "Steal some scones from the kitchen, if you wouldn't mind. And a pot of tea. Since you're up and all."

"Yes, sir."

Relief washes through me. We shared a kiss and the world didn't implode. I had a million nightmares about how this could go. I thought it'd be awkward the next day, strange, or the prince would look at me with some painful mix of revulsion and regret.

Instead, it's business as usual. If anything, Roland is *kinder* than normal. All the worry I've been carrying falls off my shoulders like a porcupine shedding its quills. I'm weightless and euphoria-high. I could shout. Dance. Fly.

Rory, who has her eyes shut and is supposed to be sleeping, can't hide her smile. *Cheeky girl.* I refocus, tighten my shoelaces, and exit the bedroom before I can make an idiot of myself.

The halls are mostly empty, save for a couple of familiar housemaids milling around. I nod to them as they pass, hoping I don't look too conspicuous. I shouldn't. I walk these halls every day without trouble. Of course, I've never spent the night with Roland before. So. That's new.

I dip through the dining room and into the kitchen. The chef is gone, probably in the back cleaning the pots and pans. A spread of the royal family's breakfast sits waiting to go out on the table. I don't realize how famished I am until the smell of freshly baked bread hits me. I pluck a scone from one of the plates (no one will notice it's missing) and bite into it as I make my way to the back. I open a silver, metal door that should lead to a meat freezer, but instead opens into a spiraling staircase. I close the door behind me and take the shortcut down to the tunnel.

The scone is reduced to crumbs by time I reach my "lair." I'm not alone. Tanner is there already, sitting in my chair, screens flickering above him. My chest tightens—did he witness my walk of shame out of the prince's room?

Unlikely. He's nose-deep in his laptop, fingers clicking over the keyboard. If he did see me, at least he says nothing, just a, "Gracing us with your presence this morning?"

"What's on the docket?" I wipe the crumbs on my trousers and look up at the monitors.

"I've been digging around about last night." Tanner

doesn't look up, his fingers continuing their crablike skitter across his keyboard. "It's strange."

"What, sir?"

"The electricity went out, the generator botched, and then it all miraculously came back. As though it were set on a timer. It appears someone rigged it up from the inside."

My heartbeat quickens and my blood responds to the infusion of adrenaline by turning to steel. "You think this was an inside job."

"But an inside job for what?" Tanner lets out a short, exasperated sigh. "Nothing went missing. Royal jewels intact. No one was hurt."

"To scare us, perhaps."

Tanner twists around in his chair and turns to face me full on now. "If it is someone on the inside… it could be a guard. One of the staff. Even a lord. You need to keep a closer eye on the prince than ever. Don't let him run off on you."

"Yes, sir. It won't happen again."

"Oh, and one more thing." Tanner reaches under the desk and lifts a masquerade mask. "We found this by the switch-board. Does this mean anything to you?"

My pulse picks up. I recognize it immediately. It's Rory's. "No," I lie.

"No matter, we'll scan the footage." Tanner gives one of his big, gaping yawns. I want to buy him a Keurig. Is it strange for one grown man to get another grown man a coffee maker? Tanner waves his hand. "As you were."

ROLAND

I've never had a woman spend the night before. Maybe that sort of thing would've been easier before my father's death, certainly. Before Helmsway Palace went on complete lockdown.

Now, I can't imagine the palace without Rory in it.

When Ben leaves the room, the door clicking shut softly behind him, I tug Rory up against me. She's noodle limp and her bare skin is warm as a tea cozy. She squeaks and nuzzles against my chest.

"When I was seven," I murmur against the shell of her ear, "my parents got me a bunny rabbit."

A grin crawls up the edges of Rory's mouth. "Did it have a name?" Her voice is rusty with sleep, and I love it.

I answer, "Lord Fluffywinkles."

"Obviously."

"Obviously. Lord Fluffywinkles would hop around the palace freely, leaving little gifts for Mum to step in. After a while, the rabbit vanished. My parents told me it escaped, but I think Mum cooked it up into a stew. I mourned that rabbit for a full month."

Rory lifts her head from my chest to look at me with those shimmering emerald eyes. "What made you think about that?"

"I thought I'd never love anything more than I loved that rabbit, up until I woke up next to you just now."

I didn't think her smile could stretch wider across her face, but it does. "I love waking up next to you, too," she says. Rory presses her lips against mine in a hard, enthusiastic kiss. My dick begins to wake up, but I ignore the low throb. I just want to kiss her. I love kissing this woman. She tastes like sleep and warmth and Rory.

"Your world... it's insane." She grins. "Lord Rabbits, masquerade balls. Kinky threesomes."

"Is it too much?"

She shakes her head. "No. But... I want to show you my world."

I scrunch my eyebrows together. "Your world?"

"Yes. Let's go somewhere. Anywhere. We can book a cheap hostel, go hiking off a waterfall, or pet a water buffalo. I think? I don't know, the last one might be illegal."

I can't help it. She makes me smile. "I'm sure they'd make an exception for the prince of England."

"It's a deal, then."

I heave a sigh and drop back against the pillows. "I can't. Leaving the party last night was one thing, but... leaving the palace is something else entirely. Mum would have a cow."

Rory sits back on her haunches and looks at me. I'm trying not to get distracted by her pert tits. "How old are you?" she asks.

"Twenty-four."

"Then the way I see it... your mother can't make you do anything."

"She *is* the queen of England."

"And you could be the future king of England." Her hand

slips over my chest. "What kind of king are you going to be? The kind of king that does whatever his mommy tells him… or the kind of king who takes what he wants?"

Her question weighs on me heavily. I've known for a long time that it's wrong to keep me here. That no good can come from being locked up like this. I don't want to disappoint my mum. I don't want to put her through more hurt after she's already been through so much. And yet…

Secretly, I know I've been itching for someone to take me away from all of this. And then there's Rory, my knight in ginger Goldilocks curls… how can I resist?

I kiss her, because her rosy lips look like they need to be kissed. She sighs and folds her naked body on top of mine.

"We're not sleeping at a hostel," I decide. "My family has a royal estate off the coast of Italy in Sorrento. Have you ever been?"

"No. But I'd love to." She's as excited as a schoolgirl now, and she clings to my shoulders. "So we're doing this?"

"We're doing this. And we're taking my private jet."

She gawks. "Your *what?*"

* * *

The RAF Airbus A330 is a hell of a way to travel.

The sleek, eggshell-white jet was originally built to fit nearly two hundred Normals, but it's since been renovated. Now it fits sixteen more-than-comfortable royals. It's equipped with a dining room, a bathroom and shower, and a king-size bed in back. Total unapologetic luxury.

It's a plane fit for a king. They call it the "Heircraft" for a reason.

Getting to the hangar was easy. I packed a duffle bag, threw on a large coat and a hat, and snuck out of my room with Rory and Ben at my side. Ben knows the schedules of every palace guard, when and where they'll be, so Rory and I hung back and giggled like naughty schoolkids while Ben stepped first around every corner before letting us know that the coast was clear. Truthfully, we probably could have walked right past them without an incident. I am, after all, the prince of England. The guards were never the thing keeping me back.

It's always been my mum. The fear of disappointing her. I left a letter for my mum in my room. Couldn't figure out what to say, so I simply wrote *I'm fine. I'm safe. Don't worry. Love you.* I signed my name at the bottom, folded the letter in half, and tented it on my pillow.

Now that we're at the hangar, it looks like a ghost town. The place is nearly empty, save for the impressive bird and a handful of very confused airline personnel. One wide-eyed man approaches us, bends at the waist, and then fumbles over apologies. "Your Highness. The queen didn't mention you were coming."

"Is it the queen's job to tell you everything?" I ask. You can get away with a lot with an air of lofty entitlement.

He murmurs another apology and then asks, "Your Highness… I must ask. Is this a matter of national security?"

I check his name tag. *Reginald.* Reginald is an older gentleman with a balding patch at the top of his head, and he's been waiting for nearly ten years for a royal to step through the hangar doors. By the look of him, maybe he's been waiting his whole life. This is his lucky day.

I put my hand on his shoulder. "I assure you, Reginald. It's a matter of life and death. How quickly can we get that bird in the air?"

Reginald's eyes look like they might pop out of their skull. He looks equal parts excited and terrified. A look of solemn duty sweeps over his face, and he says, "Right away, Your Highness."

"Good man." I reward him with a pat on the shoulder, and he immediately pops off to bark orders at his men.

Rory appears in his place. She's clutching the olive straps of her backpack and staring openmouthed at the jet. "Is that for us?"

Impressing her doesn't get old, I'll admit that. She's just so damn sweet about it, and I can't help but smile. "It is. Do you want to explore?"

Those are the magic words. She bites her lip and races up the short ladder. As soon as her flaming red hair vanishes into the plane, a boulder of anxiety that I've been keeping at bay rolls freely in my chest.

Ben stalls beside me, his eyes on the body of the jet. "Are you sure about this, sir?" he murmurs lowly so no one can hear him question the prince of England. He's holding me back like a stubborn dog pulling at its leash, its floppy ears scrunched around the taut collar. Ben has always been my conscience when I least want it.

"I'm sure," I say firmly and toss my bag over my shoulder.

I talk a big game, all right. But the second my foot hits the steps, my muscles go paralyzed. Suddenly, I can't climb the rest of the way. I can hear my mum's warnings, as clear as if she were whispering in my ear: *We're not like other people. Normals go to the pub, get a cuppa, or take a stroll without looking over their shoulder. We're not normal, dear. We're royals. And royals get killed.*

My heart abuses my rib cage with hard, thumping beats. A cold sweat breaks over the back of my neck. A sniper could be on me. On us. Right now. Any second, a bullet could rip through my forehead. Or a sniper could shoot us out of the sky. Like they shot my father down.

Through the haze of my thoughts, Rory's hand appears. She's offering it to me with a large smile plastered over her mouth. "Come on," she says excitedly. "The stewardess said they've got Cadbury chocolate in there. For free!"

She's like a child in a candy store, so full of innocence, so damned easy to please. Her enthusiasm rubs off on me. It's infectious, and my worry slides off my shoulders like a limp scarf.

"We can't keep that sweet tooth waiting," I tell her and take her hand. It's soft and warm, and her touch sends tingles through me. Rory needs me to be strong. *I can do this.* Linked hand in hand, we board the jet.

It smells strongly of mint in here, and it chills my sinuses. A stewardess with a plastic smile helps us with our bags and then offers a flute of champagne. I take it and tilt it to my lips. Bubbles burst and explode on my tongue. It's barely noon, but I need the liquid courage.

They're preparing the jet for takeoff, so I take my place in one of the plush white seats. The wide belly of the jet sits three across, and I instinctively take the middle. Ben would tell me it's because I need to be the center of attention at all times. Truthfully, I'm more insecure than that; it's a primal comfort to be pinned in on both sides. Is it possible to crave fresh-aired freedom and the tight security of a confining space simultaneously?

I try to breathe. Rory's fingers entwine in mine, and she squeezes.

Ben boards after both of us. When he takes his seat to my left, I notice that the front of his shirt is spotted with sweat as though he's been jogging. "Everyone's been vetted," he reports. "The personnel has been checked out. I did a loop around the hangar. There's no one for miles."

It's as though he's read my mind. As paranoid as I am, Ben is twofold, and I bloody love him for it.

Yet I feel inclined to rib him about it. "A bit of overkill, don't you think?"

He looks at me blankly. "You're safe."

Ben will go to the ends of the earth to protect Rory and me. That's all that matters.

The jets begin to roar, and the flight attendant announces that we're preparing for departure. My stomach clenches when the wheels roll forward.

Rory, on the other hand, squeals and keeps her eyes peeled out the window. "This is my favorite part."

Her thrill for adventure is charming. I finish off my glass of champagne, tilt my head back, and close my eyes. "Wake me up when we're there."

Cheerio, good old England.

23

RORY

Sorrento is a fairy-tale town on a cliff.

Brightly colored houses slope down the side of the hill and stop only when they reach the flat, blue-green waterline. Gulls call out overhead, and even from the top of the cliff I can still smell salt water in the air.

As soon as the jet touched down in Italy, a black car swallowed us up and swept us away toward the royal estate. We almost didn't stop here until I clambered over Roland's lap at the view and begged to be let out.

Worth it. It's breathtaking. We're perched on a platform overlooking the town, a stone wall separating us from the drop down below. There's nothing but thin, winding alleyways that hug the cliff and steep climbs between houses. Navigating this town is like playing a real-life game of Chutes and Ladders. It gives me vertigo to look down and see the roof of someone's house, and then the roof of the building below that, and below that one, but I can't tear my eyes away.

Roland folds his elbows on the stone wall and hunches over it. "Beautiful, isn't it?"

"It's incredible."

"I haven't been here in years. Since I was a boy." His irises seem to drink up the color of the sea, reflecting the Mediterranean aquamarine. He was pale on the plane, but now that we're back on solid ground, he seems reinvigorated in a way I haven't seen before. The sea breeze messes up his thick hair. Even his eyes have gotten brighter since we left the palace. They look longingly over the town when he says, "When I see something like this… it makes me wonder what else I've missed over the past ten years."

There's a small gap between our bodies, and I fill it to bump my shoulder against his. "Stop worrying about the past. Look where we are. Right now."

A grin warms his face. "I like this now."

"We have company," Ben says, and I look over my shoulder to see him standing behind us, his arms tightly crossed.

Sure enough, we're starting to attract attention. There's already a small crowd of ten or fifteen forming around the town car. They all have their phones out, cameras pointed at us. Most are calling out in Italian, words I don't understand, but I'm thrown when I hear my name.

"Principessa Rory!" A grinning, sun-tanned Italian waves at me.

I blink at Ben. "Are they… calling me a princess?"

"Yes," he says, unaffected as always.

"But I'm not. I'm… I mean… *not that.*" Now that I think of it, I don't know what to call myself. Am I Roland's girlfriend? Ben's girlfriend? Both? Neither? The redheaded tourist who got swept up in these two insatiable, love-starved men?

"Princess Rory." Roland sweeps his arm around my middle. "I like the sound of that."

He kisses me fully on the mouth. Because Prince Roland is shameless and never holds back. And me—the girl who should know better about falling for English royalty and making a display of herself in front of the entire world… I melt like butter on a hot day against his lips.

Ben interrupts us, the voice of sanity in our ears. "We need to get moving."

We make our way back to the car, but Roland pivots at the door.

"What's he doing?" Ben asks, and I can hear the note of fear in his voice.

"*Buona sera!*" Roland says to the crowd as he approaches them.

"Shit," Ben growls under his breath. He shuts the door hard and dashes after the prince. I follow after him, confused.

Everything seems perfectly fine to me. Roland is grinning ear to ear and shaking hands with every person there. He's speaking Italian—I don't know why that surprises me, but it does—and it pours from his lips melodically, fluently. I guess with all that time spent stuck in a house, I would learn a language or ten, too. I watch as he crouches down and plays a trick on a little girl that I don't need Babelfish to understand; he pulls a euro out of her ear and presents it to her. She giggles, delighted, and clutches it.

"Principessa Rory?" There's my name again, catching me off guard with the title. I turn and see a group of teenage girls. They're in summer hats and sarongs, and they're the kind of pretty, lithe girls who wouldn't have given me the time of day before, but now they're waving their phones at me. "*Possiamo…* ah… selfie?"

Selfie, yes. Everyone speaks selfie. I'm floored, but I nod and open my arms. "Yeah, of course!"

Their expressions light up, and they quickly flock around me. One of the girls holds her phone in front of us, and we all smile against the beautiful backdrop. They thank me in rapid Italian before scattering away like a startled flock of gulls.

When I glance at Roland, Ben is already at his side, hand on his arm, murmuring in Roland's ear. Roland nods and gives his last handshake and smile before he ushers me over and we go back to the car.

Ben looks visibly rattled when we pile back into the car. "So much for being inconspicuous," he huffs.

"If I'd wanted my mum here," Roland snaps, "I would've invited her."

The boys are having a tiff. Again. I let them work it out.

I have to admit, I didn't quite understand the gravity of being with a royal until now. The way people flock to Roland… that was expected. But me? I'm no one. I've been on my own for so long, I can't remember the last time someone told me what to do or where to be. Roland is chauffeured, kept at a distance, and gently coddled, as though he's a carton of eleven eggs and one unpinned grenade.

There's a nagging unease gnawing at my stomach as I turn my attention out the window. The coastal town whisks by, each house more colorful than the last, like seashells swept out with the tide.

* * *

UNSURPRISINGLY, the Pennington Estate is picturesque. The "Villa Leon d'Oro," as Roland corrected me, is styled to be part Moorish, part Venetian, which gives it a Gothic, old castle feel. It sits at the very edge of a sheer cliff face and looks like it could topple down at any moment. The villa remains sturdy, proud, and it's not until we get closer, winding up and down the curving cliff side, do I see the imperfections. The white paint has chipped and cracked, no doubt battered by the seaside storms. Bits of tree and foliage have overgrown around the sides, bursting out at odd angles. It strikes me then that Roland isn't the only one who hasn't been here in ten years—*no one* has so much as touched this place since the royal family tragedy.

The driver drops us outside the front. I come face-to-face with a black iron gate with a lion's head twisted in the metal, propped up between two white columns.

"Home sweet home," Roland says, his tone saccharine as he climbs out of the town car and shuts the door soundly behind him.

The lion imagery doesn't stop there. Once we're through the gate, I spot twin stone lions lounging on either side of the entrance. They're decrepit now, and one even seems to be missing an ear.

Roland scales the steps in twos, unlocks it, and throws open the double doors. Particles of dust blow upward when he drops his bags.

"It hasn't had any upkeep in a while," Roland adds as a side note. "So pardon the dust. Literally."

"I'll have a maid come by," Ben says, already on his phone.

"We can fix it ourselves," I murmur. "It just needs a little loving."

I step inside and look around in awe. The curtains are pulled as though the house is in mourning, and the sunlight from outside leaves bleary yellow splotches against the fabric. A white marble staircase winds up to the second floor. The den is a patchwork of old lounge chairs, landscape paintings, and antique vases. A beautiful decorative rug depicting Dionysus's followers hand-feeding him grapes from the vine takes up an entire wall.

There's something incredibly romantic about an extravagant villa abandoned by time. I can't help but fall in love with it.

"There's a pool outside, if my memory serves me right,"

Roland says. "I say we break open a bottle of limoncello and start there."

"Rory." I'm so into exploring the house that Ben's hand on my arm startles me. When I turn, he holds out a phone for me to take. "A gift for you. It's prepaid. From the palace. Perks of being a *principessa*."

I take the phone and turn it on. Already charged and everything. Leave Ben to think of every detail. "This is… a lifesaver. Thank you."

Ben adds with emphasis, "You can call anyone. Internationally."

Immediately, the realization hits. *Oscar.* I've emailed him back and forth, of course, but I haven't been able to speak to him in months. The thought of hearing his voice makes my throat nearly close up with emotion. I yelp and swing my arms around Ben's neck, yanking him down from his annoyingly tall frame to hug him. "Thank you, thank you!"

He grunts and gently peels me off before nodding to the sliding glass doors. "There's a closed patio out that way. You can get some privacy there."

I plant a noisy kiss to the side of his face and then bound off through the sliding doors. As promised, it opens up to a flat pool outlined with stones. The pool doesn't look as bad as the rest of the place, and I wonder if the locals haven't been dipping their toes in it while the royal family is away. Dead leaves cover the floor, and I crunch over them to get to the low, pale stone terrace.

Down below me, shimmering blue water crashes against the cliff. To my left, I can see the town of Sorrento tucked away. To my right, the sun starts to set.

I pull out my new phone and dial Oscar's number. It's one of the numbers I still know by heart. It takes a couple of rings, my heart pounding in my throat with each one, before I hear his voice.

"'Lo?"

It's him! I try not to scream with joy. My hand flies to my mouth to stifle my laugh. I give him our standard greeting: "Bonjovi, Otter."

There's a moment of hush from his end before he says, almost tentatively, "Ror? Holy shit—is that you?"

"Yeah… it's me." The Italian coastline shimmers in my vision as happy tears brim my eyes. "I miss you."

"Don't get all blubbery on me yet. Say something funny."

His voice sounds deeper than I remember it, but there's something else, too. He's a little raspy, and I can hear a low, rattling sound every time he breathes. I sniff. "What do you call an airplane that flies the prince of England?"

"What?"

"An *heircraft*."

"That's stupid. You're stupid."

"Your face is stupid."

Every insult is laced with an affectionate note. I know—he knows—what we're really saying. *I miss you. I love you. I needed this.*

"How are you doing?" I ask.

He sighs shallowly. "My least favorite question."

"I know, but… did they put you on the oxygen tanks yet?"

"Rory. You're calling from who-knows-where. I don't want to talk about tanks. Where are you?"

"Sorrento. It's this… little cliff town off of Italy. Here, I'll show you." I pull the phone away from my face, find the camera, and take a panorama of the view in front of me. Then I text it to Oscar and put the phone back to my ear. "You got it?"

A second later, I hear his phone buzz. And he whistles. "Damn. That's beautiful. Are you sure you're not in front of a green screen?"

I laugh. "Pretty sure. I'm at… uh. The prince's private

abode."

"So it is true."

"What do you mean?" I ask innocently.

He scoffs a laugh. "Did you think I didn't know? You're trending, Rory. Hashtag-Cinderella-Story. Hashtag-Princess-Rory. Hashtag-Red-Hair-Don't-Care."

I laugh and cover my eyes. "Oh God. Those are terrible."

"What's Prince Roland like up close?"

"Uh… honestly? He reminds me of you." I hear it and I wince. "Not in a weird way. Just… you're both so charming and silly and…"

"Annoying?"

"Lovingly annoying."

"Must be a charmed life. Being a kept woman in the palace."

"Uhm… it's amazing." I draw my fingers through my hair. "It's sort of… taken on a life of its own. I don't know if you'd believe me if I told you."

"I'd believe anything coming from you."

He's right about that. I could always talk to Oscar. I bite my lip and then come out with, "I'm sort of… dating two guys. The prince and his bodyguard."

"At the same time?"

"Yeah."

"Do they know about each other?"

"They're together, too. His bodyguard is wildly in love with him—I basically hooked them up—and now the three of us are a thing."

"Slut."

It catches me off guard, and I can't help but laugh. "Dick."

"Do they love you, Ror?"

That throws me off balance even more—he sounds sincere now, thoughtful. I cradle my phone to my ear and say, "Yeah… I think they do."

"Then make sure you're not just in it because it's easy."

I knit my eyebrows at that. "What do you mean?"

"You're always looking for an escape hatch, Ror. Just because they're into each other doesn't mean you can slip out quietly one day and no one will ever notice. If they love you like you say they do… then that's real. You've got to give it a chance."

His words sink into my bones. Somehow, Oscar always manages to see straight through me. He tells me what I need to hear. "I will," I tell him.

"Promise?"

"I promise."

"All right." He shifts gears. "You want to talk to Mom and Dad?"

"Yeah… sure."

Oscar wrangles our parents and puts them on speakerphone. Mom brags about how I'm blowing up on "the social media," and Dad wants to make sure I'm wearing enough sunscreen in Italy. I close my eyes and just listen to the murmurs of their voices for a while, their familiar inflections and loving quips at one another. This trip, my endless adventure around the world, March On… it all would've been easier if I hated my family. It would've been easier if I'd been raised with an evil stepmother and had only a few mice to call my friends.

But I love my family. I love my brother, above all. It's harder than anything to leave them. Times like these, I want to buy a plane ticket back and cut my trip short here and now.

Only I don't. I know what I'm doing is important. I know they're proud of me for doing it—especially Oscar. It takes all the strength in the world, but eventually I tell them, "Hey… I've gotta go. But I've got basically… unlimited minutes here, so I'll call you soon. Okay?"

"Love you, Ror!" comes the wave of voices from the other end of the phone.

"I love you, too," I say. "Love you lots."

It's almost too silent when I hang up the phone. I let out a deep sigh and listen to the waves crashing below, the gulls cawing ahead.

I will not cry, I will not cry.

I miss my family back home like crazy. It helps that I have a bizarre, crazy, loving little family back inside the villa. I didn't expect Roland and Ben to turn into something, but… here we are. And for the first time in years, I'm allowing myself to depend on these two voraciously loving men. Who knows? Maybe they can even be a permanent fixture in my life. It's been so long since I've had something that lasts… This feels scary, new, and exciting all at once. Like how I felt when I bought my plane ticket out of Michigan with barely enough money in my pocket, a stuffed otter in my bag, a little spunk, and a lot of determination.

I need to distract myself from the emotions rattling around in my chest, so I click through my phone to visit my March On site. Even though I've been neglecting it as of late, it's gotten an insane amount of hits since I last signed in. Apparently, my little unofficial sex tape with the prince of England has made my site go viral. Whodathunk? The good news is that my donation meter for the Cystic Fibrosis Foundation is higher than ever. If accidentally showing off my blowjob skills to thousands of VidO viewers is what it takes to find a cure… then a girl's gotta do what a girl's gotta do.

All the same. My page is littered with comments. Some are supportive, but there's my fair share of anonymous hate in there as well. It's time to take my narrative back.

I turn the camera on myself, smile, and hit Record. "Hello and March On!"

BEN

*T*he limoncello is important.

I knew it would be the first thing Roland asked for once we got back to his place. The sour, tangy lemon liqueur is strong enough to knock even the prince off his feet, and it's nearly impossible to find quality limoncello outside of Southern Italy. I knew there wouldn't be any at Villa Leon d'Oro, and if there were, it would've spoiled by now. So I rang the driver up before we left England and told him to have a bottle waiting for us. I have the paper bag in hand now, and when I take the bottle out of the bag and set it on the kitchen counter, it's still cold. Condensation leaks between my fingers and onto the azure-blue countertop tiles.

Details. The devil is in the details, and one of us has to pay attention to them.

It won't be Rory, who is as excitable as a terrier, and it won't be impulsive, spontaneous Roland, who decides at the spur of the moment to announce to all of Italy that he's here.

So much for discretion. The best-laid plans of mice and bodyguards.

I twist the metal around the neck of the bottle and the cap

pops open. I hunt around the cabinets until I find two glasses and rinse them out carefully.

"Aren't you having any?" Roland pops in beside me as I pour the yellow liquid into one of the small glasses.

"No."

I don't look at him; I just continue to pour.

Roland laughs, an airy, bitter sound. "Are you giving me the silent treatment now?"

"Only teenagers and princes give the silent treatment."

That makes his lips twist in a scowl. The prince takes a glass, tilts it to his mouth, and sips. "You've been a right prat since we got here," he comments.

I look up at him. "If it takes being a prat to keep you safe, then I'll accept that title."

I expect him to come at me with some snarky remark, but instead he stands there and stares at me. The thoughtful way he's looking at me… it makes the hair on the back of my neck stand on end. I don't like not knowing what's going on inside that head of his.

"It occurs to me," Roland postures, like a doctor giving a diagnosis, "that you may be a control freak."

I squint at him. Where is he going with this? "If either of you try to tie me up, I'll break your nose," I warn him.

"I'll drink to that, 007."

Roland finishes his glass in one fell swoop before setting it down with a clink on the counter. Then he steps behind me and corners me against the counter, his front to my back. I feel him reach around and flick open my gun holster. He takes my gun out and sets it down on the kitchen counter.

"What are you doing?" I growl. My words are husky with equal measures of lust and panic.

"Everyone is having a good time except you," Roland says. His hot breath beats against my throat. "Get off the bloody clock for once."

All at once, his hand is between my legs. I suck in a sharp breath. He's cupping my groin, fondling me. And dammit if I don't get instantly hard for him.

All the prince has to do is so much as look my way and I'm ready to burst. Like a fucking virgin. Only now he's fondling me, rubbing his palm over my length. It's embarrassing how quickly I get painfully erect, even though there's still a tent of fabric separating us. I grip the sides of the counter, and the blue tile gets slippery under my fingertips. "Fuck," I moan.

My zipper hisses open and frees some room. Boldly, Roland's fingers slip under the waistband of my briefs and wrap around my needy organ. The way he touches me… it's familiar. As though his hands were made for my dick. He's slow to start and holds me first, all five fingers wrapped around.

It has to be his first time touching another man's cock. Has to be. I've been there. I was a teenager the first time I touched another man. He was a fellow dockhand, and we jerked each other off in an expensive old schooner that didn't belong to either of us. I remember the fumbling touches. The frantic gasps. Biting back sex sounds as the tethered boat pitched side to side in the stormy waters.

I'm not a kid anymore. I'm a man, in an estate worth ten times my life savings. Roland is different, too. He's curious. Each touch is purposeful, exploring. His fingers slip up and down my cock, and I feel them tracing the ridges of my veins. When he draws a circle around my ultrasensitive head, I inhale with a sharp hiss. He doesn't pull away. Instead, he slows but continues to fondle the tip of me, painting me with my own precum.

Fuck. He's testing my limits. I know because that's exactly what *I* do. I learn a body. Find its weaknesses. Push them. I'm not used to being on this end… and I'm not complaining. I grit my teeth and brace myself as agonizing pleasure shudders through me.

"The way you kissed me last night"—Roland's breath feels hot on my throat when he speaks—"that was something."

"Was it?" My mind is swimming.

"You kissed me like you'd been waiting to do that."

"I have," I blurt out. He's sliding my cock through his fingers in long, slow pulls, and it's making me fucking idiotic.

"For how long?"

Since the first time I laid eyes on you. My pride only lets me choke out, "A long time."

"Why didn't you say anything?"

Now it's like a vice is wrapped around my throat. His body is warm at my back, though, and his hand continues to stroke. Encouraging.

"I couldn't."

"Because I'm the prince of England?"

"Because you're my best mate."

He lets out a soft noise, like a sigh in my ear, and it makes my heart pound. When he shifts forward, I can feel his hard bulge press against my rear. "I'd say we're a bit more than mates now, don't you think?" Roland says.

"What does that make you… my boyfriend?" I'm throwing darts at the wall and hoping they hit.

To my relief, he breathes a single word in my ear, "Yes. And you're mine."

I can't tell what he means by that—does *you're mine* mean *you're my boyfriend* or *you belong to me*? Maybe both.

I top. I always top. But here, with Roland's hand around my prick and his shaft against my rear, I just might make an exception. I shift back, brushing against his erection, and it makes my lion purr.

In his explorations, he finds a golden spot under my

bulbous head. My hips jerk forward, and I feel my cock flex in his hand.

"Do you like that?" he murmurs, his ministrations unceasing.

I'm breathless. My face burns. "Yes."

"If I keep stroking you right here, will it make you blow?"

"*Yes*," I gasp urgently.

He kisses my throat, and I feel his smile. "Good. I want you to lose control. Just for me. Come on, Ben." He jerks me quickly now, his thumb rubbing tiny circles *right fucking there*. "Give me everything you've got."

Normally, I'm quiet as a bloody church mouse when I reach my peak. Now? I howl. I explode in his hand. I'm a throbbing, leaking, panting mess.

Roland presses a single, firm kiss to the back of my neck, where my skull meets my spine. I shiver. It grounds me. "You came all over my hand," he observes.

"Yeah," I pant. *No shit.* I want to say something sarcastic or snippy to distance myself from the situation, but my tongue is glued to the roof of my mouth. Instead, I come out with, genuinely, "You have that effect on me." My defenses are thin. Everything is exposed, raw. My pulse is beating in the palm of his hand. For once, I'm not rushing off to recover my composure. I'm safe here. I let myself unravel.

The sound of the sliding glass doors breaks me out of my dream state. "It is sooo beautiful out there," Rory chirps. As soon as she spots us tangled up, however, her feet come to a quick stop.

Shit. I straighten up and tuck myself back into my pants. Should we have done that without her? What are the rules? I'm so fucking out of my element; I need a bloody guidebook to navigate these waters.

"Should I come back in later?" Rory asks.

Without any sense of haste or urgency, Roland unwinds

from me. "Ben, I told you not to leave the door open," he says. "We've got a little ginger stray." With that, Roland crouches down and makes little whistling, clicking noises. "Here, kitty, kitty," he coos, extending his hand toward her.

Leave it to Roland to find the most bizarre ways to include Rory. Effortlessly, he turns an awkward situation into a game.

And leave it to Rory to play along. Without batting an eye, she gets down on her knees, and begins to crawl over to us.

She meows when she reaches Roland and nuzzles her head against his thigh. Say what you will about Rory, but she goes all out. I find myself watching, mesmerized, as he pets her hair.

"Does kitten want cream?" Roland asks and shows her his hand, glistening with my cum.

Rory sits down in front of him, and her green eyes go wide. She licks her lips and mewls.

Roland offers his hand. Rory licks him clean bit by bit, her pink tongue lapping over each finger. "Good girl," Roland praises.

Bloody hell. Even with my orgasm only moments ago, the sight of them makes my organ stir to life again. I want seconds. I want her to lick my cock the way she's licking his hand.

Normally, I have better control over myself. Rory and Roland have unleashed a beast.

Once Rory has licked every drop, Roland takes her chin and rewards her with a kiss. "Thank Ben for your treat, pet," Roland commands.

Rory crawls over, sits at my feet, and looks up at me. She's submissive now, a role she falls into so easily, but still so bright and bold. Those green eyes meet mine, and she says, "Thank you for my cream, sir."

Goddamn. It's enough to make *me* purr. I lower myself so

I'm level with her. "Good girl," I say and kiss her. She sighs into my mouth. She tastes like me, and the warmth of her tongue sends pleasure sparking through my blood.

My hand slips inside her jeans, and she spreads her knees, wanting.

"Let's take this outside," Roland announces just as my thumb grazes her knickers. "And bring the limoncello."

ROLAND

*R*ory was right. It's a beautiful night.

At Helmsway Palace, I wear the crown. Here, watching the sun dip behind the cliffs with a bottle of Italy's best dangling from my fingers, wedged between two people who love me and who I love, I've never felt more like a royal.

The sun burns the sky red, yellow, then orange, its rays leaking across the oceanfront. It's been a decade since I could see the sun set without the foliage of Helmsway's garden poking out from underneath. I feel as though I'm watching it for the first time.

The estate has really taken a beating with years of disuse. None of us dare to dip a toe in the pool, but it's enough to drink and watch the skyline. Feels like forever since I've seen so much sky. The patio is decorated with an assortment of Greco-Roman columns, marble statues, and wide-hipped vases so overrun with vines that they look like leafy fountains. There's plenty of room out here, but the three of us fit snugly on a single chaise, Rory sitting half on my lap, half on Ben's.

What do the Italians call this? *Paradiso.*

"So this is what it's like to be royal, huh?" Rory breaks the comfortable silence. "I could get used to this."

A laugh puffs out of my chest with a *huh* sound. "I'm sure you could." I take a sip from the communal limoncello bottle and then pass it over to her. "There was a time when I'd have given anything to be a Normal."

"We're pretty far from normal," Ben states. The sunset spits flecks of fire into his dark irises, his eyes trained on the horizon. He's a beautiful man. Beautiful in the way a raven is beautiful—sharp, dangerous, and sleek. Strange how I never noticed it before, but now I can't stop sneaking glances at him. I wonder what he's looking for out there. A sniper in the distance, perhaps.

Rory's small body shifts in my lap so she can nudge Ben's bare foot with hers. "What about you? Did you ever want to be a prince?"

A small, bitter smile lifts the edge of Ben's mouth and shows off a glint of teeth. "I wanted to be anything but a Limehouse boy."

"What's so bad about Limehouse?" Rory asks.

"D'ay awll talk like dis, aye, mate?" I rib him, laying on a thick Cockney accent.

Ben grimaces. "Your Cockney is shit."

"Aw, I like it!" Rory says. "Why'd you get rid of it?"

Ben lapses into silence for a moment. It used to irritate me when he would take forever to form a single sentence, but now I've grown to like watching him think. You can see the wheels turning in his head as he hunts for just the right word. "When I came back from my tour... it took me a while to find employment," he says. "The palace was my last shot. I knew they weren't going to take in a dirty, desperate Cockney kid. So I had to improvise. I had a... friend from up North. He helped me practice his accent, and I used it in the interview. They hired me on the spot."

I've never heard this story. I blink with surprise. "You weren't afraid they'd see right through you?"

"I was terrified," he said. "But it was that or go back to Limehouse and become a fisherman or a pickpocket. So I took the risk."

I hand him the bottle of limoncello. He's earned this. "You have stones, mate," I tell him.

A grin flickers over his mouth. He takes the praise and the limoncello.

"Do your parents still live there?" Rory asks.

Ben shakes his head. "I sent them my paycheck every month until they had enough to get out. They have a flat in Shoreditch now."

A stitch of pain tightens in my chest. *I don't know anything about Ben.* Six bloody years he's been my shadow, working side by side with me, and he never told me about his family. I would've bought them a flat. Given them money. Invited them over for tea. I feel a wave of nostalgia wash over me, as tangible as the salty ocean breeze that blows over the railing to kiss my face intermediately. I suddenly long for all the millions of moments I've missed out on because I never bothered to ask.

It's always been about me, me, *me*, hasn't it? The bloody prince of England prancing around in his invisible clothes.

"You could've asked me for help," I tell Ben. "You always can."

"No," he says firmly, "I couldn't. It wouldn't have felt right. It was something I had to do on my own."

"To hell with doing everything on your own." I don't mean for it, but I can feel my throat tightening, the frustration seeping out. I gesture jerkily between myself and Rory. "You have not one, but *two* people who love you to pieces. Accept that. That's an order."

There I go. The spoiled prince, losing his temper. Getting

what he wants at all cost. Ben has set the bottle of limoncello on the stone floor, and I swipe it up and take a swallow from it. I mean to wash down my intolerable pride, but even the limoncello tastes too sweet suddenly and the citrus coats my throat.

Ben says nothing in response. He distractedly picks at a loose thread on the knee of his trousers. There. I've successfully gone and ruined our peaceful pool time. The worst part is, I can't stop it. Even the stitching on his bloody trousers is coming apart, and he won't ask for a single cent of help. It makes me furious.

Rory isn't any better—no. She's worse, her clothes ripped to pieces. But there's something charming about Rory's disarray. She wears it like a badge of honor. Ben wears it with shame. But I can't tell him that or he'll snap at me, so I slip a hand down Rory's thigh instead. I hold her leg and rub my thumb over the open threads fraying across her knee.

"We have to get you new trousers," I tell her.

"Why?" she says, and there's that bright smile that melts me. "I like these. They're comfortable."

"And covered in holes."

"They're breeze holes." Rory grins.

"I believe that's what they make skirts for."

"Quit picking on her," Ben growls. He's on edge. He sees right through me.

"I'm not. I'm giving her what she wants."

"You have no idea what she wants."

"Maybe because she never tells me."

"Are we still talking about me?" Rory chirps, confused. "Because I'm an open book…"

"No, we're not talking about you," I snap. "Ben is being a twat."

Now, he turns to stone. "I am what you want me to be, sir."

"Sod off with that," I snarl. Rory shifts in place, no doubt uncomfortable. She's literally caught in the middle of us. "You only show me what you want me to see. *Yes*, I've been a selfish prat. But you hide from me. You're as complicit in this as I am."

Ben's jaw looks so tight, his teeth might snap. He won't look at me, his eyes fixed on the horizon. "You never asked."

"I'm asking now. What do you *want*, mate?"

"I want you to quit calling me *mate* for one."

"What do you want, *Ben*?"

"I want you!" His confession spills out from him exasperated, strained. "I've always wanted you."

"You have me! And Rory. Are you so used to having nothing you can't recognize when you have everything?"

Ben lifts Rory and drops her solidly in my lap (she squeaks like a dog toy). He pushes off the chaise and launches to his feet. "I'm going inside," he announces.

"What's up his arse?" I scoff.

Rory's lips twist downward. She climbs off me and gets up to her feet. "I'll be back," she says.

Just like that, everyone's abandoning ship. I feel like I've swallowed a rotten apple whole and now it's rolling uncomfortable around in my stomach. I mask my discomfort with a sneer and shake the limoncello. "Fine. More for me."

Yes. Everything for me. Ben is gone, Rory is gone, and I'm the all-powerful king of no one. I lick my wounds and sip sweet liquor.

RORY

The glass door hisses when I slide it shut behind me. Ben is pacing, but he stops to look up at me. He has a cigarette pinned between two fingers, unlit, as though he meant to smoke it but couldn't bring himself to go back outside and face Roland again. When his eyes find me, the line of his mouth thins. He lowers his tall limbs into a white leather chair.

I sit down beside him. I don't say anything.

"We'll have to go back to the palace soon," Ben says. He flicks his cigarette distractedly. "The queen has no doubt noticed we're gone by now."

"Is that what you're worried about?" I ask him. "Going back?"

Those dark eyes meet mine. "You know this won't last. We don't fit in with his royal life."

It's something I don't want to think about, something I've been ignoring, but once he says it, I feel a swift reality check punch to the gut. We're have our own slice of poly-paradise here in Italy, but once we go back to Helmsway Palace? What will it look like then?

"You don't know that," I say.

"Yes. I do. And I can live with that," Ben continues. "I don't need spotlight or fanfare. But Roland… his mother has him wrapped around her finger even now."

"He came here. With us. Even though he knew she wouldn't approve. That's a start."

"I've wanted this for a long time. Now that I have it… I'm terrified of losing it."

Every muscle in Ben's body is tensed. He's in fight-or-flight mode. I set my hand on his thigh. I need to bring him back down to earth with me. "You *will* lose it if you keep yourself locked away. Do you remember what I said the first time we met?"

He looks at me blankly. "You told me muskrats were going to attack the palace."

I laugh. "Yes. That. I also told you that your smile turned me on."

There it is. That warm smile nudging the edges of his lips. It cracks his stiff demeanor and softens his edges. "How do you do that?" he asks. His tone is quieter now that the crisp panic has flown from it.

"Do what?"

"You're so… open. Effortlessly."

"I guess… ever since I was little, I realized life is too short to pretend. It's better to die regretting the things you've done than the regretting all things you were too afraid to do. You have to take what you want while you can."

"What do you want?"

The cigarette has stilled between his fingers. His strength has returned to him, and I feel it. He's looming and the look in his eyes is the same look he gives me when he tells me to get on my knees. He's in control, and it's hot. My mouth waters with want, and I swallow before I speak.

"Honestly… I miss my family. But being with you two…

for the first time since I left home, I feel like I'm part of something."

"You are. You're our beating heart."

"If I'm the beating heart and you're the overthinking brain, then Roland is…?"

"The stubborn prick?"

A chuckle vibrates from my chest. "Roland is… so out of his depth right now. This is the first time he's left home in years. I remember how terrifying it was to take that first step. Believe me… it's not easy. I think we should probably support him right now."

"Agreed."

Ben takes out his pack, tucks the unused cigarette back inside, and pockets it once more. He's in steely control again. And—jeez. I love watching him like this. He walks with the confidence of an alpha, a pack leader, and I just want to feel his fist in my hair and his teeth in my skin. Is that so much to ask for?

I must be ogling, because Ben shoots me a strange look. "Are you coming?"

"Right. Yes." I scramble to my feet and salute him. "Aye, aye. Right behind you, sir."

"*Sir*. I could get used to that."

I don't know if it's the way his smile slices across his mouth or his easy dominance that makes me so aroused, because I'm suddenly soaked. I let out a quick breath and bounce outside behind Ben.

When we step back outside, Roland is just where I left him—sprawled out on his chaise, one knee popped up lazily, the other bare foot hanging off the edge, and the nearly empty bottle beside him. He's staring out at the sunset pensively, but he turns his head our way when the door hisses. The fading light bounces off his blond hair and halos his head. *God*. He's positively ethereal.

"The rebels have returned. With no guillotine? I'm disappointed."

"No guillotine." I plop down on Roland's chaise and squeeze in beside him.

Ben unfolds his long legs on the lounge chair. "You were right," he says as he stares off at the tail end of the sunset.

"Oh?" Roland's interest is clearly piqued.

"I need new trousers."

Roland scoffs. "You look great. They're just bloody trousers."

It's the closest thing to an apology these two will get. I almost roll my eyes. *Men are so stubborn.* But then Roland continues.

"I'm the outdated prat," Roland says and holds out a hand. "Pocketknife."

Ben gives him a strange look. Then he reaches into his pocket, pulls out a switchblade, and hands it to me. I drop it into Roland's waiting palm.

"Cheers." Roland flips the blade out with his thumbnail. Then he presses the blade against his knee. I almost tear it away from him, but he doesn't dig in deep enough to reach skin. He's ripped a shallow slash in the fabric, revealing his leg underneath. The cut is too clean, and the split threads don't fray, so he saws a large, gaping hole into his pants. Then he puts the blade back, hands it off to me, and shows off his bared knee. "There," he announces. "Now I'm part of the club."

I swallow back a lump in my throat. I'm touched by Roland's gesture of solidarity. He probably has hundreds of pants to choose from—heck, he probably has Amazon Royal Prime and can get the exact same pair of pants that day. But the fact that he even thought to tear up his clothes to stand with us instead of towering over us... well. I can't remember the last time I had a man who was willing to go to the ends of the earth to make me comfortable.

Ben's touched, too. I can see the small flicker of emotion cross his face, like a spot of sunshine of a cloudy day. Ben shows his own brand of gratitude, however, when he says simply, "If we're ripping clothes, why stop there?"

Roland's teeth glint when he smiles. "What'd you have in mind?"

Ben slides off the chair. He stalks over in front of us and holds up his hand. "My knife."

Roland hands the pocketknife back to Ben. He flicks it open, grabs Roland by the front of his shirt, and hovers the blade over the collar.

"How much did this shirt cost?" Ben asks.

"Six hundred pounds," Roland replies.

Ben makes a noise that's not quite a laugh, as though astounded by the sheer lavishness of Roland's lifestyle. "You have no concept of money, do you?"

"Not in the slightest." Now Roland has that fire in his eyes, that look that goes straight between my thighs. "Rip it."

Ben uses the pocketknife to saw through Roland's neckline, but the pocketknife is pretty dull. He doesn't get far before he drops it on the chaise, grabs either side of Roland's shirt, and rips. The fabric tears like paper under his grip, satin fluttering on either side of Roland, revealing his sleek, muscle-hard chest and stomach.

Holy hell. My clit is pounding a drumbeat against my panties. The boys are turned on, too. I can tell. The intensity in Ben's dark eyes, the noticeable rise and fall of Roland's chest. I've started to read their signs well enough to sense when there's a shift in the air. It buzzes around us like an electric static that everyone can feel.

"This isn't going to cut easily," Ben hooks a finger over the hem of Roland's pants, plucking it like a guitar string.

"Right." Roland fumbles to get his belt off and then his pants. Now, he's in nothing but a ripped shirt and his briefs. I'm happy to report that it's a *damn* good look on him. My fingers twitch with the sudden urge to feel his skin.

"I want a turn," I say and hold up my palm.

"Be my guest."

I put the knife between my teeth to adjust my position and straddle Roland. Pocketknife in hand now, I tell him, "Stripping the prince of England. How many women get to say they've done that?"

"Just be careful where you aim that thing," he says, pointing at the blade. "These are royal goods."

I can see the headlines now: "Kinky American Cuts Off Prince's Cock." That's not happening. I snort a laugh and say, "Yes, Your Highness."

"Furthermore," Roland continues, "I won't be the only half-dressed one."

With that, he hooks his fingers under the hem of my shirt. "May I?" He's the prince of England, he can have anything he wants, and yet with me, he asks for consent. Honestly, it's a turn-on. Buzzing, I nod and lift my arms. He pulls my shirt over my head, and it flutters in a pile of fabric beside us. I then adjust to shove my pants off and toss them to the side.

"Much better," Roland states, his eyes feasting on my chest. "Continue."

I bite my lip, lift the elasticity of his briefs, and make a nick in the waistband. The fabric frays and splits under the edge of my blade. It's not as clean of a cut as Ben's; my line is jagged and zigzags all the way down. It occurs to me then that he really is incredibly trusting of me to allow me this close to his junk with the switchblade. When I glance up at his dazzling blues, there's nothing but his boyish humor and warmth.

"Don't get distracted now," he says. There's a second pair

of hands on me—Ben's strong, calloused grip—and those rough fingers delicately roll my bra straps down my arms. I shudder when his soft lips hit my bared shoulder.

My bra topples. Roland cups my bare breast, and his thumb grazes my nipple. It hardens immediately under his touch and lights my nerves on fire.

I quickly retract the blade, afraid I'll slip and nick Roland's thigh. A breathy laugh bursts from my chest. "Not fair."

"Focus." That growl is all Ben, and he bunches my hair up in a tight fist. The strain on my skull recenters me. I cut down the second leg of his briefs as Roland flicks my nipples and Ben's lips trace my throat. My boys aren't making this easy on me, and my body hums for them. I'm almost done, though, when I see how aroused Roland is. His white briefs barely cover his half-hard shaft, and the fleshy tip pokes out from the ruined cotton. I'm thirsty for him and the sight of him draws a low throb from between my legs.

I'm shaky with need. My hand twitches and I gasp when I see a small, crimson nick on Roland's inner thigh. "Oh, shit." I drop the offending pocketknife. "I'm so sorry."

I don't know what I thought would happen, but the thought comes to me—so he *is* human, he does bleed. He's so godlike, so untouchable, that it's striking to see him bleed the same blood as the rest of us mere Normals.

"Leave it," Roland says. There's this new look in his eyes, a near-feral glow. The orange sunset bounces off his irises, giving him that purple hue. He tugs my head down so my lips meet his and kisses me roughly. The hunger in his lips... oh my God. It turns me on. There's nothing practiced or proper about my animal prince. It takes less than nothing to rip his briefs from him, and now he's completely naked underneath me. I straddle him, arms and legs tight around him, and sigh into his kiss. The nighttime sea breeze is cool on my bare skin, but his body is furnace hot, and I leave no space between us.

"I need you inside of me," I whisper. His organ is stiff on my stomach, and it's killing me to have his perfect manhood so close and yet so far.

"I'm crazy for you." His breath hits my lips.

Ben's hands find my hips. "Let's get rid of these," he says. Then I feel it, the blade press against my thigh. The sting makes me freeze. My breath gets stuck in my throat when Ben tickles my thigh with the very tip of it. I feel tension on my panties when the blade catches on the side and then a sudden release when it snaps.

Oh hell. That shouldn't be as hot as it is, but it sends a flood of warmth through my middle. My heart pounds furiously in my chest as he goes for the other side. Again, the blade at my thigh, a snip—and that's all it takes. Ben grabs the useless fabric and yanks it from between my legs so I'm bare. The soft cotton tickles my feminine folds on its way out.

The sensation of them snipping my clothes away until I'm completely naked and vulnerable in front of them… it's a rush. My head spins. Roland reaches over the chaise to grab his pants and pulls a condom out. He unpacks it, rolls it over his hard length, and then guides his cock inside of me. I moan. Ben kisses and fondles me from behind. My crimson patch of hair meets Roland's chestnut curls as he fills me completely. Ben claims my throat with his lips and grips my hips, guiding my pace as I ride the prince. I hook one arm behind me around Ben's neck and plant another hand on Roland's chest.

I have a prince underneath me and a bodyguard literally guarding my back. When did this become my life? It feels so unreal… and yet so right.

Roland has his tongue down my throat when I hear Ben

spit. I feel Ben cup my rear and press a saliva-lubed finger... *there*. He just holds it against my asshole and then murmurs in my ear, "Is this okay?"

It's hard to think, let alone speak. I'm lust-drunk. But I manage to nod and murmur, "Yes... that's good."

Ben's teeth make little dents in my neck, and he rubs circles against my secret place. Then he probes inside and—oh. With Roland's thick organ penetrating me and now Ben's finger, I whimper. It feels amazing in a way I never expected. He's scratching an itch I didn't even know I had, and now, with the both of them exploring me, my pleasure spikes. I feel dirty. So dirty. So filthy and used and... *theirs*. Completely theirs.

Ben crooks his finger in a way that I can *feel* him petting the thin membrane between his finger and Roland's cock, and it nearly does me in. I'm sweating now, overheating and on edge, but I need more to push me over. I'm not normally this kind of girl. I'm not normally this kinky, this desperate, this greedy. But these two men send me to places I never dared to go before, not in my wildest fantasies. Finally, I can't hold back.

"I want the both of you in me," I beg. "Please."

Ben rewards me with a kiss to the side of my face. I melt into it before he pulls back, finger and all.

"Stay," he says.

It's an easy command to follow. As Ben pulls away, I lean forward against Roland. His body is hot, his arms cradle me, and his shaft hits me deeper than ever in this position.

"I want to consume you," Roland purrs, his voice like velvet on my skin.

"Lucky for you, I want to be consumed." I grin against his mouth.

Our tongues meet, warm and wet. I run his silky hair through my fingers. I love that this strong, powerful man lets me set my own pace over him, grinding against him so I can keep him in, deep, deep, deep. A gull caws in the distance, the waves lap against the cliffs below, lulled by the swollen moon slowly on the rise, and I steal deep, dark kisses from my British prince. I don't want to leave his arms, not ever.

Ben is back—I only know because his fingertips run feather-like down my spine and make me shudder. He maps the small of my back, between my round cheeks, and manipulates my little hole again. I know what's coming next, and the thought makes me throb around Roland's manhood.

Ben takes his hand away briefly, and when he replaces it, his finger is gooey with lube. Now he slides a finger inside me easily and then inserts a second. He's testing my limits, stretching me. I push back into his hand. I can't get enough.

"Are you sure you want this?" Ben murmurs in my ear.

I want this. God, I want this so badly, I can taste it. I want to be part of them. I want them to be part of me.

"Please," I whimper. "I want you. All of you."

Ben's fingers slip away from me, and I push my hips forward against Roland to make up for the absence. But then I feel Ben press against my tight hole… and he feels so big here, so, so big. I clench at first, uncertain that I can take him all. But my body wants him, craves him, and slowly, inch by inch, he eases his monster instead of me. I gasp loudly and arch back.

"Is that okay?" Ben asks as he cups my head. I feel droopy and limp in these men's arms.

"Yes…" I moan. "It's… so good. I can feel you. Both of you."

It feels so bizarre at first. It should be impossible to feel this full, full of them, full of love, filled to the brim. They shower me with affection, using their lips, their hands, and I lose track of who is touching me where. All I know is my skin is on fire and I've never been more aroused in my life.

They're moving in tandem, like a wave, and I'm sucked into the riptide of their bodies. They moan, growl, suck my skin hungrily, and touch me reverently. I'm their pet, their toy, and their princess.

All thoughts have fled. Any other day, I'd be plagued by homesick thoughts, guilt, distraction, fear—a swath of conflicting emotions battering around my head. Here, trapped between these two British alphas, my mind goes blissfully blank.

Their love for each other is palpable. And then there's me. The glue. The beating heart between two lungs. Here, in sync, we're perfect and unstoppable. Even our hearts beat together—one tangled being.

"You're beautiful," Roland whispers in a breathless mantra. "Beautiful, beautiful…"

"I can't hold back," I breathe. My voice feels tight in my throat.

"Then don't," Ben demands. "Cum for us, pet."

My orgasm explodes from me. My throat is nearly pinched shut, and I only get out a strained whimper and a series of, "Oh God, oh God, oh God…" I'm pulsing around them, both of them, as their hard members thrust inside of me, milking every throb from me. They release too, together, it seems; Roland tosses his head back with a shout, and Ben bites my shoulder and groans there. I can feel them dripping in me, out of me, and my greedy body continues to throb, holding them inside of me. My skin is so hot, but my throat has finally opened up and I pant for breath, dizzy with satisfaction.

"I love you," Roland says in a reverent moan, "I love you, I love you."

"I love you, too," I whisper.

"I love you both," Ben murmurs last.

I know this is the part where sparks are supposed to go

off—we did it! We said those three magic words for the first time… all three of us! But it feels so natural, just like having them inside of me feels so natural, and there's a warm, satisfying comfort about the romantic nothingness of the proclamation. We were just *meant to be.*

We crumple together, one lazy mess of bodies on the chaise. We're dirty, I'm covered in their fluids, but I can't move. My muscles have dissolved, and my bones are rubbery and useless. Ben kisses my back, my hips, and Roland covers my face with his lips. I bliss out from my two affectionate, dominating men.

Staring at Roland, his blue eyes vibrant, I realize just how vastly different my relationship with these two men is. Roland is fire and passion. It's impossible not to fall crazy, deeply in love with him. Ben is a slow burn. He's the calm in the middle of the storm and anchors me to the ground. Together, they balance me out. It's weird, but it doesn't even feel like I'm in two different relationships. They make one complete boyfriend—my yin and yang boys.

Could this be my life?

For the first time in a long, long time, I don't want to be anywhere else.

"How are you?" Roland asks, stroking my hair from my face.

"Good," I tell him. I must look crazy, my hair all over the place, eyes half-lidded. "Really, really good."

I giggle. I can't help it. My endorphins are in overdrive.

"That was the best sex I've ever had," Ben states. "Hands down."

"Same," Roland sighs. "We should do that every day."

"I'm not sure my body could take it," I chuckle. What is wrong with me? I've come down with a fit of the giggles. Everything seems incredibly funny right now.

"Ben will take middle next time," Roland says. "Won't you, mate?"

Ben huffs audibly, and I bark a laugh.

We catch our breath, and the men extract their softening organs from me. My body feels empty now, so I cuddle in close and soon the three of us are snuggled up, a pile of limbs.

"Hell," Ben says after a long lapse of comfortable silence. "I wish we could use the pool."

"That would require getting up." Roland opens his mouth in a lion's yawn. "And I'm in no state."

"I'll test it." I feel invigorated with my second wind. I clamber over their naked bodies and off the chaise. Even under the black blanket of night, the stone floor retains the sun's warmth under my bare feet. I walk over to the edge of the pool and dip my toe in.

It's nice. Not too warm, not too cool. Minus some leaves floating around, it's really not that bad.

"Verdict?" Ben asks.

I turn and wink at them. "Pussies."

I jump into the refreshing water with a splash. One after the other, they pile in after me.

"My sister in white. Whodathunk?"

I turn from the oval mirror, and my wedding dress flutters around me. My brother sits behind me. His tall, stick-thin body has been fitted into a handsome tuxedo suit. There's a white flower pinned to the arm of his wheelchair. He looks great.

I beam and lift the hem of my dress in a faux curtsy. "What do you think? Too much?"

"Definitely." He nods, his messy ginger hair flopping

around his ears. "But it's your wedding day. You're allowed to be too much. Speaking of."

He nods to my hand.

"What, this?" I ask innocently. I show off my hand. Two matching engagement rings are stacked together on my ring finger. One diamond for each of my fiancés. I'm the luckiest girl alive.

"*That*," Oscar shakes his head. "They spoil you."

We're in a room that I've decided is my bedroom, though it looks nothing like my old room at my parents' place. But my dream logic takes over. White, wooden-paneled walls line the space, and a window nook fills the place with bright light.

"Are you sure you're ready for this?" Oscar asks. He has my sea-green eyes, always questioning.

"Yes," I tell him. "No more running. No more hiding. This is the life I want."

"I'm just glad I get to walk you down the aisle," Oscar says and then half shrugs. "Well. Roll."

I laugh and take his hand in mine, linking our fingers. He's so real, my brother. "Me too," I whisper. I squeeze his hand in mine when—

I hear a sick, gut-wrenching crunch.

Two of his fingers have popped out of place and twist at a jarring angle over my hand. I gasp and pull away to help him, but his whole arm comes with me.

The doll arm hangs limply from my hand. Oscar blinks at his empty sleeve, unfazed. "Oh," he says simply. "That's a bad look."

I open my mouth to scream out for help—*someone help him, please*—but no sound comes out. My throat closes and my voice only comes out in small, scratchy squeezes.

Help! Save my brother! Please!

2 7

———

B E N

*R*ory thrashes in her sleep.

Her head swivels back and forth on the pillow. Her eyebrows knit in pain, her mouth open, and she emits squeaks and whimpers.

I reach through the blue darkness and take her small shoulder in mine. "Rory," I murmur. "Wake up."

Her whole body shivers. She's panting like she's run a marathon.

Roland, on the other side of the king-size bed, sleeps like a log. *Of course*. A bloody dragon couldn't wake sleeping beauty.

"*Rory*," I repeat and shake her now. "Open your eyes, love."

Her eyes fly open suddenly at my command. The whites of her eyes swim as her gaze flickers around. Panic. I squeeze her shoulder again, gently this time.

"It's all right," I tell her. "It's just a dream."

She sits up and splutters for breath. Her lungs sound hoarse. "I need…" she croaks.

"Water?"

She nods, holding her throat.

"Come with me."

I link my hand in hers. She flinches at first, as though my touch frightens her, but then she lets me lead her through the dark bedroom, down the winding stairs, and into the kitchen. Moonlight pours through the tall windows, swathing everything in indigo blue. I flick on the artificial kitchen light, which changes the room to pale white.

"Sit on the couch," I tell her. Rory coughs and wheezes as she sits down.

I pluck a glass out and fill it with water from the sink. I move to Rory and hand the glass to her.

She tilts it to her lips. The glass shakes in her hand. Once she's sipped, she sets it down and rasps, "Thank you."

"What do you need?" I'm on red alert. This isn't a normal nightmare. Normal nightmares go away when the sleeper wakes up. This is leeching off her.

Rory motions to herself. "It's… nothing. Just having a… little… panic attack." She screws her eyes shut and groans. "My heart is beating so fast. I just need to… mm. Slow it down. This happens all the time."

"Does it?"

She cracks an eye open. "It used to. I haven't… in a long time. I'll be fine."

I don't like this. I don't like feeling helpless while the woman I love gasps and chokes inches away from me.

"Maybe you can… take me in the car," she rasps. "And we can drive. Just drive."

Her eyes are wild and unfocused, staring ahead. She's looking for an exit.

"Do you mind if I try something?" When I phrase it as a question, it sounds like she has a choice.

She shakes her head. Her hand is stuck on her chest as though she can reach inside and physically slow the hammering of her heart. "Please," she says.

Our clothes are scattered all around the estate. My belt is curled up on the floor from I can't even remember when. I pick it up and stand over her. "Lift your hair," I say.

She looks at me like I'm crazy. I can't blame her. She can barely breathe, and I'm going to choke her.

"Do you trust me?" I ask.

At that, it clicks. She obeys and lifts her hair from the back of her neck. I loop the belt around her throat and then slide one end through the buckle. It catches around her neck like a collar.

"On the floor," I demand.

Rory shifts off the couch and gets to her hands and knees on the floor instead. No more protests from her. She's obeying me instinctively.

Good. This is right where I want her. "Sit, pet."

She plops her bum down. I crouch in front of her so I can better see her expression. Her gentle moon eyes melt me. I wrap the loose end of the belt around my fist and tighten it slightly. The buckle constricts her throat, and she gasps.

"How does it feel?" I ask.

"Tight."

"No, how do *you* feel? Confined?"

"Yes."

"Scared?"

She shakes her head. "No. Safe."

"You are safe." I want to tell her that, over and over. *You are safe, you are safe, you are safe. I won't let anything bad happen to you.*

She seems to get it. She's stopped panting. She's stopped panicking. Instead, she's submissive. Compliant.

"My panic attack," she notes, incredulous. "It's gone."

"Yes. It is."

She looks at me like a child looks at a magician. Pure wonderment. "How did you know to do that?"

"I saw it in your eyes," I inform her. "When I first took you to the palace. And again, here. On your knees, licking my cum from Roland's hand. You crave submission."

She looks lost for a second, and her gaze swims before refocusing on me. "You're... really good at that."

"How long have you been having panic attacks?" I ask.

We must look crazy—having quiet pillow talk on our knees in the den with my belt around her throat. It's the only way I know how to communicate.

"In high school... when my brother's sickness started getting really bad. That's when they started. But... physical illness trumped mental illness, and my parents only had enough money to take care of one of us." A lopsided smile cuts across her lips. "Imagine if you'd been my therapist. I could've cut this stupid habit long ago."

My stomach clenches. I don't need to think about bending barely legal Rory over a reclining therapist's chair with my belt around her throat. I dab my lips with my tongue and change the topic. "How do you normally stop it?"

She shrugs with one shoulder. "They stopped when I started traveling. I guess I...felt like I was doing something important. As long as I had a purpose, as long as Oscar could see the world through my eyes...then there was nothing to be afraid of. Now..."

"You have cabin fever?"

She let out a light, humorless laugh. "Something like that."

"You're important, Rory. All on your own. You don't need to run anymore."

The moonlight reflects off her eyes when they get shiny and wet. "Thank you," she says as a tear slides down her cheek.

I catch it with my thumb and press a gentle kiss to her mouth. She's so soft, so pliable right now. Completely under my control. My blood sings. I crave this. I need this.

"Do you want to go back to bed?" I ask her.

She nods. "Yes, sir."

Cupping the back of her head, I press a final kiss to her forehead. I loosen the belt from her throat and pull it over her head. Even without the collar, her eyelids droop and I can tell she's still in a submissive state.

Our pet. I'll protect her. No matter what. Even if I have to protect her from herself.

"Come." I take her by the arm to help her off the floor and lead her back to bed.

The bedroom is swathed in midnight darkness. Rory crawls into bed first, aligning her body with Roland's. I follow after her.

Now Roland wakes up. Finally. I can't see much, but I hear him murmur, "Hey there. Can't sleep?"

"I'm okay now," Rory whispers. Their lips smack together softly. The bedsprings creek. Rory gasps.

"Good kitten." Roland's voice is deep in the dark. "Good kittens get pets."

Rory lets out a wanting, needy moan. Whatever Roland is doing to her, she likes it. A grin twitches at the corner of my mouth. Rory's hair smells like coconut shampoo. I pet her hip with my fingertips, and she shudders.

"You spoil her," I inform him. We are parents who can't agree on how to properly raise our child.

"Can you blame me? Look at that cute face."

Rory's breath comes in short, sweet pants. She takes in a sharp breath. It's a wonderful warning that she's on edge. The bed is trembling. "Please," she whispers.

I reach around and clasp my hand around her throat. "No begging."

Just like my belt, the pressure of my hand flips a switch in her. She's still vibrating with want, but now she's quiet.

Submissive. She'll do anything, *anything* we want when she's in this zone.

The bed stops shaking. Roland's long hair brushes the back of my fingers. He kisses her wetly before he whispers, "Go to sleep, kitten."

I tilt her chin toward me and take my turn to close my mouth over hers. Our girl sighs sweetly. When I lift my gaze, Roland is there. Even in the dark, I can't miss his blue eyes. He closes the circle, leans over, and claims my lips in his.

"You too, mate."

"Mm" is all I can say. My cock twitches. She melts for me. I melt for him. Only a couple of days ago, I was trapped in my lair and watching them through the camera lens. Now, the three of us share one bed.

But something this good can't last forever. They fall asleep together as careless as newborn kittens. I watch the ceiling and wait for the bottom to fall out.

* * *

I WAKE up to the smell of toast burning.

I hold Rory in closer, and she sighs softly against me. She's cuddly soft. My fingertips brush against Roland, who is pressed up against her. The two of them in bed, the birds chirping outside, the smell of breakfast downstairs…

Wait. *Breakfast?*

Who the hell is downstairs?

Immediately, I'm awake. I jump out of bed, yank my pants over my hips, and take my gun out of my holster.

"Ben?" That's Rory's voice, lit with panic. "Is everything okay?"

Roland chimes in, "What's going on?"

"There's someone downstairs." I flip off the safety on my pistol. "Stay here."

I exit the bedroom and put my back against the wall. Quietly, I make my way down the staircase. I can hear someone moving about, a yellow light leaking out from the open kitchen. My focus becomes laser sharp. I crouch down under the first-floor ceiling so I can spot the intruder.

Even with his back to me, I recognize that distinct white hair. I exhale slowly, put the safety back on, and lower my gun. With that, I shake it off and let my bare feet clomp downstairs and into the kitchen.

"*Buongiorno,*" Tanner says. He's sitting on a stool at the kitchen island, tearing into a croissant. He motions to the paper bag. "Would you like breakfast? Couldn't help myself and bought the lot of them."

"You could have phoned," I tell him.

"Could I?" Tanner turns to me and narrows his eyes. "You realize the queen is seconds away from calling this a kidnapping, don't you?"

"Tanner?" That's Roland's voice behind me; he and Rory stumble down the stairs, half-clothed and bed-headed. My jaw clenches. They're terrible at following orders. "Did my mum send you?"

"Yes, Your Highness." Tanner stands now respectfully. "She's worried about you."

"I'm fine," Roland says curtly. "You can see that."

"All due respect, sir... the queen of England didn't send me here to relay a message." Tanner glances over the three of us. "Vacation is over. Get dressed and pack your bags. It's time to go home."

28

ROLAND

*I*taly fades away into the clouds as my private jet climbs higher.

Arrivederci, Sorrento.

It was a limencello-infused, sticky-kiss dream. But eventually, a prince has to return to his castle.

Even if his castle is also his prison.

I curl my fingers at my lips as I watch the clouds zip past in puffs of white. Rory and Ben have vanished into the aft cabin. Tanner sits in the back, and every now and then I hear his newspaper flutter as he turns a page. I tap my signet ring against the window just to hear it click.

Rory falls into the seat in front of me and whirls it around so we're facing each other. Gravity has a weird effect on her. It seems to pull her down more rapidly than anyone I've ever known, making her ginger hair fly out around her. For such a small girl, she throws her body around like a wrecking ball.

"Ben's taking a nap," she announces. "Apparently he didn't sleep well last night and isn't worried about snipers when we're 40,000 feet in the air. Did you know you have a full-size *bed* back there?"

The edge of my mouth lifts. Rory always knows how to make me smile. "Yes. I'm aware."

Rory cranes over to glance once at Tanner before she turns her attention back to me, dropping her voice so we can talk privately. "You look anxious."

"That's because I am."

"Is it about your mom? I know it's hard going back, but… she's your mom. She'll forgive you."

"Going back isn't the hard part." I turn my gaze to meet Rory's. "She's not going to take it very well when I tell her I have no intention of staying at the palace."

"You don't?" Rory chirps.

I shake my head. "How would you feel about running away with me?"

For a second, Rory gawks. "Running away… from the palace? Can you do that?"

"I'm the prince. I can do whatever I want. We'll leave the palace. All of it. We can spend a month on the Greek Islands. Soaking in the sunshine. Sipping martinis on the beach."

Rory's nose crinkles. "I don't want martinis."

"No?"

"No. I want adventure."

"We'll hike the Nepalese mountains, then. Meet some Buddhist monks. Explore the ruins."

Her eyes seem to glitter at that. "Now you're talking."

"I don't care where we are," I explain. "As long as I'm with you and Ben, I'm happy. We'll shag our way through every country."

Rory fidgets in her seat and rubs her hands over her skirt. "Just… don't jump into this. It's not all peaches and cream. Before I ended up at the palace, I'd been three months without a private shower. That's showering in communal bathrooms with a plastic curtain separating you from strangers. I got bitten by bugs and lay awake at night praying they weren't venomous. I got ripped off by probably every taxi driver in the world. Without fail, I've gotten lost in some of the sketchiest places where no one spoke English. Are you sure you're up for that? Up until now, everything's been handed to you on a silver platter."

"And look how well that's turned out for me," I interrupt bitterly. "I'm tired of living that way. I never wanted my life handed to me. I see that now. I look at you and… you make me hungry. I want to see the world with you, Rory."

"Have you talked to Ben about this?"

"Not yet. But he'll follow us."

"Why? Because you order him to?"

My mood darkens. "No. Of course not. Because he loves us, and he'd follow us to the ends of the earth. That's *Ben*."

Rory stares out the window, her eyes following the streaks of white. She's quiet for a long moment, contemplative, but then finally, she utters a single word. "Okay."

My muscles tighten with surprise. "Okay?"

A small smile graces her lips. "Yeah… where do you want to go first?"

That smile. I want to kiss that smile. I hook my hands underneath her knees, draw her forward, and close my mouth over hers. I can taste the curve of her lips. Here, my mouth still brushing hers, I murmur, "Right now… I don't want to be anywhere but right here."

Rory gets up and curls into my lap, and I wind my arms around her as the plane purrs underneath us.

* * *

REGINALD DOESN'T SPEAK to me when we get to the hangar bay again. He's traded in his personable smile for a deep scowl. I can't blame him. He was duped by the prince of England, an arrogant boy used to getting what he wanted. Is his job on the line? I certainly hope not. I'll put in a good word if it is. Pull some royal strings. No one should have to suffer for my pride.

"Your Highness," Reginald grumbles with mandatory politeness. "Welcome back to England. Did you enjoy your stay?"

"Quite," I respond as I step down the stubby ramp and onto British soil. "All except the surprise ending."

Reginald grunts out, "Very good, sir."

Rory follows behind me, Ben in the back. At the bottom of the stairs, Rory collides into me with a squeak. She's like a baby giraffe learning to walk.

"Careful," I tell her and perch my arm around her shoulders. "I don't want to have to peel you out from under the plane tires."

"Careful yourself," Rory says. I'm not sure what she's talking about until my eyes fix on the motley crew ahead of us. Three or four secret service agents swarm around my mother, all in black. They look like they're part of a funeral procession.

My stomach clenches. The look on my mother's face is nothing short of murderous. Her bloodred lips curve downward like a saber. I remove my arm from Rory and let it fall at my side. The only thing that could make this worse would be flaunting Rory in front of my mother.

"Mother." I step forward and smile broadly. "What a delightful welcome!"

"Silence," she hisses. She tilts her chin barely a centimeter toward her bodyguards. "Kindly escort my bratty son and his incorrigible friends back to the palace. We can't afford any more runaways."

A full-on militia comes around behind me. Out of the

corner of my eye, I see Rory shrink and Ben go on full alert.

"After you, sir," one of the guards grunts roughly.

I may as well have iron cuffs around my ankles. My feet drag heavily through the stone doorway and back to Helmsway Palace.

29

RORY

*B*en and I stand outside the closed doors of the sitting room like chastised children. Growing up, I was never grounded—my mom and dad mostly parented out of guilt—so it feels strange to have to huddle out here and wait for Roland. It's especially awkward when the ruckus from inside the sitting room spills very clearly out.

The queen, who is just about the most composed, quiet woman I've ever met, shouts shrilly at her son. "I didn't know where you'd gone! Or who you'd gone with!"

"I don't have to give you every bloody detail of my life!" Roland's voice booms back at her in their explosive verbal ping-pong.

"Yes, you do! You're the future king of England—act like it."

"Letting my mum boss me around… that's kingly, is it?"

I look at Ben. He stares dully at the bare wall across from us as I play with my fingers. "Does this happen often?" I whisper.

"Every full moon," Ben replies, his eyes unmoving.

"You could've been hurt!" the queen cries out. "I've already lost your father. If I'd lost you, too—"

"Oh, will you sod off about that!" Even I flinch at that. Roland rails at his mother, "I lost my father, too, and I sure as hell know he wouldn't want me living like a bloody hermit! I won't postpone my life because he can't live his!"

"Roland!"

I jump in my place as the double doors fly open with a bang. Roland storms out, his hair whipping around his shoulders, eyes burning, jaw so tight he looks like he could split marble between his teeth. Ben and I stand to attention, but Roland barely looks at us. "We're leaving," he announces curtly.

I pop off the wall, far too eager to be away from here. "Where to?" I ask.

Roland only replies coldly, "A long-overdue family reunion."

* * *

THERE'S an echo in the royal vaults.

Even standing still, not making a sound, the whole place vibrates with a low, whale-song hum. It's so grand and austere here, with frescoes lining the walls and ceiling that date back centuries, and I find myself barely breathing. Ben stands beside me, forever composed, his hands clasped together in front of his lap. Even royal ghosts don't spook him.

Roland kneels in front of a long line of ruby-stoned tombs stacked up on the far wall. His palm lays flat on the stone that reads in flowing engravings: PRINCE CONSORT DUNCAN HUGHES.

Roland's head is bowed, his hair pulled back with a violet ribbon. He hasn't said anything in a long while. Well.

176

Minutes, maybe? But even thirty seconds of silence makes me uncomfortable. I keep a respectful distance for as long as I can, but… finally I can't let him suffer in silence.

I kneel beside him and cross my arms in front of me. "You must miss him," I say.

"Yes and no," Roland replies. His voice is soft, somber. Apparently, he saves the shouting matches for his mother. "I don't remember a lot from that time."

"What do you remember?"

"The timbre of my father's voice. Racing toy boats with him in the pond behind the palace. He always let me win."

I can see it in my mind's eyes, the handsome king and his little prince, decked out in a tailored sailor suit, pushing their tiny boats along. The image makes me grin. "He must have loved you very much."

"Bizarrely… I miss my mother more." Roland's gaze lifts from the floor and flickers across the gravestones. "The way she used to be. Something in her died that day and never came back. I used to think that if I just did what she wanted… if I stayed inside, kept up with my studies, if I could even just get her to smile… then maybe we'd be a family again. It's all I've ever wanted."

His hands dangle at his knees, so I reach across and take one of them in my own. He doesn't pull back, so I squeeze. "You have a family now. You get that, right?"

Roland finally looks back at me. Some of the warmth has returned to his eyes, and the corner of his mouth lifts in a small smile. "Let's go out," he says. "I can't stand the thought of going back to my mother right now."

"Are you sure that's wise?" There's Ben—the quiet party in the back. Our conscience, only occasionally chiming in to remind of things like *reason* and *responsibility*.

Roland releases my hand, rises to his feet, and steps away

from the tombs. "Lighten up, Ben," he says and pats the other man on the chest. "You look like someone died."

Just like that, Roland is back to his old tricks. Shoving his damage under the rug and masking it with good humor. Who am I to say anything? We're two animals with the same laugh-so-we-don't-cry instincts.

Ben looks less amused. His lips crease with disapproval.

"He'll be fine," I assure him. I try to sound confident enough for the both of us.

"Right," Ben says, but his eyes never leave the prince.

"Posse, assemble!" Roland calls back, his voice echoing in the cavernous halls. "To the pub!"

I swallow. The prince is falling apart, the bodyguard is at the end of his tether, and I'm frantically trying to keep us all in one piece… *How can this go wrong?*

30

BEN

We end up at a club called Liberation, and I'm trying not to lose my shit.

Rather than slip in inconspicuously, Roland strolls right up to the bouncer and shakes his hand. The poor bloke looks like he's seen a ghost. There's a line around the block, and everyone whispers and snaps pictures on their phones as the bouncer ushers the three of us in.

Now everyone knows we're here. In the palace, I have a roster of permitted guests, background checks, and access to security cameras. Here, I'm blind. The club is a maze of dimly lit rooms, a wide dance floor, and strobe lights. The sofas and bar tables are all outlined in gaudy neon colors, so they pop out from the shadows. If they ran a black light through this thing, I doubt it would pass health code.

Roland, naturally, is as happy as a clam at high water. First a couple of people notice him and want to take a picture. Then a couple more want autographs. Before long, he's amassed a small crowd and they're lining up shots.

I hang in the corner of the bar where I can keep an eye on Roland. A crowd of gutter punks and hippies create a semicircle around Roland and a beefy Irish bloke. They stand at either side of the table, hawk eyes on each other.

A leggy blonde stands at the middle—she's clearly designated herself some kind of referee. "First to the middle gets the lime! And…" She throws up her arms. "Go!"

Immediately, Roland and the bulldog start to down shots, starting from the end of the table and working their way in. The crowd cheers as they flip over each cup, racing toward the center.

In the chaos, Rory appears beside me. "What's he doing?" Rory asks. She's holding a blue-tinted drink, her second of the night.

"Mourning," I answer.

"He looks like he's having fun," she tries.

Roland gets to the middle first and bites the lime. The club explodes in cheers. "God bless the bloody queen of England!" Roland shouts.

Rory's lips draw into a grimace. "I'll be right back," she says.

I watch as Rory wiggles through the crowd to get to Roland. He immediately scoops her in his arms and covers her mouth with his. He's drunk and overly affectionate. Rory's body goes rigid when the crowd *ooooohs*, and my hands clench into fists. She unwinds herself from Roland, pets his hair, and murmurs something I can't hear over the pounding beat of the music. He nods and follows her like a puppy to the dance floor, where they fall into a swaying movement.

I've mapped all the exits. I know every bartender and waitress by sight. My eyes scan the room, but it's hard to make heads or tails of this crowd. The only good news is that there's certainly no one hiding a gun in those skinny jeans. My eyes catch on a bulky man who moves to the bathrooms, and for a second, he almost looks familiar.

"So, Tall, Dark, and Strange." A woman steps side by side with me. "Are you strictly a voyeur, or do you participate as well?"

She's more skin than clothes, an hourglass of a woman fitted into a leather miniskirt and a matching blouse that crisscrosses over her chest. Her blonde hair is cropped at her shoulders, and it bounces when she turns her head. It occurs to me in an out-of-body way that she's just the type of girl I would've taken back to Helmsway Palace for Roland and me to feast on, back in the days before Rory. Now, I can barely muster up the energy to give her the time of day.

"Voyeur," I say shortly.

She rolls her eyes. "The clean-cut ones are always the kinkiest." She lingers, not taking my hint. Her eyes scan my suit. "So you work with the prince, eh?"

"What gave it away?"

She smirks. "He always this much fun?"

The tempo changes. Prince Roland bounces up and down on the dance floor, and Rory jumps with him, laughing, pumping her fist in the air. "Not exactly."

"He and his lady friend. They're awful cute, aren't they?" She shifts her weight in her hips, and her arm brushes against mine. "Must get boring, watching them have all the fun while you play third wheel."

"Boring isn't the word I'd use."

"Right you are, mate." She reaches out and traces her nail around my ear, pushing my dark hair back. "Bet you're anything but boring, aren't you?"

I grab her wrist and hold her back. "I'm on duty," I inform her. "In other words: *shove off.*"

"Touchy." She tugs her hand back and steps away from me, her wedges wobbling toward the dance floor. "Oi!" she shouts and catches my attention. When I turn to her, she bites on her grin. "Since you're a voyeur and all..." She pulls back the thin straps of her blouse, and her round breasts spill out. Her blouse cradles her perky orbs, and she bounces them a couple times for show. Then she covers them once more, blows me a kiss, and turns back to the dance floor.

Jesus fucking Christ. I'm certainly we've fallen into some level of hell. I need to get out of here. And I need a smoke.

3 1

ROLAND

I want to replace my heartbeat with the thump of the bass.

The music is so loud in here it dulls out my screaming thoughts. The alcohol numbs the anxiety burning in my blood, and as I make a fool of myself on the dance floor with Rory... for a second, I feel almost peaceful. We're jumping together, and I spin her and pull her against me. Her laugh rings out in my ears and vibrates through my soul. My adrenaline rushes, my head spins, and I swallow Rory up in my arms and laugh.

This is freedom. This is the world I've been kept from for so long. I want to immerse myself in it. I want to experience it—all of it. I crave it the way an addict craves heroin; my nerves feel frantic and fuel my desperation.

So I jump higher. Push harder. Until my heart is beating so quickly, I can barely tell it apart from the music. I'm no prince. No royal. I just *am*. I can forget myself here. And it feels so goddamn good.

Sweat drips down my neck. As I toss my body around the dance floor, my gaze swims over the bar.

There. Right there. My mother stands at the edge of the dance floor. Her hair is pulled into a bun, a black funeral lace covering her face. All sound dims until all I can hear is the rush of blood in my ears. My father stands beside her in his proud military uniform. Proud family. Idiot son.

"Roland!" Rory's voice, like a shard of sunshine on a rainy day, breaks through my imagination. Her hands rest on my chest, and all I can see is *her* now and those big, soft eyes, filled with concern. "Are you okay?"

I try to find my family again, but they're gone.

Loneliness is like an ice pick in my heart. The pain is unbearable and constant. I wind my arms around Rory and crush her against me. Her body is warm, soft, and I crave her heat.

"Don't leave me, okay?" I blither like an idiot in her ear. "I can't lose you. I can't bear to lose another person I love."

"It's okay," she murmurs. "It's going to be okay." She runs her fingers through my hair. I'm magnetized to her touch, and I lean in even as she pulls away. "I'm going to get you a cup of water, baby… Go find Ben, okay?"

I nod. I feel dumb, sweat slicked, and my throat is thick and clotted. She cups my face and presses a sweet kiss to my mouth before she pulls away, vanishing into the crowd.

Ben is easy enough to find at least. He sticks out like a sore thumb, the three-piece suit at the far end of the crowd. His gaze is askance, eyes caught on something else when I come to him.

I throw my arm around his shoulders. "You having fun, mate?"

Ben goes rigid. His jaw is tense. "No."

I already feel better in his presence, though. Safer, even from my own hallucinations. "We're here to have a good time," I persuade him. "So lighten up."

I'm messy, I'm drunk, and I'm absurdly brave. I lean in and brush my lips over his.

Ben? He nearly rips my bloody arm off. He grabs me, shoves me off him, and hisses, "What the hell are you doing?"

"What's your problem, mate?" I snap back.

His jaw is tight. "You're drunk," he states. "We're going home." Ben's eyes swim over the club. "Where's Rory?"

"She went to the bar to grab a water or something..." I'm stumbling, my alcohol content catching up with me fast, and the ground feels less solid under my feet.

Ben's eyes never settle. "No," he says. "She's not."

My heartbeat picks up in my chest again, old anxieties prickling my skin. "What do you mean, she's not?"

I've never seen Ben panicked. When the strobe lights flash across his face, I can see that he's gone white as a sheet. "She's gone," he states.

RORY

The edge of the bar bites little indents in my forearms as I fall forward against it. The sonic boom of dance music rattles my brain free from my skull. Normally, I'm a fan of loud music—Oscar can attest to this, for all the times he'd had to bang on the wall between our rooms to get me to turn down my music. I always said his grandpa was showing. But this makes even my ears pop.

I'm sweaty and my skin sticks when I bend my arm to wave down the bartender. "Can I get a water?" I shout over the din. I don't know if it's my second cocktail or the endorphins from dancing with Roland, but the room feels crooked under my feet. It was fun dancing with Roland—the prince can't dance, not really, but damn, does he look good trying. Who am I to talk anyway? My signature move is jutting my hips forward, turning my arms into wings, and flapping around. There's no point in dancing if you can't have *fun*, after all.

And Roland needs fun. Heck, we all need fun. Italy was amazing, and I think we're all just… reeling. Trying to find our footing again in the real world.

I can't imagine what this must be like for Roland. A taste of the outside world for the first time. I'm reminded of every time (and there *have* been multiple times) when I had to serve as the DD for a twenty-first birthday. Somehow, I always became the designated driver, designated decisions maker, and designated *don't send that picture* girl. Freedom can be a double-edged sword, and I've held back enough ponytails to attest to that.

If I have to hold Roland's hair back at the end of the night —so be it. A rite of passage, in my opinion. Why *doesn't* the prince of England get to have a crazy, judgment-free night every now and then?

But there's a nagging in the back of my head. The responsible voice (which sounds oddly like Ben?) murmurs, *Because you know he's hurting.*

The whole thing makes my head spin. The bartender slides a glass of ice water over, and I have the good sense to add, "Actually, can you make that two?"

I pluck the paper covering from the straw and take a sip. The cool liquid feels good going down my throat and washes some of the fuzz away from my brain.

For his effort, I reach into my pocket and pull out a couple pence. It's the least I can do. As I'm rummaging around, a voice behind me crystallizes in the cacophony.

"You're here with the prince, aren't you?"

The voice is gravelly, but the words are polished, articulate. He's short, stout, with an egg-shaped bald head. Middle-aged, maybe—he looks even more out of place than we do as he moves next to me.

I have no idea who this man is. A reporter, probably. Someone trying to dig up some dirt on the royal family. I shrug and keep my answers short. "I guess so."

My gaze veers away to the bartender, who is still filling my glass. *Damn that slow water drip.*

"Rory, right?" he says conversationally, as though we're old friends. "Rory March. You have that little… blog of yours."

I blink at him. Unease rolls over my skin like fish scales. There's something…off about him. "How do you know me again?"

He turns to me and smiles, an eerie jack-o'-lantern smile. A pink, fleshy scar runs lengthwise from his ear down his jaw. "Because I've been looking for you all night, Miss March."

Every bone in my spine goes cold. I grab my water and twist away from the bar. "I have to go—"

"Yes. You do." His meaty hand wraps around my arm like a vice. In his other hand, he flashes an item under his long coat. A gun glints in the flashing lights, and fear hits me like a lightning bolt.

I want to scream. I want to shout for Ben. Roland. But I can't. Between his threat and my fear, my voice has dried up in my throat.

"You're coming with me," he informs me. He shoves me to the exit, the muzzle of his gun pressing sharply against the small of my back.

33

———

BEN

 see her.

Rory.

Her hair blares siren red at the door.

She's not alone. There's a man with her. Stocky build. His hand is on her arm, and he pulls her outside. She turns before she goes, her hair fanning out behind her.

Panic in her eyes.

A knot tightens in my stomach.

"Door," I tell Roland and start toward the exit.

He stumbles behind me. "Rory—"

"Someone's taken her. They just left."

I don't have time for this. I don't have time to explain myself to a drunk, royal pain in the arse. I shove my way through the bumping and grinding bodies and burst out the door. I didn't realize what a bloody sauna it was in there until I'm licked with a rush of cool nighttime air. Sweat has caked on the back of my neck, underneath the collar of my shirt, and under my arms, and I feel it blaringly now.

My vision focuses on the cars parked on the side of the road, waiting for one to light up. The club coughs up Roland

189

with a gust of hot air. "Who would take her?" he asks as he runs his hands through his tousled hair.

"Someone after you, I imagine."

"Shit," Roland sighs. "I cocked this up, didn't I?"

I perk up when I hear her. A scream echoes down the alleyways.

"This way," I say. I'd love to shove the prince away, keep him protected in a locked car or a quiet space, but that's not going to happen. I don't know how many of *them* are out here. For all I know, Rory is just a clever distraction to get to the prince.

So he has no choice but to tag along with me.

There are very few people out and about this late. A businessman shuffles home. A couple walks hand in hand. Neither seems to be moved by the scream—that's London for you.

I jog down the street and flatten against the wall. Roland takes the hint and comes to a quick stop. When I look around, I see two shadows vanish around the corner.

I gesture Roland forward and we move quickly, quietly after them. He's taking her away from the cobbled side streets and narrow, twisting alleyways. I don't understand why he's still on foot. If this were a true hostage, he'd have a getaway driver. A quick exit. But this—

It's almost as if he wants us to catch up with him.

We've come to the end of the main street. The Thames sloshes nearby. I follow the twin clicks of footsteps to a bridge that crosses over the river. Adrenaline rushes through my blood. I'm blade sharp and focused. I reach into my jacket to grab my sidearm and pull back the hammer, disengaging the safety.

"Stay here," I murmur to Roland. "And don't make a noise."

He crouches in the bridge's shadow. I step off the brick

ledge, point my gun forward, and step through the tunnel. My shoes click on the walkway. I'm not hiding anymore.

Neither is he. The kidnapper stands in a yellow pool of light from the streetlamp. Rory, stiff as a board and wide-eyed, is clamped in a headlock. He holds a long blade underneath the soft skin of her throat.

My finger rests on the trigger. I don't have a clear shot, not with the way he's using Rory as a human shield. I wait for my moment and take a step forward.

"Let her go," I tell him.

"Yeah," he says. "That's not going to happen."

Her eyes look scared, frantic. I can't look at her if I want to keep my cool, so I focus on him. He's a stout man in clothes that are just slightly too baggy, fitting him awkwardly. His most prominent feature is a pink scar that runs down the side of his face—

I recognize this man. He was at the masquerade ball. The realization shifts uneasily in my chest. *He's been hiding in plain sight this whole time.*

"Let her go," I repeat, "or I'll shoot."

"And risk hurting your sweetie?" He digs the knife against her throat, indenting the skin. She twists and gasps like a worm on a hook. Chills run up and down my spine, and he smiles, her red hair pressed to his face. "I don't think so."

"She's not the one you want." That voice. It echoes boldly through the tunnel. I hear the clip of footsteps behind me. Roland steps into the light, his palms up above his head.

"Roland, what are you doing?" I hiss.

"This is about me," Roland says, his eyes on the other man. "Yes? You want me. Not her. So let her go… and you can have me instead."

"*Roland,* get back here." My blood is buzzing with frustration. I should've left him behind. He's too drunk, not thinking straight, being a bloody heroic idiot…

"Please," Roland says. I hear the strain in his voice. This isn't a drunken, messy decision. He wants this. This whole masochistic night of his has been culminating into one redemptive sacrifice. "You want a hostage? I'm your man. I'll do anything you want. Just let her go."

The kidnapper's eyes flicker between Rory and Roland. If he takes a step toward Roland, I decide, I'm going to shoot him point-blank.

"You want your girl?" the man growls. "You can have her."

He shoves Rory. She pitches forward with a yelp. Roland grabs her in his arms before she falls on her face.

Then the kidnapper reaches for his gun.

I fire. A single squeeze of the trigger. It hits his arm and he drops his gun with a yelp. The second shot misses him completely. Before I can fire off a third, he throws his leg over the railing and jumps. I hear a splash as he hits the Thames.

Roland has Rory. They're safe. For now. I rip my jacket off, then my sidearm holster, and drop them on the ground. "Stay here," I tell them as I kick off my shoes as well.

"What are you—?"

That's all I hear from Roland before I straddle the railing. The water bobs not far below me. High tide. I'm guessing it's about fifteen, twenty meters down before I hit the bottom. I push off the side and into the river. The cold, black water splashes up and swallows me.

The channel is narrow, and it wouldn't be hard to swim to the other side, hop on the dock, and hide in one of the small craft boats. I scan the choppy river until I see him. His white head stands out like a mooring ball, bobbing through the water to get to the other side.

I propel myself forward. I need to catch him before he gets there. I see him turn around, spot me, and pick up the pace. This far down river, I get nothing but mouthfuls of salt water as I jet after him. We're about midway across before I grab the bulky man by his shoulders. He veers around and throws a punch. Using land tactics in the water—bad idea. I dodge it, lock my legs in his, and push him back so he dips under.

He's gasping when I pull him back up, eyes buggy like a trout.

"Who sent you?" I shout.

"Go ask the queen yourself!" he growls. We twist and spin, water splashing around us in the struggle. I kick, grab at him, and I feel my hits make contact, hear him grunt. Then he grabs me by the back of my head, and I barely have time to catch a breath before he shoves me underwater.

I'm a good swimmer, but this man is twice my size and twice as strong. When he pushes me down, I know I'm not getting back up. As much as I try to twist out of his grip, he's there. I might as well be pinned under the hull of a ship. He's unrelenting, solid as a tanker. I reach up and grab his arm, digging in. The cool air I crave kisses my fingers, but my head remains trapped under his hand.

So I stop fighting it. I sink. I fan my arms behind me and draw myself deeper under the water. Constricted around me like a boa, my attacker has no choice but to sink with me.

If I'm going down, he's coming with me.

We're both submerged and only getting deeper. When he realizes what's happening, he tries to pull off me, but now I latch to him. I know this river. It's not incredibly deep, but if I wind myself around him, it doesn't have to be. A man can drown in two inches of water if he can't find the surface. We're no longer fighting each other. We're fighting the pull of the river.

I can see nothing but darkness. I can hear nothing but the rush of water filling my ears.

Oxygen is precious at this point. It burns in my chest. My

lungs are at half capacity at best. I hold on to every bubble of air, only releasing it in small increments. I focus all my attention on keeping him locked in my arms and keeping my breath in my body. His elbow slams hard into my ribs, and sharp pain licks through my bones. I've broken a rib, probably, maybe two, but nothing hurts more than the bubble of air that escapes my lips.

I've got less than a single breath left inside of me. The pressure is intense, and my eardrums feel like they might burst. I can feel my lungs straining, wanting desperately to expand.

We thrash together in the river. Our bodies spin, turn, until I can't tell if I'm upward or down. I ignore the ache in my lungs, the pain in my body, the burning in my eyes. I cling to his body with everything I have.

I can't let him resurface. I can't let him finish what he started. I have to keep Rory safe. I have to keep Roland safe. I have to...

His body goes limp. Just like that, my arms feel weightless, as though I'm holding nothing more than a pile of laundry. He burps out a bubble of air, and his heavy, dead weight sinks to the floor.

I release him. The white of his skin gets sucked into the cold darkness.

Never try to outswim a Limehouse boy from the docks.

I go into full survival mode now. My limbs are growing heavy and threaten to follow him. My chest is on fire. I scratch at the water and climb. I think I'm going toward the surface, but I can't be sure. For all I know, I could be going deeper. There's nothing but inky blackness above, inky blackness below. I scramble and my desperate lungs gulp in seawater. I feel my consciousness fading to a black, noisy hum.

Just a little more, I think. Just a little farther...

I kick and claw my way up until I break the surface. The murky, sour London air is the sweetest thing I've ever tasted. I choke on it, gasping, coughing, as my lungs suck it down greedily.

My head is spinning. I'm incredibly disoriented. There's a dock a couple of meters away. I push my sluggish muscles, even though my very blood burns with the lack of oxygen, and swim to the dock. It creaks as I climb up on it, and I savor the solid wood under my hands and knees. I retch, my stomach expelling salt water. Even the act of clenching my gut sends shooting pain through my ribs.

Okay. Get it together. I'm shaky, but I'm alive. I have to find Roland and Rory. I have to make sure they're okay. I find a ladder, and my fingers scratch on the barnacles as I climb it. My bare feet leave wet traces on the walkway as I make my way down. The tide pulled me down the river, and I pass a few streetlamps before I see them—two figures crouched down under the lamplight.

I pick up the pace until I've reached them. Rory is wide-eyed and panting lightly in Roland's arms. "Are you okay?" I ask.

"I'm fine," Rory says, but her vision is unfocused and her face is white.

Roland cradles her against his chest. When he looks up at me, his eyebrows knit. "Where's the guy?"

I half shrug. "The river took him."

If he reads between my lines, he doesn't make a note of it. Roland simply nods once in confirmation. I had a job to do. I did it. That's all there is to say about that.

Roland's eyes lock on mine meaningfully, and he tilts his head to the side to motion me around. I step beside them when I see it. The handle of a knife sticks out of Rory's side, right above her hip. For a second, I don't understand why she isn't screaming, and then I realize—she's in shock. She probably can't even feel it. Even as the fabric on her shirt turns crimson, she remains utterly unaware.

"She's fine," Roland says, his voice hardened. He's staying calm for her sake. Now is not the time to frighten her anymore. "I called an ambulance," he adds to me, under his breath.

I nod. My stomach constricts. I'm sick with worry now. I sit down beside them, collapsing gracelessly on the ground.

Dear God, I pray quietly, *please let Rory be okay. Please. Please.*

In the distance, sirens begin their pitchy wail.

3 4

ROLAND

I can't tear my eyes away from the windows. My graze follows the stained glass depictions of an eagle stretching its gold-tipped wings with the royal crown above it. The words *Per ardua ad astra* encircle the bird.. *Through adversity to the stars.*

The King Edward VII's Hospital is discreet, private, and just about the best comfort and care one can get. The walls are polished hardwood, which makes the whole place feel less like a hospital and more like a country club. Nurses occasionally walk by with muffled voices and clicking heels, but no one disturbs Ben or me.

I'm incredibly sober at this point—fear is a hell of a hangover cure. I still clutch my small plastic cup of ice water. Ben sits quietly beside me. His clothes are still sopping wet, even though he now has a terry cloth over his shoulders, and every now and then, I hear a *plink* of Thames water hit the ground.

He's holding his side. He hasn't let go of it since we got here. "Are you sure you don't want to see a doctor?" I ask him.

"I'm fine," he says shortly. His gaze is also fixed ahead.

Neither of us has said a lot to each other in the past hour. We're just waiting for those damn doors to open. I need to hear something—anything. I need to know Rory is okay.

Around the corner, I can hear a light bustle of commotion. I don't pay much attention to it until a familiar voice floats our way. I brace myself as the sharp sound of heels on hardwood grows louder.

My mother rounds the corner and comes to a stop beside me. She's wearing a black dress, black heels, and a black clutch. I nearly wonder out loud what funeral she came from, but verbally suggesting anything close to death feels like a bad omen, so I hold my tongue.

"How is she?" Mum asks, her eyes darting sharply over me.

I scoff and turn away from her. "Don't act like you care now. You hate her."

"I certainly never wanted her dead, darling. There's a difference."

The curtness in her voice makes my teeth grind.

"Roland," she presses. "I need a word."

"And I need to stay here," I argue. "Rory needs me right now."

"It will only take a moment."

She has a quiet command in her voice that leaves no room for argument. Ben turns to me. "I'll let you know if they open the doors," he says.

I nod with gratitude. I don't want to leave my spot, but I set my cup down and rise to my feet. Reluctantly, I follow my mum around the corner. There's no one but nurses and doctors to overhear us here, and in my mum's world, that makes us as good as alone. *Normals* are barely people to her, after all.

"I've come here to tell you one thing," she says, cutting straight to the chase.

I cross my arms over my chest. "Speak."

Her cerulean eyes meet mine. "This could have been prevented," she states.

"So you're saying this is all my fault?"

"No. I'm saying this could have been prevented."

She stares at me with the haughty look of someone who knows they're right. My stomach tightens at her words. I feel as though the hospital has gotten ten degrees colder.

I know there is truth behind her words. If I hadn't gone out… if I hadn't gone to the club… if I hadn't been such a bloody selfish idiot…

I tighten my arms on my chest.

"Think on it," she tells me.

"Roland." There's Ben's voice—saved by the Ben. He peeks around the corner, his hand on the wall. "Rory's awake."

RORY

’m drowning in cushions. The mattress swallows me like a big, fluffy cloud, and I sink into it. My head is fuzzy, my skull extra heavy, and it feels like a watermelon on a stick when I try to lift it. There's a bleeping sound, a whoosh, and a woman in a white pencil skirt and folded hat smiling at me.

This is a bizarre resort, definitely.

"Welcome back, Miss March," she says cheerily.

"Did I go somewhere?" My mouth is dry, like I've been chewing on chalk.

"Nearly, miss. How are you feeling?"

I put my hand on my forehead. "Like my head is a balloon with too much air." When I shift my arm, a sharp pain stabs my gut and bolts up my side. I gasp and move my hand to my hip. I touch the rough edges of a bandage.

"You won't want to be touching that much," the nurse explains. "Your stitches need to heal."

Stitches. Oh. That's like a splash of ice water. Memories come flooding back—I'm not in a resort. I'm in a hospital. And not by accident, either. I remember his grip on my wrist, so tight it hurt. The scar that ran down his face. His cold knife against my throat. That dry, raspy voice: *Be still, little slut. Wouldn't want to have to stick ya.*

My heart trembles in my chest, and I can feel the panic rising. My eyes flee to the door and back to the nurse. I imagine him bursting in here any second, while I'm weak and my bones are too heavy to fight him off. "Is there... um. Does that door lock?"

Her lips press in a sympathetic, reassuring smile. "No one comes in here without our approval. Okay?"

"Okay." Logically, I know I'm safe here. My heart doesn't listen to reason, however, and it continues to beat out of my chest. "Roland and Ben... are they okay?"

"They're just fine, miss. Prince Roland is right outside, waiting to see you. Would you like that?"

My throat tightens already. "Please."

"Yes, ma'am. I'll send him in right away."

The nurse clicks out with poised steps. I bite the inside of my lip and try to keep my composure when the door reopens.

Roland slips around the door, blond hair in disarray, his grin crooked on his mouth. "Hey, kitten," he says. "How're we holding up?"

He calls me *kitten* and immediately the air leaves my lungs. It's okay. I'm safe with him here. Cold relief sweeps through my blood, and my anxiety defuses.

"Oh, you know." I shrug. "Besides a little stabbing, I'm fantastic."

A single, abrupt laugh escapes his chest. He shakes his head and sits down on the side of my bed. "Leave it to you to find the humor in any situation." He pushes my hair back, and I nudge into his touch. His kitten is practically purring.

"The guy... did they get him?" I ask.

Roland nods. "He won't come after you again."

"It just seems like such a nightmare," I sigh and lean against his chest. "When you stood in front of him… I didn't know what was going to happen."

"It's okay." Roland's arms go around my shoulders. He hugs me to him. His voice is strong and exactly what I need right now. "Everyone's okay. That's the important part. I'm more worried about you."

He's not lying about that part. The bright, boyish humor has gone out of his expression. His eyes are raincloud gray and just as stormy.

"Are you okay?" I ask.

"I'm fine," he assures me. His gaze fixes on the wall, and his jawline seems sharper than ever. He reminds me of the man I saw when I first met him—a prince locked up in a cage of his own design. A man whose very bones seemed bolted together, every motion rehearsed and robotic.

I rest my hand on his leg. "Hey. Look at me."

He does and there's a chip in his façade. For a second, his eyes brighten and his features soften. His throat unlocks, and a sigh escapes. "No," he confesses. "I'm not okay."

"So talk to me."

His lips press together. Such plump lips. I want to kiss them then. I want to kiss every gray cloud out of his day.

"I didn't want to do this now," he says. "I was going to… wait. Until after you got better, at least. Didn't seem right to… rub salt in the wound. So to speak."

"Salt in the wound?" My head is spinning, and I don't think it's from the painkillers. "What are you talking about?"

Then I see it in his eyes. Oh no. No, no, no. It's *that look*. Equal parts reluctance and regret. The look of a guilty dog who just ripped up your favorite shoes. Roland—for all his practice—can't help but wear his emotions on his face.

I sit up straighter against the sturdy pillows. "Roland… are you breaking up with me?"

"This isn't easy," he states.

"No, *algebra* isn't easy," I counter. "This is out of the blue."

"It's not you, Rory," he says and rests his hand on my shoulder. "Truly. It isn't."

But now his touch stings, and I shrug out of it. "I don't understand," I say lamely. My heart feels like it's fallen straight into my gut and is boiling in my stomach acid.

"The time I've spent with you… well. It's the happiest I've ever been." There's a tremor in his voice as he speaks. "You've shown me just how big this world can be. You're the most courageous woman I know. I love you, Rory—"

"Why?" The breath has gone out of my lungs again. I feel useless and limp when I look at him.

To his credit, he doesn't look away from me. He doesn't dance around the subject or try to pump me full of more sugar-sweet nothings. "I can't imagine a world without you in it," he tells me. "Life with me… it's dangerous. And I can't put your life on the line like that."

"Every day is dangerous." I throw up my hand. "Crossing the street is dangerous."

"This isn't crossing the street!" His eyes go vibrant when he loses his temper, and I close my mouth. The lion roars and you shut up. He seems to remember himself and rakes his fingers through his mane quickly, soothing the beast. "You were stabbed. That's not a risk I can take."

I know I should back down in the face of his anger, but his frustration only piques mine. "Life is *about* taking chances," I argue. "Scary chances. If Ben hadn't taken a chance, he'd still be a dock boy in Limehouse. If I hadn't taken a chance and left the States, I'd have never met you. Taking that risk—that plunge of faith—that's what makes life so amazing."

"Maybe for Normals." The temperature of his voice has dropped to something low and cold. I'll take his temper any day over this quiet resignation. "Not for me. I take chances, people die."

"No one died."

"Not this time." He looks at me, and those blue eyes are full of pain. It breaks my heart clean in half. "What about the next time?"

I wind my fingers through his and squeeze. "We'll figure it out."

"I already have." Roland untangles our fingers and retracts his hand. He leaves my bed and gets to his feet. "You need to leave London. There's no telling how many people are out there like the man we ran into tonight. I'll make sure you're cleared to use my private jet. They'll take you wherever you want. Back to Michigan. Anywhere."

Roland presses a small, lingering kiss to my forehead. I feel my hair move when he sighs against me. "Take care of yourself, Rory," he murmurs.

With that, he makes to leave. He twists his signet ring on his finger as he walks to the door. My throat tightens and my heart hammers in my chest. I feel paralyzed. "Roland," I finally get out. He stops at the last second and turns to face me. My lower lip feels swollen and trembles. "Please. Don't do this."

I swear, his eyes go glassy for a second. But then he blinks, and the hardened mask falls over his face once more. "I'm sorry," he says.

With that, Prince Roland walks out of the hospital room and out of my life.

BEN

The second hand ticks by on the wall clock. The queen and I wait in silence outside as Roland visits with Rory.

Queen Selena doesn't deign to sit. Instead, she stands and waits, arms folded. Her dress hugs to her like rubber, and I wonder if it would even allow her to sit and stand back up.

"A dead man was found in the River Thames today," she says, abruptly breaking the agreed-upon silence between us. "Would you know anything about that?"

"No, ma'am," I lie. Dripping wet. Holding my broken rib.

"Hm," she huffs. And that's the extent of our conversation.

I'm staring at the door. I'm trying hard not to overanalyze this situation, but it doesn't escape my notice. Barely a couple hours back in England, and Roland and Rory are an item and I'm... left holding the door. I try reasoning with myself. I knew my place. I knew this was how it would be. I knew we would revert back to our old ways once we got here. What's the saying?

Two's a company; three's a crowd.

Still. It kills me to have either of them out of my sight, even for a moment.

Three hundred seconds tick by before the hospital door opens again. I stand quickly, even though the effort sends bursts of pain through my chest. The queen stiffens her spine.

Roland looks weary. I see it in his eyes. White-hot panic bubbles in my blood. But then he gives the two of us one of his charming smiles. "She's doing okay," he says. "Knackered. They've got her on painkillers. But she's fine."

"Thank God," I sigh with relief before I can stop myself. The queen shoots me a queer look from the edge of her vision.

Roland waves her away. "Mother, give us a moment, please."

"I'll wait in the car," she announces as though it was her own idea. She sniffs. "I hate hospitals anyway."

Ah. The last time she was here was probably—right.

With her dying husband.

I feel a wave of empathy for her, a twinge of regret that I didn't say anything to make her feel a little more at ease… but what *do* you say to warm the heart of an ice queen anyway? I let the moment pass, and the queen vanishes, the click of her heels growing quieter as she makes her way down the hall.

Roland crumples into his seat once more with a hefty sigh, so I take my place beside him.

"You're off," I tell him. It's a statement, not a question. He can tell me what's wrong with him or not, but now he knows that I know.

I expect him to come back with some snide comment or cutting quip. Instead, Roland is abnormally quiet. He sits with his thoughts for a moment, not even looking at me. Finally, he murmurs, "I broke it off with Rory."

There's a second after you've been slapped, when the pain vibrates through your face with a prickly tingling. I feel that now as I stare at him. "What? Why?"

"She could have died, Ben." Roland's voice is hard and polished. That stone-cold Pennington denial.

"You're right." Sarcasm drips on my tongue. "What better way to protect her than to release her onto the London streets on her own?"

"I can't lose another person I love." The sharpness in Roland's voice makes me hold my tongue. "I can't."

"You had no right," I growl.

Roland turns to me finally and blinks with surprise. "Pardon?"

"She was *ours*," I snap. "You don't get to make that call."

"Watch your tongue," Roland hisses.

"Should I bow to you now?" I stand. I need to stand over him. "After everything I've done for you... the years I've spent going above and beyond my station to make you happy. Everything I've done has been for you. And you can't do this one thing for me."

"Ben." Roland stands now, as patient as a parent. "You're not listening to me."

"I am listening to you. For six years, I've done nothing but listen—"

"Ben, you're fired."

My words dry up on my tongue. My heartbeat pulses in my ears, feverish, and I must look like a fucking idiot, staring at him with not a damn thing to say.

"I meant what I said," he continues, coaxingly. For once, he's the calm and collected one, and I'm the one spinning out of control. "I can't lose another person I love. That includes you. You put yourself in front of the line of fire for me, time and again... and I couldn't bear it if I lost you."

"You couldn't bear it," I repeat.

"No," he shakes his head. "I couldn't."

"And it's all about you, isn't it?"

Roland's shoulders sag. "I'm just trying to protect you."

"Stop protecting us," I tell him. "I'm your bodyguard. That's my bloody job."

"You *were* my bodyguard," he corrects.

I put my hand on the door to Rory's room. "May I be dismissed, Your Highness?"

"Ben. Don't hate me."

"Is that a royal decree or a request?"

He looks gutted. "A prayer."

My eyes flicker over him. I'm a python, venom swollen and ready to strike. "Then you should probably get on your knees next time you want something from me." With that, I push through the door and into Rory's room.

There's a blast of cold from her room. Machines beep and whir around Rory's bed. She looks very, very small in the billowing blankets and pillows. Or maybe it's that she's been crying that makes her look small. When I step in, she wipes her face and sniffles. She tries to smile, even though there's no hiding the red blotches around her eyes. "Hey."

"How are you?" I ask.

She shrugs meekly. "I've had better days."

I step around her bed and take a seat in a circular chair beside her. "Roland told me that he broke up with you."

"He's trying to protect me," she sniffs. "I get it, but—"

"He's a bloody idiot."

She chuckles politely.

"He broke it off with me, too," I inform her. "Fired me, actually."

Rory's big eyes widen at that. "Oh no… Ben. I'm so sorry."

Leave it to Rory to feel bad for me when she's the one in the hospital bed. She reaches out and catches my hand in her own. I shiver. She's made a crack in my hardened composure.

"Now I'm out a boyfriend," I say. "Out a job. And out a place to live." I look at her and add, "I hope I'm not out you, too."

A tear goes unchecked and slips down the slide of her face as she nearly loses it again. "No," she says, her voice shaky. "You're never out me."

I reach over and brush her tear from her cheek. "You're never out me, either. I promise."

That draws a single, relieved sob from deep in her chest. "Thank you," she sniffs and clutches my hand. "I really needed to hear that."

"It's what I'm here for."

I hand her a tissue, and she blows her nose. "I have an idea about a place we can stay," she says as she dabs her eyes. "Local. Under the radar. But you're not going to like it."

ROLAND

hey hate me.

Good.

Hate me. Loathe me. Make me the villain. The devil. The spoiled boy prince in his castle.

Hate me, but stay alive.

They think I'm selfish. Proud. They're wrong. *Selfish* would have been keeping them to me. Selfish would have been taking them to bed, night after night, and forcing them to give up their lives to live in mine. Selfish would have been putting them in danger every day simply because my heart ran away with me.

This is the least selfish thing I've done in my whole life. I want them with me so badly I can taste it. But my life isn't normal. I'm the prince of England. Even the prince of England, it turns out, can't always get what he wants.

I leave the hospital in a numb daze. There's a long black car waiting for me right outside. The driver nods to me. I step into it and close the door behind me. My mother barely gives me a glance.

"Are we waiting on anyone else?" she asks.

I stare out the window. "No."

"James, take us home," she says. The car coughs as it starts up and pulls out into the street. "I know that was hard for you, darling." My mum turns her attention to me now. "But you did the right thing."

"You were right," I tell her. "All this time, I thought you were protecting me from the outside world. I didn't realize you were protecting them from me."

Mum doesn't say anything for a moment. When she does, it's simply, "I'll make you a pot of tea when we get home. You'd like that, wouldn't you? And some blueberry scones. Just how you like them."

Tea and scones aren't going to fill this emptiness in my chest. As the hospital gets smaller in the distance, I want to scream for the driver to stop the car. I want to run back to the hospital. I want to take Rory and Ben in my arms. I want to kiss them. I want to tell them I love them, over and over, so they never forget it.

The car turns the corner, and King Edward VII's Hospital vanishes from sight completely.

I've been alone for ten years. I can do it again.

Only *alone* never felt quite this lonely. Before I knew what it was like to love with my whole heart and feel their love in return.

My throat is tight, and my lungs vibrate with effort to keep from screaming out. I twist my signet ring around and around on my finger, battling my surging emotions, until I feel…

Nothing. Nothing at all.

RORY

Brekson sits behind the desk at Free People Hostel, sipping his coffee and reading the local paper. The safety pins clipped to his earlobes wiggle when he jerks his head over the paper to look at us.

"Look what the cat dragged in," he says, folding up the paper and tossing it aside. "Long time no see, kiddo."

"Do you have room for two?" I ask. I approach the desk, Ben stepping quietly behind me.

Brekson's eyes flicker between me and Ben, then back to me, back to Ben. He sniffs, seems to decide not to ask, and says, "Sure do, pumpkin."

He takes two keys from underneath the desk and tosses them to me. They each have little tags on them with a three-digit number. "Those'll get you into your lockers; you'll need a $50 deposit each. How long did you say you were staying?"

Ben takes out his wallet, produces four fifty-pound notes, and sets them on the desk. "Keep the change," he says.

Brekson's eyebrows lift up his forehead. "Aye, aye, Captain," he says. He pockets the money and doesn't ask about our duration again.

Ben takes his time up the stairs, favoring one leg. Each room in the hostel has its own cute name. Ironically, we've landed in the Hufflepuff Room, the same room I was in before. Ben touches my side as I put the key in the door. "Do you think they'll let a Ravenclaw in here?" he asks.

He's trying to make me smile. It works. I shrug. "They let a Gryffindor in, so... just try not to outsmart everyone else in the room."

I unlock the door, and we push inside. There are a couple bunks with clothes and personal items splayed over the beds, but it's mostly empty. Everyone is out and about, sightseeing. There's a quiet Korean girl in the back of the room, but she has headphones plugged in. She glances at us when we enter and nods once in acknowledgment before turning back to her iPhone.

Our bunk is by the door. "Top or bottom?" I ask.

"Bottom," Ben says. He tosses his duffle bag on the floor.

Fair enough. He probably shouldn't be climbing up and down the ladder anyway. We made a brief pit stop at the palace, where a doorman handed us our personal belongings. Talk about a royal send-off. But I have my bag now—that's the good thing—and I shove it on the top.

As I do, I notice Ben crouch down. He's untying his shoes, and as he does, he discreetly slips something underneath his mattress. I see the black muzzle of his gun vanish, and it makes me shiver.

His dark eyes meet mine. He's caught me staring. "Precautionary," he explains.

"I know." You can take the bodyguard off the payroll, but you can't get him to stop guarding.

I leap off my ladder, and my feet hit the floor. "Okay." I motion to the bed. "Sit."

Ben obliges. I kneel between his legs and roll the soft cotton of his shirt up. Stacked abdomen, slim waist... Out of the corner of my vision, I see the Korean girl sneak a peek, and honestly, I can't blame her. I keep lifting his shirt until… there. A huge, ugly, black-and-blue bruise covers the right side of his rib cage and draws spidery lines up his chest.

"It looks worse than it feels," he tries, but I doubt it.

"Stay here." I drop his shirt back down. "I'm going to get some ice."

I get up and leave the room. I know these hallways by heart by now, and my feet lead the way. I put a couple of coins in the bathroom dispensary, and it spits out a hand towel. Then I pop down the winding staircase to the kitchen, where I crack the ice tray and dump the cubes into the towel. My hands and feet move on their own, mechanically. I like having a task, something to keep my idle hands busy.

I know if I stop moving, I'll start thinking about Roland again. And I can't seem to keep myself from crying when I think about him anymore.

It feels so strange to be back here. The last time I was in the hostel, I was full of boundless energy, ready for the next adventure around the corner. Now, I feel like I'll shatter apart if someone so much as looks me in the eyes for too long. I don't like this. I don't like feeling weak.

I busy myself some more. I rummage around the kitchen and find a rubber band. I twist it around the towel and— voilà. A handmade ice pack.

When I come back, Ben has stretched himself out on the cot. It's comically small underneath his tall frame, and his feet hang off the foot of the bed. His eyes flick toward me when the door opens, and I hold up my palms. "Only me."

I sit down on the edge of the cot and roll his shirt up again. Ben helps, peeling it over his head and tossing it to the side.

It looks bad, and I cringe just staring at the bruise.

"Okay... tell me if it hurts," I say and very gently lower the pack of ice onto his purpling bruise.

Immediately, Ben sucks in a sharp breath and hisses through his teeth, "Ah... fucking... cunt."

I flinch and retract the ice pack immediately.

"No," he says quickly, "I wasn't... calling you a cunt. It hurts, that's all."

"Do you want to use a safe word?"

He scoffs a pained a laugh. "Just put it back. Sorry. I won't call you names again. Promise."

I twist my lips together dubiously, but I lower it to his ribs once more. He swallows so hard I can see his Adam's apple bob and his fingers curl around the bedsheets, but he doesn't swear at me again. Anxiety bounces around in my stomach. I don't like hurting him, but I know it's for his own good.

"Okay," Ben says after a second. He replaces my hand with his and cups the ice pack to himself. "It's numbing out. I've got it now."

"Are you sure?"

He nods. "Thank you."

I tuck a strand of hair behind my ear. "Is there anything I can do?"

He lifts his good arm, opening a spot in the bed for me. "You can get comfortable."

I lower myself into bed and press a kiss to his jaw. Ben holds his ice pack to his side with one hand and wraps the other arm around me. His fingers nudge under my shirt, and I wince when he brushes against my bandage.

"Sorry," he murmurs.

"No, it's okay. Just... higher." He rests his hand on the small of my waist instead, and he draws little circles there. "We're a mess, aren't we?"

"Definitely," he says.

"Would distraction help?" I ask.

"Please."

I have a couple of shows I've downloaded to my phone for times of crisis. I've seen them all about ten million times, but they're classics.

"Are you a *Friends* fan?" I ask.

Ben shakes his head. "A what?"

"Seriously? *Friends?* It's like... American *Harry Potter*. I mean, they're not wizards, but... popularity-wise."

"I'm dying with anticipation," Ben says dryly.

I reach into my bag. I pull out headphones and Otter Oscar and tuck him behind my iPhone. The otter angles my phone up, and I snuggle back against Ben. I plug in the headphones; one bud for me, the other bud for Ben.

"Can you see?" I ask.

"Yes." His breath beats against my hair.

I press Play.

It only takes a couple of episodes for Ben to fall asleep behind me. I can tell because his body—normally wound so tight—relaxes against mine and his breathing becomes even, a slow patter on my neck. Ben's ice pack melts a wet spot in the bed, so I move it from his side and drop it to the floor. People file in and out of the suite, mostly young travelers in their early twenties. They all have that fresh-from-the-club vibe, and most stumble unevenly to their bed and pass out.

I'm wired. I can't even think about sleep. The stab wound was numb from whatever painkillers they were giving me at the hospital, but now it feels hot and throbbing. They gave me some Vicodin when I left, so I check the time on my phone to see when I need to dose up again. It's nearly three in the morning—time to take another pill.

I carefully shimmy out of Ben's embrace, leaving him asleep in bed. Then I rummage through my bag until I find the two little orange prescription bottles, one for antibiotics and the other for the pain. I tiptoe out of the room and down the hall. The hardwood floor stops abruptly at the bathroom and turns into square tiles, which feel cold under my feet.

The communal bathroom is empty, but it is a bizarre time of night to be out and about. I stand in front of a sink and roll my shirt up my side. I let out a small hiss of pain when the fabric of my shirt catches on the dried blood at the edge of my bandage. Crap. This sucks. I take a paper towel out of the dispenser, run water over it, and dab it around the bandage to clean it up.

When I see myself in the mirror, I nearly freeze. Oh my God. I look like something out of a horror movie. Toward the end of the movie, where the heroine has been through hell and back again and hits rock bottom before the exorcist saves her. My hair is a frazzled mess. The skin under my eyes is puffy and blue. And the bandage on my side… it's huge. A solid three inches of white.

The back of my throat gets saliva thick. I feel sick looking at it. I've been stabbed. *With an actual knife.* I could've died. I can imagine that phone call, some officer from Helmsway Palace, maybe. All official and British when they called up my parents and delivered the news. They'd be devastated. And Oscar…

It would kill him.

My heart is pounding, and I feel that flush of heat crawl up my neck. A panic attack is coming on. I quickly shove my shirt back down so I don't have to look at the bandage. My hands are shaking, and it's hard to twist the cap off my prescription bottle, but I finally do. I pop my antibiotics and a Vicodin—one less than the doctor prescribed, but my stomach never did well with medications. I flip the tap and bend over the sink to let the cold water dribble over my lips. I wipe my mouth and rush out of the bathroom.

My vision is pulsing, and the hallway narrows and widens

with each rapid beat of my heart. I quicken my pace like a child chased by nightmare monsters. I stumble into the room and dive into Ben's cot.

"Ben," I whisper.

His eyes fly open immediately. He's not exactly a deep sleeper. "What is it?"

There are people in the room. Even through everyone seems to be asleep, I don't want to draw any attention to myself. So I murmur, just loud enough for Ben to hear, "Choke me. Please."

Ben doesn't ask. Maybe he sees the panic in my eyes. Maybe he just *knows* how badly I need this.

"Get on your back," he commands. In the dark, his voice is low and velvet smooth.

I submit to him and settle on my back. The bed groans as he leans on his elbow and closes his hand around my throat. As soon as his fingers touch either side of my jaw, I feel a blanket of bliss fall over me. Ben tightens his grip and my airway constricts. His arm is like a rope pulling me to safety, and I hold it to me. I hear a soft, grateful hum leave my throat. The lack of oxygen makes my brain feel fuzzy... but I'm safe here. I'm safe. So safe. My fear dissolves in my blood and is replaced with calm, peaceful submission.

I don't know how long Ben holds me here. When he does finally release his grip, I gasp like a newborn. The air tastes cold and fresh in my lungs.

"Better?" he asks.

I nod. I don't realize I've been crying until I feel my tears wet the pillow. "Thank you," I whisper.

"For what?"

"Being here. I can barely get through this without Roland... and I miss him so much it hurts. But... I don't know what I'd do if I'd lost the both of you."

He leaves his hand on my throat, but his grip is loose now. I love it. It feels like a collar. I'm safe, as long as I'm his.

"I'm not leaving you," he tells me. As my eyes adjust to the dark, I can see the dark of his irises fixed on me.

"Let's go away," I whisper. "There are cheap flights to Scotland from here. We can just… go."

"I'll go wherever you go," he says, and the back of my eyes burn again as fresh tears spring free.

I grab his face and pull him into a kiss. He presses his lips back against mine and roughly invades my mouth with his tongue. I feel so open to him, and my lips part easily. I taste his tongue and my own salty tears.

One touch from Ben and my shackles of anxiety fall away. I'm free. But even this euphoria has a dark undercurrent. I miss Roland so much—and so does he. I can taste it in the way he kisses me. We crush our lips together, forgetting to be gentle with our damaged bodies. We're missing a third piece and making up for it with a collision of desire.

"Be quiet," Ben says as he tugs the button of my pants loose. I nod in understanding and hang around his neck. I feel his hand slide down my pants and underneath my panties. My mouth falls open, and I stifle a gasp when his rough fingers slide over my slit. I must be slippery, because his touch glides back and forth, igniting every nerve between my legs. When he finds my clit, he flicks it mercilessly. I almost cry out, pleasure burning through my veins with every touch, but he shoves his tongue in my mouth and extinguishes any sound.

"There's a condom in my bag," he murmurs and pulls his hand out from between my legs. "Side pocket."

I'm buzzing all over. I twist over the side of the bed and grope underneath it for his duffle bag. I find the strap and tug it forward. As I undo the zipper, Ben's hand ventures under my shirt. He slips under my bra and rolls his thumb over my peaked nipple. I bite my lip hard to keep myself from whimpering. Every pinch sends another needy pulse between my legs.

It's not in one side zipper, so I hunt blindly through another until my fingers brush the square foil. Eureka! I tug it out and roll onto my back, holding it up between two fingers like a victory flag. "Boom."

"Good girl." He takes it from me and rips the foil between his teeth. That shouldn't be hot, but it makes me lick my lips. I feel the mattress under us move as he reaches down to adjust the condom over himself.

Ben kisses me. I sigh into his mouth as he shifts over me. He only gets part of the way on top of me, however, before he finishes our kiss with a sharp gasp. Moonlight bounces off his jawline, and I can tell it's tense. His injury is acting up.

"You're going to have to be on top," he mumbles.

"Okay." I pet his hair back.

Honestly, this is probably not the smartest time to have sex. What we both need is a good night's sleep, a lot of rest, and definitely no physical exertion. But there's an emptiness inside of me that only intimacy can fill, and I know Ben feels it, too. His strong hands and demanding lips heal me like nothing else. Ben fucks his pain away. I just need to be close to someone.

We trade places—Ben gets on his back, and I shrug out of my pants and underwear before straddling him. If anyone looked our way now, we'd definitely be caught, but I care about that less and less with every passing second. My need for him is urgent and so palpable I can taste it like metal in my mouth.

There's not a lot of space between this bunk and the one above it, and I have to hunch over to keep from bumping my head. With my legs wrapped around his hips, I reach between his legs, take him in my hand, and stroke him. Ben—

the silent, controlled one—barely makes a noise. If I strain my ears, I can hear his quickened breaths. But his cock responds to me with vigor, growing swollen and thick in my hand even under the latex. It sends a thrill throughs me, and I want to keep touching him and finding new ways to make him twitch.

But I want him inside of me more. My pussy is greedy and achy. I lift myself awkwardly in the small space and guide him inside of me. As I slide down his stiff pole, I can't help but gasp. *Oh God.* He feels so good inside of me. At this angle, he feels insanely deep. I grip one of the wooden slats that hold up the bunk above me and start to rock over him.

The tip of his cock grazes a place inside of me that makes me crazy. Every time I rock back on his shaft, it sends pleasure tingling through me. I have to dig my teeth into my bottom lip to keep Ben's name from spilling out of my mouth over and over.

I need this. I need to forget everything about the world. Soon, all I can think about is every inch of him inside of me. When I grind forward, my little clit lays flat against the base of him. The stimulation makes me drench myself, and I feel a hot flush blossom all the way up my face. My shirt is still on, but my bra is pushed over my tits from Ben's fondling, and every now and then the fabric grazes my nipples. I feel that all the way to my molars.

Even in this intense pleasure… I feel like I'm missing something. I'm spoiled now, accustomed to four hands instead of two. Two lips, two cocks, two hard, needy men. As if he can read my mind, Ben's hands slip up my thighs. He cups the round orbs of my ass and guides me to a faster pace over him. I obey. The mattress squeaks underneath us with every thrust, and it's painfully obviously that we're having sex now, but I'm too desperate to care. All thoughts dissipate when Ben's hand ventures farther. He slips between my cheeks, and then his finger presses me *there*.

I can't help the moan that escapes me now. His finger is spit-wet, and it circles my dark hole a couple times before easing inside of me. I grip so tightly to the wooden slat above me that I'm afraid I might break it. The sensation of Ben inside of me, both holes, filling all of me… it's exactly what I need.

My cunt clamps down on Ben's organ. I gasp and grind out my orgasm on him, pulsing and pulling at his manhood and his finger. I feel his iron-hard shaft throb inside of me, and a noise escapes him that sounds like half a moan, half a growl.

As our orgasms wind down, I hang over him, my hands on either side of his head. Ben pulls his finger out from me, and I whimper a small protest at the emptiness. We kiss here for a while, soft, lazy, satisfied kisses as he goes soft inside of me.

"That was amazing," I whisper.

"It was."

"I should uh… go clean up."

"I'll follow you."

I want him inside of me forever, but I shift off him. We fumble around our bags blindly for a moment, and I use the light on my iPhone to give us something to see by. Ben slips on a pair of boxer briefs, and I toss my bra in my bag and use the length of my shirt to my advantage, wearing it like a dress. Ben snags a toiletry bag, I pluck out my toothbrush, and we slip out of our suite and make our way to the bathroom.

After being in the dark for so long, the fluorescent lights nearly blind me. I squint around—no one else here. We're all alone. I take advantage of this rare moment of privacy to check into a stall, drop my panties, and try to clean up the fluids dripping down my legs. I can hear Ben disposing of the condom in the trash bin.

"Pretty sure this is next-level relationship status, by the way," I tell him. "If you can jump straight from the sex to the cleanup phase, you're practically married."

"Need any help mopping up your pussy, sweetie?" Ben plays along.

I laugh and it echoes off the narrow stall. "I've got it. Thanks, honeybun."

I clean myself off, flush the toilet, and step around to the sinks. There's a line of about five sinks, side by side, and Ben has already stationed himself at one. Feeling domestic, I take the one beside him.

"Can I borrow your toothpaste?" I ask.

"Be my guest."

I squirt some of his toothpaste over my toothbrush and wash out my mouth. I feel weirdly giddy, like a little girl at a sleepover.

"What do you think about *Friends*?" I ask, my words jumbled as I speak with my mouth full of toothbrush.

Ben, also brushing his teeth, has a little more decency than me. He spits in the sink before saying, "It's good."

"Who's your favorite?"

"I'd fuck Chandler," he says without missing a beat.

I nearly cough on my toothpaste foam. "Chandler? No one wants him!"

"I do."

I roll my eyes. "I was always a Ross girl."

"Obviously," he scoffs. "You're a hopeless romantic."

"You say that like it's a bad thing."

"It's not." He's incredibly earnest suddenly, those dark eyes on me. He turns my chin to face him, and my toothbrush pops out of my mouth. He presses a small minty kiss to my lips. "It's my favorite thing about you."

Somehow, I got a gay best friend and a sensual lover rolled into one. I don't know how that happened… but it did. His rough hands choke me when I need to hurt and cradle me when I need affection. Ben should be all I need… but he's not.

And I'm not all he needs. We're not whole together. Not without Roland.

Sadness barrels into me like a freight train. Suddenly, my vision blurs and I'm crying again. For the hundredth time today. Boo-hoo, poor me. Concern flashes over Ben's expression. "What's wrong?"

"I just… hold on." I spit in the sink, wash my mouth, and wash my face. The cold water feels good on my tear-hot eyelids, and I keep holding my hands over my face. "I miss Roland," I choke out. I hate myself for saying that. I hate myself for admitting that I miss one lover when my other lover is right here in front of me. When did my life get this complicated?

Ben takes my wrists gently, and he lowers my hands from my face. I know I must look a wreck—my lower lip feels swollen, and I'm doing my best to keep it from trembling.

"Rory… I miss him, too," Ben sighs. "Incredibly. You don't have to hide from me."

"I told myself I wouldn't fall in love while I was traveling, you know? I knew it would just lead to heartbreak. I knew it and I did it anyway. God." I drop my head. A teardrop hangs on my eyelashes. "I feel like such an idiot."

"Hey. Look at me." Ben's eyebrows press together, intense. "You know the lie I told myself?"

I sniff. "What?"

"I told myself I would never let Roland know how I felt about him. I held it inside of me for six years. It nearly ate me alive, but I swallowed it. Without you, I would've taken it to my grave."

"Do you regret telling him?"

"Not for a second. A wise woman once told me that it's better to die regretting the things you've done than regretting all the things you were too afraid to do."

"Did you mean it?" I ask, looking into his coal-dark eyes. "Will you really come to Scotland with me?"

Ben nods. "I meant it. We can leave tomorrow, if you'd like."

"Okay." I rock forward and lean against him, resting my head on his chest. My heart feels stone heavy, and my eyes are so puffy they're nearly swollen shut. I'm tired of crying. I'm tired of feeling this heartbroken. "I just… need to leave. I need to get out of London."

"It's going to be okay, love," Ben reassures me. He holds the back of my head and presses a kiss to my forehead.

BEN

*R*ory cries herself to sleep.

I'm sure between the crying, fucking, and whispering, we've kept everyone else up all night. We're terrible houseguests. Truthfully, since I left the military, I'd hoped I wouldn't have to bunk with a room full of people again. It seems that's not the case. I could have asked my parents if we could stay with them for a night, and I'm sure they would've said yes. But that would've involved telling them that I got fired from the palace. I'm not ready to face their disappointment and barrage of questions. Plus, we're safe here. No killers or assassins will come looking for us here.

No matter. We won't be here long anyway.

Rory's got plans for Scotland. Which is fine by me. Without Roland to tether me, there's nothing for me here.

Rory snores lightly, her lips parted, her cheek flattened against my chest. Now that she's fallen asleep, I'm wide-awake again. Rory's phone lies charged on the side of the bed, so I pick it up and pop her headphones back in. I flip through her video library. She has a cornucopia of movies here. Mostly feel-good movies—romances, comedies—and a couple of travel documentaries.

Then I find her own personal stash. Her March On videos. They're posted on her website, so I decide it's definitely not snooping, and I click on one at random. There are a couple of shaky moments as she adjusts the camera shot; this video must be unedited. Helmsway Palace comes into view. Nighttime, but the doors are wide open and a warm, white light glow spills down the steps. Rory brings herself into frame. Her pink dress hugs around her chest and clings to her sides before billowing out around her hips—it's the night of the masquerade ball. The wind brushes her red, curly hair into her face, and she pushes it back. She has an excited, nervous grin that stretches from one side of her face to the other.

"Hello and March On!" she says. "Your fearless leader, Rory March, reporting for duty from Candyland."

A chuckle escapes me before I can stop it. I can't help it. She's bloody adorable.

"Really! Look at this dress!" she continues. "When was the last time anyone saw something so pink?" She angles the camera down to scan the dress and wolf whistles at herself. "But wait… check this out." She lifts the hem of her dress to show off her combat boots and then twists the camera back to her knowing grin. "This Bo Peep isn't going down without a fight. For those of you who are wondering… yes. I got invited to the Helmsway Palace annual ball by Prince Roland. He's… um." She fidgets and tucks her hair behind her ear. "It's nothing romantic—don't get ahead of yourselves, internet friends with your internet gossip. We're just friends… getting to know each other. That sort of thing. Anyway!"

She brightens again and slips on a black eye mask with

dark raven feathers popping out of the sides. She gestures wildly toward the palace. "Who wants to come inside?"

Rory carries the camera up the steps with her and holds it in front of her as she enters the doors. The camera gets a sweeping, rare view of inside the palace. Lights twinkle off the chandeliers hanging above the party. The room is flooded with people in wild, extravagant dresses and tailored suits, all toting their strange and bizarre masks. There are long buffet tables, one topped with a full pig, oriental rugs patterning the floors, and old kings and queens staring down from their larger-than-life portraits.

I've walked down those halls every day for years. Yet it seems like I'm seeing it all for the first time. Even I have to wonder at it. Helmsway Palace, truly, is a world built in a dream.

"Holy cow..." she whispers, her voice barely audible, as though she forgot she was on camera. "It's like a fairy tale."

"Excuse me, ma'am." The crisp, British voice seems to startle Rory. The camera jerks and fumbles as Rory moves to hide it.

"Hi!" Rory chirps. "Yes. Rory March. I'm on the list."

"Are you filming, ma'am? There are no cameras allowed."

"What—me? No—I mean... this is just a project..."

Their conversation continues as Rory tries to talk her way out of getting kicked out.

I pause the video. I pinch the screen outward, enlarging the video and scanning the stilled image. There's Prince Roland, hanging off to the side. The corner of my mouth twitches upward—the man looks like he might faint. I remember that day, the jumble of nerves he'd twisted himself into. And there I am, standing stiff beside him.

I look like a prat. Nothing new there. I scroll on through the rest of the party guests. This was the first time I spotted the scarred man... I know he's somewhere here. He was wearing a waiter's outfit, I remember that. I hunt for the waiters and roll my finger up and down the screen until... *There*. I've found him. He's caught in the middle of the room. I'd recognize that man anywhere. The stocky build, those strong arms that pressed me down underwater...

Swallow that memory back. March on.

I hit Play. Rory is prattling on to the doorman, and I follow the scarred man as he winds his way through the crowd of guests. He comes to a halt and catches a woman's attention. She turns to him and—

My blood runs cold as river water. No. Not any woman. It's Princess Iris. The dress is unmistakable, a rush of blood red. I watch as the princess turns away from her guest to engage the scarred man in a conversation. They speak intently for a moment. The princess looks perturbed. Then she reaches out, touches a hand to his shoulder. The scarred man nods and leaves, vanishing into the crowd once more. She turns away as well and plucks a cigarette pack out of her purse.

I stop the video. My heart pounds away in my chest. I've paused on Princess Iris's face. She looks distant, her eyes staring off in a faraway gaze.

What did they talk about? What does the queen of England's twin sister have in common with a man who tried to kill her nephew?

This is insane. Conspiracy-level shit. I should put the phone down. I should mark it up as a bizarre interaction and let this rest.

Instead, I replay the video, over and over again, until the pieces start fitting into place.

40

ROLAND

As soon as we get back to the palace, my mum breaks away from me to vanish into her room. She's retreating. My little "escapades" have taken it out of her. She's a snake that needs to burrow underneath the ground and recharge. She'll remain in bed for days and won't come out until she's ready. It was the kind of thing that used to drive me insane as a child—*Mummy's gone, Mummy's broken and it's all your fault*—but now it's just a fact of life. Like splinters and bad weather. It *will happen*, no avoiding it, and all you can do is keep trudging through.

Perhaps it's not a bad idea. I feel like sleeping away the winter myself.

As I slump down the hallway, Iris meets me. She follows at my side and moves her hand to my shoulder. "I heard what happened at the Thames," she murmurs. "We're all very happy you're safe."

"Is that what *we* are? Happy?" My voice is clipped, disinterested.

She sighs. "Don't worry about your mother. She'll come

around. You know how she is. She just needs to have a fit every once in a while. I'll take care of her."

"Fine."

She twists her head side to side. "Where's Rory?"

"How the bloody hell should I know?"

"Lover's spat?"

"I don't want to talk about it."

I grab the handle of my bedroom door and twist.

"Roland." I lift my eyes just enough to look at Iris. Her Pennington blues reflect back at me. "Everything will be okay. You'll see."

But it won't. Not anymore. I push into my room and close the door behind me. Closing out Iris. Closing out my mum. Closing out the world.

The maids have come and gone while I was away. My room is clean, my bed made, and a sanitizing lemon scent hangs in the air. My eyes immediately snap to the one item out of place. Rory's pink masquerade dress is washed, dried, and folded neatly on the foot of my bed. I lift the dress and run my fingers over the fabric. I remember how her body responded to my touch, feeling the hardened peaks of her nipples through the lace of her dress. I lift the bundle of dress to my nose and inhale. Even washed, there's still a hint of her left. Her unique blend of earthy tones. My wild woman who smelled constantly of fresh rainfall.

My heart aches like an open wound.

What have I done?

I've made a terrible mistake. This is all wrong. I can't go back to the way things were. I can't pretend I don't need her in life. I miss Rory. I miss Ben. I need to go to them. I need to apologize. I need to wrap her in my arms and never let her go.

I rush to my door and twist the knob. It doesn't budge. I push my shoulder into it, but it's no use.

It's locked. That solid security lock. *What the heck?*

A switch must have accidentally flipped somewhere. Tanner will hear about this. I reach into my pocket to phone him, but all I feel is loose fabric. I check my other pockets.

Shit. Where the hell is my phone?

I bang the door. "Hello? Is anyone out there?"

"Roland." A familiar, flower-soft voice bleeds in through the wall.

Thank God. Iris.

"Iris… I'm locked in. I need you to call Tanner and tell him to fix the bloody door."

There's a small spot of silence on the other side. I wonder if she hasn't heard me. Then her voice, gentle and calm: "I'm afraid I can't do that."

The hairs on the back of my neck rise. "What do you mean?"

"It's for your own safety, ducky," Iris sighs. "Perhaps we could have worked something out, but you're just so… unpredictable these days."

My blood runs cold. No. No, no, *no.* They can't lock me in here. They can't. My breath goes short, and my vision vibrates, the blood behind my eyes pulsing. The walls seem to be beating, drawing in closer. *This room is a bloody tomb.*

"Iris!" I shout. "You can't do this!" I bang my fist on the door. Pure, animal Pennington rage courses through my blood. My temper rears its ugly head. "Let me out!" I roar. "Let me out!"

I unleash my fists on the door, but they don't budge. If they want to cage me like an animal—*fine.* I will be an animal! I rip the bedside table off the floor, the contents scattering to the ground, and throw it against the door. The wood splinters, but the door remains unscathed. I smash lamps. I tear up curtains.

Only when my hands are bleeding and my lungs burning do I stop. My room is a mess, and the clutter does nothing for my claustrophobia. I grab my hair by the roots, fall to my knees, and howl.

I'm locked in the palace. For good, this time.

41

RORY

*T*ea can cure anything, Roland once told me. He was naked, we were postcoital sore, and his lion's den of a room engulfed us. Ben had brought in scones and a pot of tea, and we all sat up, enjoying breakfast in the prince's bed. *War, sickness, a prolonged eternity of boredom,* Roland continued. *Fix a cuppa, turn that frown uppa.*

I'm not sure if it can cure heartbreak, but I figure it's worth a shot. My eyelids are swollen, my wound is throbbing, and I feel hungover. Ben isn't in bed when I wake up, and his gun is gone, but his duffle bag is still tucked under the mattress, so I know he hasn't run off on me. I rummage through my own bag to pick out some clothes.

Nearly everyone has already left for the day. The Korean girl in the far end of the room sits on her cot, headphones in ears. She shoots me a glare when she sees I'm up.

Oops. I'm normally a better suitemate. I try an apologetic smile and a cheery, "Good morning!"

She doesn't even respond; she turns back to her device. Well, I deserved that one.

As I pull clean clothes out, a folded-up map pops out of

my bag. I unroll it out onto my lap. It's my old bus map, most of the routes to Scotland already circled. A tremor of excitement runs through me. This is what I'm good at. I fish a pen out of my bag, open up my phone, and start looking up flight schedules. I jot down a couple of times on the corner of my map, along with the corresponding flight numbers. Then I hunt down bus schedules, hostels, and price match. I've got the process down to a science, and it's not long before I have a couple of options mapped out.

I'm already feeling more like myself when I put my work down to freshen up. The bathroom is bustling now with morning activity, and I manage to snag a sink to wash up. I shimmy into a stall and maneuver out of my sleepwear and into a clean, dark pair of jeans and an oversized band shirt.

No more *Principessa Rory*, thank you very much. I'm back to plain old Rory March for a while. And honestly? It feels good.

I've reached phase two of the breakup: the angry, indignant phase. *Screw Roland.* Screw Roland, screw his martyrdom, screw his self-importance, and screw his stupidly handsome face and soul-crushing blue eyes.

Now for that cuppa.

I pack everything up back in the room, except for the map, my wallet, and Oscar. Those, I tuck in a lumpy purse that I hang over my shoulder. I shove the rest of my stuff in my locker along the far wall and head downstairs to the common area. There are a couple people up and about, working on their laptops, reading, or chatting over breakfast. I find the beverage station. I fill the electric teapot with water, stick it in, and pick out a tea bag as it boils.

"Make me a cuppa while you're at it."

I glance over my shoulder and see Ben sitting alone at a circular table. I don't know how I didn't notice him before—maybe it's because he doesn't look quite as out of place as he did the first time we had tea together here. He's dressed down in loose jeans and a soft coal-gray shirt that cuts off around his bulging biceps.

Ben has an assortment of papers scattered in front of him. As he studies them, he scratches the side of his face absently. He hasn't shaved yet. He's got morning stubble. It looks really good on him. Really, really good. I'd-like-to-feel-that-bristle-against-my-inner-thighs good. My sex pulses and my legs squeeze together at the thought.

Dear God, Rory! Focus!

"Yes, sir." I wink and make a second cup.

I expect one of his small amused smiles or that smoldering *you're being a naughty girl* look from his dark eyes. Instead, he barely looks up when I set the cup down in front of him. "Thank you," he murmurs.

I take the seat across from him and wrap my hands around my mug. I try another tactic to get his attention. I unzip my purse, pick the map out, and spread it out across the table. "I found a couple cheap flights to Edinburgh," I inform him. "Most of them are about sixty euros one way, but if we take the red-eye, it's practically half the price. Most of the buses are shut down at that point, but there's a shuttle that'll take us into the city—"

"That's great," Ben says. His tone is curt, distracted, and his eyes flicker up to me. "You should book it."

I should. I try not to flinch. My heart drops like a stone into my stomach. I try to remain upbeat and tuck my hair behind my ear. "Yeah, I mean… I can. No problem. But am I booking for one or two? Because… last night you were pretty clear about the whole *where you go, I go* thing, but now I feel like I'm talking to Frosty the Snowman here…"

Ben's lips thin and he finally diverts all of his attention to me. "I found something last night," he tells me. His voice is all official. Bodyguard Ben mode.

Okay. I can deal with this. He's not mad at me; he's just locked up in his head. I relax my stance and nod. "What kind of thing?"

"I couldn't fall asleep, so I started watching your March On videos."

A grin lifts the corners of my mouth. "You were watching my videos?"

"Yes." Plain. Simple. As though that's the obvious answer. It's such a small, sweet gesture, and I feel my heart grow wings again. "I found the video you took the night of the masquerade ball."

I sip on my tea and sigh at that. "I could barely use any of the footage I got from that. You bodyguards are a piece of work."

"The man who kidnapped you—he was there. At the masquerade."

Chills run up my spine, and I feel goose bumps tighten the flesh on my arms. The thought of him there, only a couple of feet away from me while I danced and laughed with Roland… it makes me queasy. "Are you sure?" I chirp.

Ben picks a page out of his folder and turns it toward me. It's a blown-up image from my video of that night. I can see the man with his bald head, stuffed into a tuxedo. I try not to look at him for very long. I don't want another panic attack, not now.

Ben taps the image, redirecting my attention. "Here he is, speaking with Princess Iris."

I blink at the image and then back at Ben. "They know each other? How?"

"That's the question of the day. So I watched the rest of your videos, did a little research, and I found a couple of other interesting images."

Ben lines up a few other printouts in front of me. One is from Sorrento; I recognize the brightly colored stone walls and beach hats. It's an image of the small crowd of people taking our photos. Roland's arm is wrapped around my shoulder. I look incredibly happy. So does he. The memory feels like warm sun on the back of my neck, and it draws a little smile from me.

Ben points to a woman in the crowd wearing a slim dress and a black hat. "I found this image off an Italian paparazzi gossip blog. This woman was at the bar the night you were kidnapped. She flashed me. I think she was in on it, possibly trying to distract me—"

I nearly choke on my tea. Jealousy is a petty, completely inappropriate emotion to be feeling right now, but it rears its head up suddenly. "Rewind," I say. "A woman showed you her tits, and you didn't think to mention this before now?"

Ben narrows his eyes. "I rejected her. Obviously. And you got stabbed. When exactly should I have told you?"

Right. He has a point. Still. I pout. "Her distraction worked. *Obviously.*"

Ben sighs. "No. It didn't. Our drunken prince distracted me. A mistake I won't make again. Can we move on?"

"Please."

"Right." Ben procures a final image. Two mug shots, side by side. "So I did some sleuthing and I found them. Martin Hindel, fifty-four, arrested in 1987 and again in '94. His charges included assault, robbery, and—you guessed it— kidnapping. The woman is Sara Ryan, thief and con woman."

I blink at the images. My brain is pounding with all this information, and the printouts blur before my eyes. "Don't they do background checks on everyone who comes into the palace?"

"Yes. Extensively. So you have to wonder what two felons were doing near the royal family, unless—"

"Unless they were invited," I blurt out, finishing his thought.

Ben nods slowly. "Exactly."

"But that doesn't make sense!" I toss up my hand. "Why would Iris send a couple felons after her nephew…?"

"That's what I intend on finding out." Ben quiets me and reaches across the table. He slips his hand over mine and traces his fingertips over my wrist. "Which is why I can't come with you to Scotland right now."

My throat tightens. "But…"

"I know what I promised last night," Ben continues. "And I intend to follow through on that. You should go. Just in case things get hairy here. Get settled at a hotel. I *will* meet you in Edinburgh. I promise you, Rory. I just need a couple of days to sort this out. As much as I… hate his bloody guts right now, I can't leave if Prince Roland is still in jeopardy. Hindel is dead, but the woman…" Ben's eyes wander. I can practically see all the worst-case-scenario thoughts flickering through his brain. He fixes his gaze back on me and says firmly, "I need to make sure he's okay."

I nod at that. "I understand," I tell him. I thread my fingers between his and squeeze his hand. "You promise you'll find me?"

Ben's dark eyes soften at that. "I swear to it." He stands suddenly, leans over the table, and pulls me into a kiss. His kiss is strong, unrelenting, and it nails his point home. *I'm not letting you go,* his lips say, and I believe them.

When he seals the kiss, he pulls back and picks up a pen. Then he turns my map toward him. "Are these all the flights?" he asks.

I nod. He draws a circle around the last flight and turns it back to me. "Twelve forty-five. The red-eye. I'll be on that one."

My heart is still hammering, but it slows at that. The black circle on the page has the same effect on me as Ben's hand around my throat. It's *security*. My anxiety bubble pops, and I settle when I look into his eyes.

"Okay," I say.

Ben's shoulders sink with relief. He picks up the pages he's scattered about the table, then sticks them back into his folder. Watching him, my heart begins to patter again.

"Ben?"

He turns his gaze away from the pages and looks back up at me.

"Be careful."

A smile inches across his face. "Don't worry about me, kitten," he says and closes the folder.

* * *

"Now boarding Zone 3 for Flight 106, heading to Edinburgh," the voice crackles over the loudspeaker.

The chairs are hard semicircular plastic bits that are curved in such a way that make it impossible to get comfortable. My giant backpack takes up the whole seat next to me. I curl up against it, rubbing Oscar's soft, velvety ears.

This is usually my favorite part. Onward to adventure! I'm probably the only person in the world who still loves traveling through airports. They're the closest things we have to portals. You enter in one country, you exit in another a few hours later. It's amazing, really, how quickly someone can turn their life around.

So why this sinking pit in my stomach?

I've got my phone charging in the outlet beside me. My one-way plane ticket juts out of my pocket. I haven't been this nervous since my first flight out of Michigan.

"Now boarding Zone 4," the loudspeaker announces, voice bored. "Zone 4 for Flight 106."

A tingle runs up my spine. Zone 4. That's me. I pluck out

my boarding pass and stare at it. "What're we going to do, Oscar?" I sigh.

"I'm telling you, we put it right on the bloody belt!" I glance up to see a man in a suit yelling at an attendant. She folds her arms over her yellow-and-orange neon vest as he jabs a finger at her. "How incompetent does the airport staff have to be to lose a bloody suitcase?"

His hair is slicked back, his three-piece suit barely ruffled, and his Rolex gleams from his wrist. The attendant is doing her best to soothe him, but his face only gets redder by the second. A little girl—maybe five or six, wearing a spring dress dotted with daisies—tugs on his blazer and wails.

"Daddy!" she howls. "Misses Kitty! They lost Misses Kitty!"

"Debbie, sit!" the businessman snaps at his daughter as though she were a dog.

Debbie throws herself into the seat beside me, as dramatic as a 1920s starlet. She wails into the seat, her blonde pigtails bobbing with every heaved sob.

People are starting to shoot the family glares. Sure, maybe she is a spoiled little girl, but… shouldn't every little girl get to be spoiled? I can't help it. I hate to see kids cry. I pick up Oscar and push him toward her, as though his otter feet are walking over the divider separating our seats.

"Hello, little girl!" I say, curling my tongue on the roof of my mouth to give Oscar a pitchy voice. "Why are you so sad?"

Debbie climbs into her seat, sits down, and scowls at me as she wipes her nose on her sleeve. "I'm six. I'm not a *baby*."

Well. Called out by a six-year-old. I can cross that item off my bucket list. I abandon my plan and drop the cutesy voice. The little girl sniffles beside me, so I try a more honest approach. "You lost your friend, huh?"

Her bottom lip wobbles. "My *best* friend."

"You know, Oscar has been my best friend for years," I tell her, turning the stuffed otter around in my hands. "We've been on lots of adventures together, all over the world. He's protected me no matter where I go."

"Misses Kitty keeps me safe."

"Do you think Oscar could protect you? Just until Misses Kitty comes back?"

The little girl stares at Oscar, and then she reaches out to take him. I hand the stuffed toy over. She hugs him tightly to her chest.

I can't help but smile at that. "Stay brave, sweetie," I tell her.

"Debbie!" her father snaps. "Come!"

The little girl scampers after her father, clutching her newfound friend. I smile as I watch them go.

"Last call!" the loudspeaker squawks.

Time to take my own advice. I have to make a choice. I look down at the bold black lettering on my boarding pass. *Stay brave, Rory.*

42

BEN

The golden Angel of Justice gleams brightly from her post. Spotlights illuminate her from underneath and cast sharp, crooked shadows on the stone memorial. Beyond her, the Helmsway Palace gates loom like prison bars.

It's chilly tonight, and I suck the end of my fag. The smoke warms my lungs, at least. I tug the sleeve of my coat and check the time.

My watch blinks up at me. 18:13. In two minutes exactly, the guards will change shifts. I'll have approximately thirty seconds to make it in unnoticed.

I lean across the railing and scan the area. It's mostly empty, minus a drunken couple staggering across the bridge. The man's footsteps stomp clumsily above me, and the woman laughs shrilly.

I touch the gun at my hip. It's loaded and ready. I don't want to use it, but sometimes you don't have a choice in the matter. I'd rather not show up empty-handed.

I check my watch again. 18:14. Okay. Time to move. I flick my lit smoke into the river.

Fuck you, Thames.

Just as I'm pivoting to head in, I hear a squawk. "Ben!"

I jerk around and grab my pistol in the same motion. It's halfway out of the holster when I come nose-to-nose with Rory.

Well. Nose-to-chest. The girl is at least a foot shorter than me. Amazing how something so small could be so much trouble.

"Bloody hell, Rory," I hiss. She has no idea how close she came to eating my lead. "What are you doing here?"

"I couldn't let you do this alone," she explains frantically. "And I tried to call you, but you weren't answering your phone, so—"

I lift my palm and lower it slowly to gesture her to be quiet. *Inside voices.* She swallows her words. "Aren't you supposed to be on a plane?" I chastise quietly.

Those emerald-green eyes shimmer in the moonlight. She shakes her head. "I've been running ever since I left the states. I'm not running from this. If Roland's in trouble, we're going to help him. Together."

Admittedly, my heart softens at her words. I do feel better now that she's here, the pins and needles suddenly swept away by her whirlwind presence. I can't tell her that, though. Instead, I press my lips together and demand, "Follow me. And be quiet."

"Aye, aye," she salutes. I turn and head down the walkway parallel to the river. She follows me like a puppy. "What are you going to do?" she asks. "Are we breaking in? How are we going to get through the entrance—aren't there guards everywhere—?"

I cut her short and stop underneath the bridge. "We're using a key." I pluck my key card out of my pocket and swipe it on the hidden sensor. Sure enough, it hasn't been deactivated yet. The light goes green and the door hisses open.

Rory's mouth falls open with surprise. "Dumb luck."

I motion her in. "I'm full of it. After you."

43

ROLAND

The fireplace crackles and burns. I perch on the edge of a footstool and toss a pillow cover into the fire. Immediately, the fireplace bursts into a ball of orange and smoke. The fabric burns quickly, and just like that, the fire tames once more, coughing up a puff of gray in its wake.

I destroyed everything I could get my hands on. Now, my beast is spent. For the moment. And my rational brain has kicked in.

There has to be a way out of here. *There has to.*

No more temper tantrums. It's time to get to work. With my hair tied back in a ribbon to keep it from singeing, I've spent the better part of the night playing with fire. Literally. If I set off the fire alarm, I've decided, someone will have to bust open the door and come get me.

Or I burn alive. There's *that.*

It scares me how little that thought bothers me.

Without Rory and Ben, nothing else matters. Not the crown. Not this prison of a palace. Nothing.

I chuck off another pillow cover and watch it burn. Just

then, a noise outside my door catches my attention. I hear footsteps and then… a familiar voice.

Could that be—? It sounds like Ben. His voice is a low mumble, and I can barely make it out, but it sounds like he's asking someone for the time. My skin buzzes, and I leap to my feet.

I nearly call out for him. *Help, I'm trapped in my own room and I can't get out!* Sounds like a bloody infomercial. The moment I open my mouth, however, I hear a brief struggle followed by a soft *thud*.

My heart hammers. The lock scratches, clinks, and then the door opens. Relief pours over me. My guard is unceremoniously slumped on the floor, unconscious, while Ben and Rory stand at the door.

I could kiss them.

"You're a sight for sore eyes," I sigh.

Rory rushes to me, and I immediately take her in my arms. She smells like springtime and honeysuckle, and it makes my heart ache. I don't want to let her go—not ever.

"I shouldn't have left you," I tell her. "I'm so sorry."

"It's okay." Her voice shakes. "We're here now."

A thump distracts me, and I relax my grip and look up. Ben drags the bodyguard into my room and props the poor bloke up on the love seat. He wipes his hands over his pants. "What happened here?" Ben asks, scanning the destruction that is my room.

I half shrug. "I'm redecorating." I point to the limp guard in my love seat. "What happened to him?"

"Nasty fall," Ben states. "He'll wake up soon. We need to go." Ben is all work. There will be time for long embraces later.

Urgency spikes through my bones, and I extract myself from Rory. "Not without my mum. Iris… she's lost it. I think she's after the crown."

Ben nods, his expression lacking surprise, and I realize he already knows. Of course he does. And they came for me anyway, even knowing the danger that was involved. My heart trembles, and I want to weep with gratitude.

"Can she do that?" Rory asks. "Just…take the crown?"

"After my mum dies, she's next in line," I tell her.

"You two stay here," Ben says. "I'll go find Iris."

"No," Rory pipes up beside me. "We came here together. We're finishing this together."

"I second that," I agree.

Ben seems to recognize that there's no use fighting two stubborn people, so he checks his pistol at his side. "Stay behind me."

RORY

We leave the bodyguard tied to a chair in Roland's room. I put a glass of water next to him. You know. Just in case he wakes up and needs hydration.

Ben leads us out of the bedroom and down the hallway. We walk quietly, against the wall, and stop frequently every time Ben signals us by lifting a palm. Every time he stops us, we pause only a couple of minutes for the guards to turn away before Ben ushers us down another hall.

It seems like forever until we hit the sitting room. Roland darts to the fireplace. He removes a globe from the mantel and hits a button engraved in the wood behind it. The wooden paneling beside the fireplace clicks and swings ajar.

"A shortcut," Roland explains. "This goes straight to my mum's room."

One by one, we slip through the narrow passageway. This secret tunnel becomes shorter the farther you move through it, and we have to crouch by time we reach the end. It stops at a grate.

"Everything will be fine, dearest sister." The voice sounds

jarringly close through the grate… and then a pair of long legs step in front of us, only a couple of feet away. I find myself holding my breath to keep quiet until the legs walk past.

"It's Iris," Roland whispers. We're all crammed together, and his rapid, panicked breaths hit my ear hotly. "She's with my mother."

I hear the clicking sound of spoon on porcelain. "Drink some more tea, ducky. You know that solves everything."

"Thank you, Iris." The queen's voice sounds strangely soft and strained, and it makes me shiver.

Roland flips the latch and pushes out of the tunnel. Ben and I climb out after him and stand behind him.

"Mum—put the tea down," Roland orders.

"Roland?" His mother blinks blearily. She's sitting on the edge of her bed in a long white nightgown. With her hair down, long blonde tresses curling like waves, she looks meek and doe-like. Beautiful still, but… well. *Normal.* "What on earth are you doing here?"

"Ah. Roland." Iris's red lips twist in a grimace. "Just the man I wanted to see."

"Drop the weapon, bodyguard." A woman in a dark suit seems to emerge from the wallpaper behind us and points a pistol at Ben's head.

My heart falls through the floor. So much for the element of surprise. Ben looks like he's swallowed an apple core. He scowls and hands his weapon off to her.

"Sara Ryan, is it?" Ben says.

"Handsome *and* clever." She smiles cruelly. "I like that."

"You two know each other?" I venture.

"She was at the club," Ben grunts.

It dawns on me. "You're the boob flasher," I pipe up.

A low laugh escapes her throat. "I see my tits precede me."

"I'm completely lost," Roland snaps, his hands in the air.

"Why are we talking about her breasts?" He snarls at Iris, "You're trying to poison my mum and steal the crown."

"Goodness, Roland!" The queen tosses up her hand. "You're always so bloody dramatic. No one's trying to poison anyone."

Iris's lips purse together like a rosebud. "No, Selena, he's right," she says coldly. "I've been trying to kill you for *years.*"

Her words are so startling that my whole brain feels fuzzy, like I've been hit over the head with a brick. Everyone's eyes are locked on Princess Iris. Slowly, I reach into my jacket and my trembling fingertips graze my phone.

BEN

The cold muzzle of her pistol presses against my temple. My heart is banging against my rib cage. Yet the air seems sucked out of the room at Iris's confession.

Iris laughs. It cuts the tension with all the grace of a rusty machete. "Oh, why so *sour*?" She cackles. "Come, now. You had to know this was coming. Your meddling kids clearly have it all figured out."

"Poison?" The queen stares into her teacup and then throws it at her sister. The remaining tea slops against the wall, and the cup shatters into a million pieces. "You conniving, jealous *brat!*"

Selena lifts a hand to slap her sister, but Iris suddenly grabs the queen by the throat. I lurch forward, and so does Roland, but the gun twists at my head as a reminder. "Down, boys," the agent hisses.

"Don't spend all your energy at once, dear sister," Iris coos. "It'll only make the toxin work faster."

Selena gargles, and then her legs give out. She sits at the edge of the bed, and her eyes fill with tears. "Why?"

"*Why?*" Iris mocks, releasing her sister to pace in front of the bed. "You had everything! You had our parents' love and attention. You had the crown. You had a handsome husband and a strong son. You took everything and left nothing for me."

Queen Selena starts to nod off, her eyelids drooping. *No,* I plead quietly. *Stay awake. Stay alert.*

Iris cups her sister's chin in her hand. "How long did you expect me to live quietly in your shadow? Who was left to love me?"

"I loved you," Selena mumbles, her words slurring together.

Iris spits. "You pitied me. That's not love." She stands and her eyes blaze over the three of us. "So I'll take everything you love. And then I'll take the crown."

"My father," Roland speaks up, his voice a near-whisper. "That was you?"

Iris's lips twist in a grimace. "You were *all* supposed to be on that plane... mechanical failure. It would have been perfect, and the crown would have fallen into my lap. But no... you had to make me wait. For ten years, this place was a goddamn fortress... until you." She turns her vicious smile on Rory, and every muscle in my body goes stiff. "I should thank you, ducky. Without you, I would've never gotten the prince within my crosshairs.

"Of course, I didn't expect *you* there, bodyguard." She turns to me and clicks her tongue against her teeth. "The things you three get up to behind closed doors... naughty, naughty."

"All this time and you chose now to act," I say. "Why? You had access."

"Pragmatic bodyguard wants details." Iris clicks her tongue again. "Very well. Yes, I had access. I also had plenty of *motive*. Scotland Yard would have fingered me in a second. I thought about pinning it on one of the guards, trust me, but they're all just bloody good-boys."

"You're insane," Roland snaps. "You can't possibly think you'll get away with this."

"Oh, but I *have*," Iris sneers. She motions to us. "A sordid love triangle ends in bloodshed. The despondent, codependent queen takes her own life. The headlines write themselves, dearie. And now… about that bloodshed."

Iris nods to the agent beside me. I feel the muzzle align with my brains.

Fuck. This is how I die. I taste metal. My eyes meet Roland's blues. He looks terrified. I search myself for peace in my last moments, but all I find is the same thought, over and over: *Please, God, please. Take me and let Roland and Rory make it out of this…*

"Wait!" Rory's voice rings out, and I exhale. I'm glad, at least, her bell chime of a voice is the last thing that I get to hear. "Just… one thing. Before you blow our brains out."

"What is it now?" Iris hisses.

"Smile for the camera." Rory lifts her hand out of her jacket to reveal her iPhone, the camera lens aimed straight at Iris. "Livestreaming," Rory explains. "It's a bitch. Ten million people just witnessed your confession."

Iris's jaw goes slack. "No…" she whispers. "It can't be…"

Just then, the double doors fly open. Chief of Security Tanner and a crew of guards line up behind him.

"It's over, Princess," Tanner growls, his gun trained on Iris. "Step away from the queen of England."

The agent beside me does the smart thing—she drops her weapon, puts her hands behind her head, and gets to her knees. She knows when the jig is up. The princess doesn't give in so quickly. Her eyes look bloodshot and frenzied when she says, "God bless the queen." With that, she grabs the broken shard from the teacup and lunges toward Queen Selena.

Two shots from Tanner's gun are all it takes to subdue her. The once-proud woman slumps to the floor, limp. Her white-blonde hair turns crimson red.

"Mum!" Roland's voice snaps me back to attention. He darts forward and lifts his mother, who has fallen back on the bed. "Mum… oh God. Stay with me."

Rory and I rush to his side. The queen's eyes flutter open, but just barely. She sees her son, smiles, and her fingers reach out to touch his face. "I only wanted to protect you," she whispers. She seems loopy, the drugs making her sluggish. "I only wanted to keep you safe… and she was… in the palace… the whole time. Silly me."

"I know," Roland murmurs. "It's over now. Everything's going to be okay."

Rory looks sick with worry. Her eyes brim with tears, and her hand covers her mouth. I reach out and touch her arm. "You saved us," I whisper to her.

It seems to be what she needs to hear. She takes my hand and clutches it hard. I squeeze her back.

Roland cradles his mother, and we hold hands beside him until the ambulance arrives. Officers from Scotland Yard come with them. While the EMTs whisk the queen away, Roland, Rory, and I are stuck with the officers. We recount the story. Tell them what happen. Rory shows them the video. They nod, somber frowns lining their faces, but even these hardened professionals look shaken.

They jot down notes and then tell us to remain in sight. Roland collapses onto a bench, and Rory and I flank him protectively. For a long while, the three of lapse into silence. The palace, which has been so empty for so long, is suddenly buzzing with activity. Scotland Yard officers and medical professionals bounce back and forth while the help flail around frantically, looking lost.

"Are you okay?" Rory asks Roland, breaking the quiet between us.

"It's strange," Roland says. He stares ahead at nothing in particular, those blue eyes now smoky and clouded. "There was part of me that thought we'd never find the person behind this… or maybe, that there never was a conspiracy against the crown. For a long time, I thought my mum had just lost her mind. It turns out she was right after all."

"Half-right," I speak up. "She never guessed her sister. No one did."

"I've spent my whole life hiding away from some… great monster outside. It turns out, the monster was right within these walls."

I watch as Rory's hand slips over Roland's arm, and he turns to face her. Rory always has a way of grounding us somehow. "You can go anywhere you want now," she says urgently. "Anywhere. You're free."

I see the temptation in Roland's eyes. The knee-jerk instinct to run. "And you'll go with me?" Roland asks. His gaze flickers between the both of us.

I nod. "Wherever you are, we'll be," I promise him.

Some of the light comes back in Roland's eyes.

Tanner steps in front of us and clears his throat. "Your Highness? I don't mean to interrupt."

"You're not," Roland says. "Any word on my mum?"

"They have her at Edward's. She's stable."

Roland lets out a breath of relief. "Thank God."

Tanner has a bound booklet in his hand, and he holds it out to Roland. "You'll need this."

Roland takes it and stares blankly at the leather-bound cover. "What's this?"

"The royal oath. For your swearing-in ceremony as prince regent." Just then, it clicks. *Of course.* Tanner adds finally, "You're the reigning monarch now, Your Highness."

ROLAND

*M*y eyes look wild in the mirror. Electric blue and static. I resist the urge to run my fingers through my hair—it's already been slicked over my skull and tied into a tight ribbon. I settle for fidgeting with the gold cufflinks around my wrists instead.

"Relax." Rory's small hands make dents in the white fabric of my shirt as she clutches my arms. She gives me a squeeze. "You look like a king."

"Prince regent," I correct. "Just until my mum gets better."

My mother is still tucked away safely in King Edward's Hospital. The doctors expect a full recovery; the poison has been flushed from her system. But her wounds are far more than skin-deep. I saw it in her the last time I went to see her. There were bags around her eyes, and her hair looked limp around her face. She's tired. Tired of losing family. Tired of carrying the weight of the crown.

Those wounds will take far, far longer to heal. She has the best medical and mental health professionals in the world at her side to help her through it, I've made sure of that.

Until then… England needs a monarch. England needs me. And thousands of people are waiting outside to witness my transformation. The swearing in was one thing: a private ceremony for the Privy Council. Stiff shirts and bulldog frowns. But now I have to address the people of England to let them know that the monarchy is in good hands. *No pressure* or anything.

My fingers tremble and I accidentally flick one of the cufflinks out of its pocket. It pings against the mirror and clicks across the hardwood. "Hell."

"I've got it." Rory bends and scoops the tiny piece up. Wordlessly, she takes my arm and threads the cufflinks together. "You're shaking," she comments.

"I'm nervous."

"You have nothing to worry about. Just be you."

"I feel like a virgin with his first maid," I admit.

Rory chuckles. "Okay, maybe be a little *less* you."

She presses her lips to my frown. The soft warmth of her kiss distracts the frayed edges of my mind. I cup the small of her back and pull her body against mine. She sighs against my mouth, and in that moment, she's completely mine.

Hell with addressing the people. I could live between her lips. I push my tongue inside and taste her. My kitten moans, her soft breath pattering against my cheek.

"Sir." Ah. There he is. My conscience, ready to reel me in. I break away from Rory's mouth to see Ben standing in the half-open doorway.

Ben looks sharp. The stubble on his jaw has been carved into a clean line. White shirt. Black jacket. Even his trousers are new. Good on him.

"They're waiting on you," he says. He's got an earpiece perched over the shell of his ear and that no-nonsense look in his eyes. Big day and all. He barely even acknowledges the fact that Rory is tangled up in my arms. Give him a job and the man is a horse with blinders.

I turn back to Rory and press my thumb against the swell of her lower lip. "Tell them to wait a little longer."

"Should I tell them to postpone for tomorrow, sir?" Ben's tone is curt. I'm going to be in trouble if I stall any longer.

I sigh dramatically. "Daddy's calling."

"Sounds like it." Rory grins. "Go. Speak to your people."

I kiss her again, lingering this time. I want to reach under that shirt and feel her shiver under my fingertips. I want to taste between her legs. I *want* her.

Ben clears his throat.

I seal the kiss and say, "Wish me luck."

"You don't need it." Rory winks and blows me a kiss.

Ben escorts me out of my room and down the hall. The royal guards are all in red, dressed to the nines. It's a monumental moment.

"Rooster coming to coop, copy," Ben says into his headpiece.

"That's your code name for me?" I scoff. "Rooster?"

"Would you prefer Royal Pain in the Arse?"

"Yes, actually." I stop at the end of the hall. There's a curtain separating myself and the balcony. Once I step out there, there will be nothing between me and the thousands of people down below. My heart is positively racing, and I'm doing my best not to break into a sweat. This will be the first time most people have seen me—besides that little snafu with the sex tape. I don't want to be the prince who shags on camera *and* who sweats through his first official address.

I stop on my heels and turn to Ben. "How do I look?"

I'm stalling and he knows it. Still, he plays my game. "Good," he says.

"Only good?"

"Your family would be proud of you," Ben tells me.

That hits me square in the chest. My father, my mother… what would they say to see me here now? I try to sneak a peek through the curtain, but all I see are shards of white light. "You think he's watching? My father."

"Without a doubt."

"Well, then. Let's give him a show."

47

BEN

*R*ooster is walking.
Clear on ten? Eyes on twenty.

Crowd is rowdy. Calm them down. This isn't a bloody rock concert.

Check. Check. Copy. Clear.

The voices chatter incessantly in my earpiece as everyone takes their place for the prince regent's address. My skin buzzes. I'm alert, eyes and ears everywhere. After all the action we've seen over the past few weeks, I'm not taking any chances.

I push people to the side to let Roland pass. "Step aside. Prince regent coming through."

I make eye contact with Tanner. He's standing at the edge of the curtain. He nods and we flank Roland on either side as he breaks through the curtain and steps onto the balcony.

People. I've never seen so many people flooding the palace gates. There's a whole sea of them below, moving like a massive wave, and they let out a single, joyful roar when the prince shows his face.

Not prince. Prince regent. Reigning monarch, for the time being.

Roland certainly does look the part. The London breeze flutters at the loose strands of blond hair that have fallen around his face. His eyes sparkle, a perfect match to the cloudless sky above us. When he smiles and lifts his hand in a wave, I'm certain I can hear half the crowd swoon.

Dammit. Get your eyes off his perfect mouth and back on the people below.

It's impossible to watch this many people all at once, but we have a reliable crew. Guards are perched up above like hawks, eyes trained on the crowd below. I can see other suits mixed into the mass, black dots fidgeting with their earpieces and radios.

And, of course, Roland has me at his side. At the first sign of trouble, I'm prepared to throw him to the ground and drag him back to the palace in one piece.

There's a small microphone fixed to Roland's suit, and it sends his voice booming over the loudspeakers and out into the crowd. "I can't tell you what a joy it is to see you all here," Roland says. "The palace hasn't looked so good in years."

A ripple of laughter from the crowd.

"My family has been through a lot," Roland says, taking on a more somber tone. "And as always we appreciate your prayers and well wishes. When a plane crash took my father ten years ago, my life changed forever. The palace doors closed. I kept myself locked away out of fear for my own safety. I failed to recognize that it wasn't only my life that had changed, but the future of England. For years, I deprived you the chance to get to know your prince."

Roland takes in a deep breath, and it shakes in his throat. He's vulnerable now. I want to reach over and hold him, protect him, but I keep my feet rooted in my spot. The sunlight makes his blue eyes sparkle. He smiles through the pain.

"No more closed doors," he says. "As of tomorrow, Helmsway Palace will be open to the public. If I've learned anything in these past ten years, it's that you don't get anywhere in life without taking risks. Live the life you were meant to live. Don't hold back. As your prince regent, I intend to do just that."

The crowd erupts with cheers. My eyes flicker over the sea of people, and I feel a knot in my chest. They love him. I can't blame them.

I love him.

Just then, my attention is interrupted when Roland starts toward me. Panic stabs through me—did someone push him? Is he ducking an attack? He has his place markers, he shouldn't move... but he does. He closes the gap between us, takes me by the back of my head, and pulls me into a kiss.

I can't move. I can't breathe. Roland's lips are on mine, and my body forgets how to survive. The soft, warm press of his mouth entices me in closer. There millions of people watching us. There is no turning back from this moment.

Kiss him, you fool, I hear Rory's voice in my ear. *Take a risk.*

I sink into his lips. His kiss strips me of everything. I am his. He is mine. My prince. My king. For the world to see.

When Roland pulls back, I'm breathless and he is grinning. I'm positive I'm beet red, but there's nothing to be done about that now.

The crowd is still cheering. There are no gunshots. No throwing knives. He kissed me and everything is fine. Everyone is alive. The world still turns; England still loves him.

Roland shouts over the balcony, "God bless the queen! And God bless England!"

My muscles unlock. It's time to usher him back inside.

I'm grateful that Tanner is there because he helps pull my focus, and we redirect Roland back into the palace.

"You'll have to answer for that kiss, Your Highness," Tanner informs Roland, playing the role of father for the day.

"Let them ask," Roland laughs. "I'm an open book. It's time England got to know their royal family." He turns to me then and adds, "Are you all right with that?"

It's a bit late to ask now—but I'm somehow pleased he's asked at all. I nod, my head flopping. I'm still in a daze. "Yes. I'm all right with that."

"Good." Just like that, Roland is onto the next thing. He strolls down the halls with decisive purpose now. He turns his head left and right and then asks the million-dollar question: "Where's Rory?"

48

RORY

Getting out into the crowd to watch Roland from the balcony seems like a pipe dream. So I putter around the palace until one of the maids *pssts* me and gestures me over to the living room. There's a handful of help here, all in matching uniforms, eyes glued to the television.

"Pop your rear down, dearie." The maid sits on the couch and pats the spot next to her.

I sidle up next her, grateful that the palace help got to me before any of the dukes or duchesses could. I'm far more comfortable here, where people call me *dearie*, rather than squeezed in between a couple stuffy suits who address each other as *ma'am* and *highness*.

"Lookit, there goes our boy," the chef snorts.

"Awww, he looks all grown up." A middle-aged maid sniffs and dabs her eyes with her apron. "He's gonna make me cry."

These are the people Roland grew up with—his only human contact, day after day. And they're so *proud* of him. It makes my heart swell in my chest.

Roland starts to speak, and we all hang on his every word. He looks great on the TV. Confident. Bold. He looks as though he was born to be there. He's effortlessly commanding. I watch as Roland wraps up his speech and then… he turns to Ben and catches the bodyguard in a passionate kiss.

The reaction from the help is a mixture of gasps and laughs. My hand flies to my mouth, and I can't help the stupid, wide grin that explodes across my face. Oh my God. He *did* it. He went for it.

Leave it to Roland. You can give the boy a throne, but you can't stop him from being a boy. And I wouldn't want to. Roland's boldness is infectious and magnificent, and nothing can diminish his blaze.

Ben looks in a euphoric haze when Roland pulls back. Roland is ecstatic, and his enthusiasm is contagious.

"I always knew Roland fancied him," a maid declares.

"You did not!"

"Did too!"

"Someone owes me twenty quid!"

I let them squabble it out, and slip out of the room. It's only a matter of time before they turn their attention on me and start asking questions I don't have an answer for.

It's bittersweet, this fluttering in my chest. My job here is done. The palace is all a flutter of bodyguards and help rushing back and forth, and I move through them like a ghost. No one pays attention to the Normal with tattered jeans and a lumpy backpack. I move down the hall and slip into the library. My fingertips fly over the book spines until they hit the world atlas. It's stiff under my fingers, the pages blocky, and I tilt the book back. I can hear the clunky lock come undone, and the bookshelf groans open.

I've mapped out most of the secret doors in this place by now. This one should spiral down to the underground tunnel, which will let me out under the bridge by the Thames and then—

"Here, kitty, kitty."

The familiar voice stops me in my spot. I turn and see Roland and Ben standing at the entrance of the library, eyes on me.

"Oh, hey." I smile lamely. "I was just…"

Roland fills in the blanks. "Leaving the party before saying goodbye?"

"I thought you were done running," Ben says stiffly.

My shoulders droop at his tone. "I am," I tell him. "I'm not running." I lift my hand, motion to them, and drop it. "You've… found your home. Now I have to go back to mine."

"About that," Roland says. "I thought you might want to stay a little longer."

Roland steps back and motions someone forward as if on cue. I hear the sticky-tape sound of rubber wheels on hard-wood floor.

When I see him, my heart nearly leaps out my throat.

"Bonjovi, Rory." Oscar smiles at me, the nurse behind him holding onto the handles of his wheelchair.

My jaw falls. My mouth works uselessly before I get out the words "Otter? How…?"

Roland has one of his canary-eating grins, and he shrugs. "I'm the prince regent. I can pull strings."

My bag falls to the ground with a loud thud. I launch myself forward and throw my arms around my brother. "I can't believe you're here." I hug him and bury my face into his wool sweater. His red hair tickles my nose. He smells like mothballs and minty disinfectant, and honestly I can't get enough of it.

"Careful with the delicates," Oscar wheezes. All of him is delicate. He's frail under his sweater, like a pile of baby bird bones in my arms.

I pull back and wipe my nose on my sleeve. I'm a blubbering mess.

"Why don't we give you two some space?" Roland suggests.

* * *

THE COURTYARD IS beautiful this time of day. Twin rosebushes line either side of the brick walkway as Oscar and I make our way through it. At the end of the walkway, there's a stone fountain with cherubic angels dancing around the base, water spouting over their heads. I push his wheelchair over the brick road. We stop by the fountain and listen to the water gurgle and hiss.

It's a cool day; the air is crisp, but the sun is hot. I hop up and sit on the edge of the stone fountain, letting the sun bake my skin. Oscar tilts his head into the sun as well and closes his eyes. He's so pale, spotted with freckles, and I worry he'll burn.

"What are you thinking?" Oscar asks as though he can hear my thoughts.

I shrug. "I'm thinking… what a weird fountain this is."

Oscar snorts a laugh without opening his eyes. "It *is* weird. Why would angels be spitting at each other? Doesn't seem very angelic of them." He opens an eye and peeks at me. "You're worrying."

"Of course I am."

"Well, stop it."

"Okay," I say. But I can't. The pollen is out; I can feel it tickling my nose. We should go inside soon, before it gets into his frail lungs and he starts hacking—

"The guards inside are complete morons, by the way," Oscar huffs.

I can't help but grin. "Why's that?"

"One of them tried to convince me a coat of arms was from the 1600s. It was eighteenth century at best."

I chuckle and knock my leg against one of his wheels. "He probably didn't know. Not everyone is a huge history geek."

"I don't see why not," he sighs. He pauses a moment before he says, "This palace… it's remarkable."

"Yeah," I say. There's a bitter nagging nibbling the edge of my heart. "It's not bad."

"What's that tone of voice?" Oscar says, twisting his chair back so he can face me properly.

"It's nothing," I say, but there's no use hiding from Oscar. He sees right through me.

"You're thinking about leaving, aren't you?"

"You know me," I say. "Itchy feet."

Oscar's eyebrows furrow together. I've spent so much of my life taking care of him, sometimes it's hard to remember that he's the older sibling. When he gets that serious look and pulls the big-brother card, however, I shut up. "Rory… seeing Helmsway Palace like this… it's not something I ever thought I'd see for myself. I can touch these walls here. The fountain." He reaches forward and sets his hand palm reverently down on the stone. "Rough edges. Sun-warm. It's… wonderful."

"Yeah. It is."

His eyes lift to me. "You've shown me so much. I've seen the world through your eyes. I can't thank you enough for that."

A knot tangles up in my throat. "You would've done the same for me."

"I do have one more thing to ask of you."

"What is it?" I ask quickly. "Anything. Name it."

"Put roots down, Ror," he says. "Here. Home. Anywhere. Wherever you want to be. It's time to stop living for me and start living for yourself."

My vision blurs. I try to be strong for him, I don't want

him to see me cry, but it's dangerously hard to hold back. "Otter… it's not like that…"

"What is it like?" he asks. "You like them, don't you? Roland and Ben."

I nod. My head feels heavy on my neck. "I love them."

"Good. They seem like good guys. Didn't get much out of Ben—he's something of a steel trap. Prince Roland, though… we had a lot to talk about. Hermit stuff. You wouldn't understand."

Despite my tears threatening to spill over, I bark a laugh at that. He always manages to make me laugh. It gives me a chance to move my hand to my face and wipe my eyes. "How do you do that?" I ask.

Oscar grins. "It's the terrible March sense of humor, I imagine."

"Make room, March." I leap off the fountain. "I'm coming in." I wind my arms around him, hugging him close. He wraps his arms around me and cradles me in his chair. We sit here for a moment, curled up together, just enjoying being close to each other.

Finally, he coughs lamely. "Pollen," he says, which is his way of asking for space. He can only take too much touch. I climb back up to my feet. With that, he grabs his wheels and starts rolling himself backward up the walkway, forcing me to pick up my pace to keep up with him. "Come on. Let's go back in. I've got tour guides to educate before tomorrow. Who knows? Maybe they'll hire me. Tours on Wheels… it has a ring to it."

* * *

ONCE WE'RE INSIDE, Oscar makes good on his promise and detours to explore the rest of the palace. I walk beside him for a while, not really taking in the information he's giving me, just soaking in the cadence of his voice.

When we get to the sitting room, we run into Roland and Ben. The lion and the wolf. They're spread out on the pale, gold-rimmed chaise. Roland has his head in Ben's lap, but they both turn their gazes up at us when we peek in the doorway.

"Would you mind watching over my sister for a bit?" Oscar says suddenly. "She's slowing me down."

"Aye, aye, Captain," Roland says and salutes Oscar. "We'll take good care of her."

"I don't doubt it." And just like that, he jets off, leaving me in the predators' den.

I step inside. "Close the doors behind you," Ben says. His fingers sift through Roland's long hair, petting. The tall doors clatter when I close them behind me.

The excitement from the day seems to have petered out, and everyone is lazy, like sated animals after a good hunt. Even the canaries hanging in their cage are sleeping, their small beaks tucked into their chests.

"Room for one more?" I motion to the chaise.

"Always," Roland says and opens his arms.

I snuggle up against Roland. He kisses the top of my head. Suddenly, I understand what Oscar was saying about the stone fountain. Seeing is one thing, but living it, breathing it, smelling it… it's another thing entirely. I lose myself in the tactile sensations of Roland—the softness of his long hair against my cheek, the hardness of his body underneath his coat, the expansion of his ribs with every precious breath. Ben trades heads and rakes his fingers through my hair instead. My chest clenches with emotion, and I grip the hard leather lapel of Roland's coat. "What if…" I struggle with the words; my throat feels so tight that my voice is barely a whisper. "What if… I stayed here? Permanently."

"Queen Rory," Roland muses. "It has a good ring to it."

Ben scoffs. "How many queens does it take to rule a monarchy?"

I reach up and smack his thigh. He grunts, but even from this angle, he can't hide the hint of smile on his lips.

"Maybe not… queen," I venture. "Doesn't really sound like me. But *something*."

"Royal pet," Ben states.

"Mmm… royal pet," I muse. "I like that."

"Me too," Roland agrees. He parts my lips with his tongue and tastes me. I open my mouth for him easily, giving him full access. He takes it, cupping my jaw and swiping his tongue over mine, licking every inch of my mouth.

Ben's fingers tighten in my hair and tug the roots. I gasp as the sensation jolts down the center of my body and pulses between my legs. I try to clench my thighs together, but Roland nudges them apart and fits his knee between my legs. I don't mean to be this desperate, but the pressure makes me whimper and rut against his thigh.

Roland adjusts on the couch, pushing me underneath him. Now his knee is squarely against my sex, and it's impossible to hide how badly I need him. I'm sure he can feel the heat from between my legs. He kisses me for a while, working his tongue against mine until I'm a panting wreck.

"Someone could walk in," I whisper.

"Good," Roland says. He sits up, unbuttons his heavy coat, and tosses it to the ground, revealing the white cotton shirt underneath. "Give them something to say about this room on the tour. *And here, Prince Roland and Ben Tolle licked their royal pet until she screamed…*"

I giggle and shiver. The thought alone makes me tingle all over.

I reach up and grab Ben's leg for something to hold on to. I'm not the only one who likes Roland's suggestion. I can feel

Ben's erection brush against the back of my hand. I bite my lip. I want it inside of me so badly; my thoughts scatter.

"You heard your prince," Ben says suddenly. "Take off your trousers."

I unbutton my pants, draw down the zipper, and shove them down my legs awkwardly. Roland tugs my shoes, socks, and pants off my ankles, discarding them all in a pile on the ground. Now, I'm in nothing but my loose shirt and white panties.

Roland splays my legs and gets comfortable between them. He looks at me, and then a grin slices across his mouth.

"Ben, it seems our kitten has soaked right through her knickers." Ben slips off the couch to join Roland at my feet. When his fingertips trail my bare legs… it makes me weak. My throat goes dry, and I swallow. "Do you think she wants this?" Roland asks.

"Not nearly enough," Ben replies.

They launch an assault of kisses on my body then. Each takes a leg and licks and nibbles his way up my bare skin, over my thighs, and to my hips. When Roland gets to my knife scar at my hip, he brushes his lips very softly, lovingly against it. I whimper when they get close to my aching need and push my hips up toward the warmth of their breath, but they only pull out of reach. They're kissing me everywhere *except* where I need it the most. I'm so pent up, I dig my fingers into my own hair.

Finally, I feel a pair of hands tug my panties down. I let my legs fall open, lewdly exposed for them. Roland puts two fingers on either side of my pussy, spreading me wide. The cool air hits my slick, wet skin. Again, my hips flex themselves forward, needing something inside, but Ben pins my thighs down, trapping me in place. I'm helpless to their teasing.

"What a beautiful pussy," Roland says reverently.

"The most beautiful," Ben agrees.

My sex trembles with desire. I'm sure I'm dripping right onto the velvet-soft fabric of the couch, but I'm beyond caring.

Suddenly, Ben climbs to his hands and knees over me. He replaces his hands on my thighs, holding them down, and drops his head between my legs. I feel his long tongue twist slowly around my sensitive nub. His stubble grazes my inner thighs. I gasp. I want to jerk up toward his mouth, but he's keeping me in place. Instead, I suffer deliciously through the excruciatingly slow circles he paints around my exposed clit.

I barely have time to ease into Ben's ministrations before Roland's head lays on my thigh. A second tongue laps between my legs, teasing my folds and tracing my slit.

"Oh God," I whisper. "Oh my God, oh my God... that feels good... so, *so* good..."

I'm babbling. I've always felt lucky enough to have one mouth between my legs, but two? Nothing can compare to the way these two talented alpha men work their tongues over my slippery sex. They lavish me in affection, their tongues crossing, bumping, working me. The two flexible muscles find my clit and flick the small nub back and forth like they're playing tennis with it. I nearly hit the ceiling. I shout with sensory overload, and my legs begin to shake hard. I'm going to cum. I'm on the screaming edge. And then...

They stop. I nearly cry out and beg for more, until I hear it. Sloppy kisses. They're *making out* over my pussy. My blood feels like lighter fuel, and that sucking sound paired with Ben's soft moan sets me on fire.

"I don't know what I like more," Roland muses. "Eating our pet's cunt or tasting her on your lips."

"Fuck," Ben groans. His cock clearly refuses to be

contained, and I see him shift as he unbuttons his pants to give the swollen monster a little breathing room.

"How are you holding up, kitten?" Roland asks.

"More," I beg. "Please, sir. I need it."

"Good girl," Ben breathes. They dip between my legs again. They work in perfect tandem now, and I can't keep track of who goes where. One tongue presses inside of me, greedily lapping at my want, while the other goes to town on my sensitive button.

My climax hits me hard. I cry out loudly. My legs tremble and quake, my body writhing as best it can under Ben's strong grip. I'm clenching, throbbing around one tongue as the other beats against my bundle of nerves mercilessly. Even after my pulses start to ebb, he continues sucking my poor clit until another orgasm breaks free. It feels so good, my eyes water, and I repeat both their names, over and over, in a lustful babble.

Two tongues. Two orgasms. One satisfied and shaky Rory.

They lick me clean before pulling back. Ben falls ungracefully off the couch, and Roland sits back.

"Good?" Roland asks.

I'm buzzing and I twirl my fingers through my hair in a daze. "The best," I respond.

"Good." Roland climbs over me and kisses me hard. I taste myself on his mouth, salty sex lips. His erection presses against my hip, and I moan.

"I want to be inside of you," Roland murmurs heatedly.

My pussy clenches painfully. I gasp and let out a breath of a laugh. "I don't know if I can…" I reach between us block my sex with my hand. "I'm waaaay too sensitive now."

"Poor pussy," Roland coos and kisses my lips. "But I wasn't talking to you anyway."

Roland's hand trails off the couch and twists in Ben's hair, giving it a tug. Ben and Roland lock eyes. In that insane, unspoken way of theirs, they make a decision.

"I'll need lube," Ben says, with all the practicality of a den mother.

Are they going to—?

Oh. Yes. Oh my God, yes. And I get to be a part of it.

"I have some!" I pipe up, and when they shoot me a weird look, I shrug a shoulder. "My bag is full of… useful items."

"Fetch, kitten," Roland says.

Which sounds like something you'd say to a dog, not a cat, but I'm also too aroused to point out technicalities.

I have to squirm to get out from under Roland. I don't realize until I stand up how incredibly slippery I am between my legs. I feel so messy that I half walk, half hop over to my backpack. Everything is disorganized inside, nothing folded, all items shoved as tightly together as possible, and it takes a moment of hunting to find what I'm looking for.

Eventually, I pull out a small tube of lubricant and a sheet of condoms. I carry them back to my boys. They've mostly disrobed, down to their briefs, and they're making out on the couch. I don't want to interrupt; there's part of me that could just stay here, watching. They're horizontal, Roland on top, and they've locked lips and grind their hips together. Roland must be doing something incredible with his tongue, because it makes Ben groan audibly and he shudders underneath the other man, pelvis twitching upward.

God. It makes my mouth water to watch these two gorgeous, strong alpha men turn shaky and desperate under each other's touches. There's love in the way they look at each other, touch each other, and kiss each other. As though their very fingers are saying *I've got you, I trust you, I'm not letting you go.*

"Let's see what you've got, kitten," Ben says when he catches sight of me and extends a hand.

I know my place. I drop my knees, lube in my hand, condom packets gently between my teeth, and I crawl over to them.

Ben nudges his elbow against Roland's chest, pushing the other man off so he can sit up. Then Ben scratches the top of my head and coos in his low, faraway-thunder voice, "Good girl."

It makes me shiver. He takes the condoms from between my teeth, takes the lube, and inspects it. "This'll do," he says and tosses it to Roland.

With that, Ben stands, drops his briefs, and steps out of them. And—God. I can't stop staring. I want to fall to my knees in front of him. Worship at the V-line of his slim hips. Trace every stacked muscle of his abdomen with my tongue. Praise whatever god had the imaginative genius to craft such a gorgeous, proud cock.

"Let's do it here," Ben says and bends at his hips, his hands clasping the arm of the chaise. *Come and get it*, the arch of his body seems to challenge.

"Perfect," Roland replies. He kicks out of his briefs like he's in a locker room instead of one of the lavish palace spreads. My body hums at the sight of him. I want to nuzzle against that blond thatch of hair between his legs. Roland positions himself behind Ben, slips on the condom, and shoots the lube into his hand.

"You've got such a nice arse," Roland comments, the man who is never afraid to say exactly what's on his mind. "How did I not notice before?"

Ben, on the other hand, goes sunset red. How can such a sculpted man be so unused to compliments?

"You were too busy admiring your own jawline in the mirror," Ben deflects.

Roland lets out a noise that's nearly a laugh. "Perhaps.

Not anymore." I watch as his finger disappears between Ben's cheeks, and Ben swallows.

"Just..." Ben starts, but his words trail off. If we've learned anything, it's that Ben has trouble asking for what he needs. "I'm usually... on the other end. So."

"I'll be gentle," Roland reassures him, filling in the blanks without hesitation.

"Right," Ben says in a small sigh of relief.

Roland speaks Ben-language. Ben speaks Rory-language. I'm fluent in both dialects. We understand each other. Know each other. That they let me into their relationship like this... it's so sweet, so tender, so full of trust. It makes me want to cry.

Home, I think. I'm home, I'm home.

I scramble up onto the chaise to be closer to them. I press my lips to Ben's and murmur, "I've got you."

Ben seems to regain his footing with me. He pulls my hair, and he shoves his tongue in my mouth. Me, he can still control. I open for him, purring as he greedily tastes the inside of my mouth. I reach down to run the silky-smooth skin of his cock through my fingers, and he stiffens.

Ben breaks the kiss abruptly to gasp, and his forehead rests against mine. If possible, his face burns redder. "Oh, *fuck*," he swears between gritted teeth, and I know Roland must be inside of him now.

"Is that okay?" Roland murmurs. It strikes me suddenly how compassionate he is. When I first met him, Roland was the selfish, spoiled-brat prince who took what he wanted, when he wanted, with little thought to the consequences. The Roland standing behind Ben now... he's a man. He's strong, controlled, and respectful. It makes my heart pitter-patter in my chest.

"Yes, just... give me a second..." Ben pants.

"Tell me when," Roland encourages. Just the same way Ben took care of me the first time he was in my tight place.

I coax Ben to relax with my tongue lapping over his. The bodyguard doesn't give up control easily. But then he starts breathing again, his jaw slackens, and I feel his manhood start to throb in my hand.

When Ben says, "Okay," his voice is hoarse and lust-soaked. The sound makes my pussy buzz with need. My libido is catching its second wind at the sight of these two.

"Bloody hell, Ben, you feel so good," Roland moans.

"So do you," Ben sighs as his body rolls into each of Roland's thrusts.

I'm positively soaking the chaise again. I'm tingling from my peaked nipples to the arch of my feet. I can't sit on the sidelines anymore. I need them. I jump off the chaise, rip off a second condom, and peel it out of its packet before climbing back in front of Ben.

"May I, sir?" I ask as I tease the condom over the tip of his manhood. Because good pets ask for permission before climbing on their master's cock.

Ben opens his eyes, and when they meet mine, those ebony coals flash. "Yes," he growls.

I climb Ben like a tree and wrap my legs around his waist. My feet touch Roland, and my heels catch on his hips. I hug Ben and get a handful of Roland's hair. They're so tight together, I can't reach for one without holding both. And I *love* it. I lower myself onto Ben. My pussy is so greedy for him, I waste no time getting him all the way inside of me.

Ben and I gasp in unison. It feels good—*so good*—to have him angled deep inside of me. It makes my very toes tingle. My pussy clamps around him, and I struggle not to cum right away. He, too, seems to be teetering on that edge because he lets out a fierce growl. In one sweeping motion, he grips my thighs tightly around him, sets my ass down on the arm of the chaise, and passionately punishes the soft skin of my throat with his teeth. I've never seen him lose control like this and—*fuck*. It's hot.

I cry out and tug on a fistful of Roland's hair. Roland moans in return—we've all lost the ability to form comprehensive sentences. I *feel* Roland, I feel his thrusts, I feel how the forward motion of his hips sheaths Ben deeper inside of me. Roland drives into Ben, Ben drives into me, and I'm doubly fucked. The three of us move in tandem, one perfect, synchronized wave of hands and lips and sweat and sex and love and trust.

My orgasm is so powerful that it nearly blinds me, a burst of white-hot light exploding behind my eyes. My boys moan, and their bodies jerk and twitch and throb as they climax with me, the three of us reaching our peak as one.

When it's done, we collapse like dominos, Roland and I making a steeple against Ben. I kiss Ben's chest, I hear Roland's lips on Ben's throat, and Ben just pants and swears under his breath until I hear the rapid thud of his heart begin to slow. I find Roland's lips and kiss him in a lazy, satisfied way, savoring the warmth of his swollen lips. Ben shudders as we kiss, and I feel his spent organ rebound and twitch inside of me.

"I love you," Roland sighs to both of us, always incredibly affectionate in postcoital bliss. "I love you, I love you."

"Love you, too," Ben and I say in tandem, and then our eyes meet and we share a smirk, as though we're in on some secret—because *how perfect*, that I love him, and he loves him, and we love each other, and how did we get here, and *who even cares*, because this feels so right, and nothing has ever, will ever, feel this right.

"Do you want me to pull out?" Roland asks.

"In a minute," Ben murmurs, and I'm grateful for that, because I don't want to leave this, either.

Not ever.

I'm here, right where I belong. A couple months ago, you couldn't have convinced me to stay in the same zip code, let alone with the same man. Now, I never want to be anywhere else, or with anyone else. I fit, like a puzzle piece, between these two men, with these two men, belonging to these two men.

I'm theirs. And they're mine.

Their royal pet.

Forever.

Thank you for reading my debut novel, The Royal's Pet! I had so much fun falling in love with with these characters and I hope you did too. Don't forget to show your love by **spreading the word** to your friends and **writing a review!**

What do you get the prince who has everything? Find out when you sign up for my newsletter and receive a completely **FREE bonus book** featuring Rory, Ben, Roland, and a birthday surprise!

https://adoracrooksbooks.com/bonus-book-royals-pet/

* * *

Keep reading for **an exclusive sneak peek** at the steamy sequel, **THE ROYAL'S BABY**…

THE ROYAL'S BABY: SNEAK PEEK

1

RORY

I'm minding my own business at the bar, picking through a plate of a German egg pasta called *spätzle*, when the insults start flying.

My German is rusty at best, but I know enough to make out the sneered words: "Ack! Turn it off—I won't listen to that sick freak!"

I turn my eyes up to the television hanging crookedly in the corner. The local news is playing an interview with Roland Pennington, prince of England. Just the sight of him makes my pulse beat a little faster—it's so strange, seeing him the way other people see him, on TV like this. The camera loves him, and it's not hard to see why—his dashing smile, his twinkling blue eyes, his golden mane of hair. *My lion.*

The interviewer loves him, England loves him, and *I* love him. But the two German men circling the pool table in this Berlin dive bar have a different opinion, and they aren't afraid to show it.

"Shut that pervert up!"

"*Schwuchtel!*"

"Where's his American slut, eh?"

They spit and snarl, clearly having no idea that the *American slut* they're referring to is sitting barely three feet away from them, with a meal that's suddenly gone sour.

We knew we would get backlash, coming out like we did. It's been over a year now since Roland announced to the world that he has not one, but two loves in his life: Ben, his best friend and loyal then-bodyguard, and me, the American tourist who stumbled into a love story as beautiful as it is bizarre. England was supposed to be just one more stop on my way to see the world for my brother who couldn't; I'd go to new countries, take videos, and send them home to Oscar, who was stuck at home with a crippling illness. Instead of a good story, I met Roland and Ben, and the three of us fell in love. It shouldn't work, but somehow, some way, it does.

I love my two men—Prince Roland, who has so much energy, compassion, and love in him that sometimes it over-whelms me. And Ben, our quiet, sometime surly lover whose loyalty knows no bounds and who can make my body hum just by putting his hands on my throat. We've overcome insane odds and grown together. In our world, in our little bubble, it's perfect.

But as soon as I step outside Helmsway Palace (as I do, often—these traveling legs won't sit still), I remember the cold truth: that the rest of the world is still struggling to understand our love.

And some—like the two men behind me—have turned their confusion to hate.

I pinch my bottom lip between my teeth. I know I should stay out of it. I'm the prince of England's girlfriend now, which means certain things are *expected* of me. I'm no longer allowed to wear ripped jeans and Doc Martens 24/7. I have to watch my mouth and can no longer swear like a sailor on my (increasingly popular) travel vlog. And I'm *definitely* not supposed to engage with drunken, homophobic Germans who can't wrap their small heads around love is love *is love*.

Buuuut…

Your girl Rory March has never been incredibly good at following the rules.

I pay my bill, push away from the bar, and step over to the pool table. I can feel eyes on me—that would be Sam, my bodyguard, watching me from behind her Shirley Temple a couple of seats over. Traveling on my own is one thing I would never—could never—give up, so I've since made concessions to appease my overly protective boyfriends: Sam is one, and my multitude of disguises is another. Right now, for example, I'm wearing a black wig that stops short at my shoulders to conceal my trademark ginger hair. Between the wig and a black romper that is comfortable, casual, and cute, I can tell that the men at the pool table still don't recognize me even when I'm right up next to them. I motion to the table, and in my American-accented, bad German I ask sweetly, "Do you mind if I play, too?"

They exchange looks, then one grins leeringly and passes me his cue. We establish that I'm stripes, his partner is solids. The man I'm playing against is a burly, built guy, and the muscles that flex in his arms when he arranges himself over the pool table briefly remind me of my Ben, my wolf, and the hard biceps that stretch when he pins my wrists effortlessly above my head. It's been a *while*, too long, and I fidget with a present that remind me of my boys—a necklace that hugs my throat with a small cat figure on the end of it. *Their kitten.* It's a pet name they gave me when we were first dating, and it stuck. And, boy, can my men make me purr…

My daydreams scatter as the pool balls click together. My opponent stands and turns to me, smugly, and says in stilted English, "Your turn, darling."

I retract my previous thought—he looks nothing like Ben.

Similar builds, maybe, but Ben's dark eyes are full of aching love and compassion. This man's face, though handsome at first glance, is ugly with lines of anger and superiority etched into his jack-o'-lantern mouth and *anything-you-can-do-I-can-do-better* eyes.

What he *doesn't* know is that during Prince Roland's decade of isolation in the palace, he became very good at two-person games—darts, chess, and yes, pool. As a result, I went from not knowing which end of the stick to hit the balls with to becoming *pretty damn good*, if I do say so myself, after multiple games of what we called *strip pool*. We also left a couple of unsightly stains on the pool table, which…sorry to the maid who had to clean up after us. Really. Sorry.

I bend over the pool table, relax my grip on the cue, and line up my shot. I can almost feel Roland's hands teasing my hips, his breath on my neck, his cocky smile on my throat: *Sorry, am I distracting you?*

Yeah, babe, you are.

I exhale a breath, steady my focus, and tap the ball. The cue hits with just the right force and I sink a ball in the hole. And another, and another. We go a few rounds back and forth—my opponent's smile drops, he talks less, and when he does say something, it's in a German mutter I don't understand. The whole game doesn't last ten minutes before I sink my final ball in.

"Well," I say cheerily as I pass the cue over. "Not so bad for an *American slut*, am I?"

I linger just long enough to see the recognition dawn on their faces as their mouths fall open. On my way out the door, the second German—the bigger one—starts after me with a single, growled "Hey!"

But my bodyguard, Sam—all five foot one of cucumber cool—is already between us, and she peels back her black blazer just enough, I know, to reveal the firearm holstered at her side. "I wouldn't," she warns him.

The threat is enough to stop him in his tracks. Meanwhile, Sam and I make a swift exit out into the street.

It's late December and Berlin is freezing. The entire city is covered in a coat of white snow. I've got a parka with me, and I pull it over my shoulders as the wind bites my cheeks. The chill or the dark of nighttime sobers me up, and we walk past buildings covered in surreal, post-war graffiti. I heave a sigh and see my breath crystalize in front of me.

"I'm sorry," I say to Sam. "I know I forced you to Hulk out, and I shouldn't have—"

"You absolutely *should* have," Sam insists. "Please—they were being complete pricks. Badass bitches like us have got to put little boys in their places sometimes."

And *this* is why I love Sam. I thought it would suck not having Ben as my personal bodyguard—and there are late nights when it *does*—but then there are moments like this. I grew up with a brother, and now I have not one, but *two* boyfriends; Sam is the female empowering *attagirl* that I need on my shoulder. My sister from a British mister. Ben handpicked her himself, which is all I need to know about the strength of her credentials, but I don't think even he realized what a source of gal-pal comfort she'd be to me.

Or maybe he did. My boyfriends have a way of knowing what I need most—even when I don't know it myself.

"I only wish he'd put up more of a fight," Sam huffs. "Would've liked an excuse to break his nose."

I hook my arm in hers. "Since I failed to provide you a good bar fight," I tell her, "how about a minibar nightcap?"

"It won't make up, but it's a start."

We laugh and Sam hails a car to our hotel.

· · ·

***

I'm STAYING at Hotel Adlon Kempinski—another one of my concessions to Ben and Roland's rampant paranoia. It's hard to believe that, not so long ago, I was backpacking across the world, hopping from hostel to hostel and cataloging my experiences on my vlog, *March On!* (a play on our names, Oscar and Rory March). My adventures started after my older brother, Oscar, was diagnosed with cystic fibrosis, a condition that left him wheelchair-bound and incapable of leaving the house, let alone the country. So I traveled for him. I went from country to country, getting lost, making friends, and most importantly, documenting everything for my brother so he could see the world through my eyes.

I still travel, but things are different now. Instead of a hostel, I'm granted access to five-star hotels all across the world. It's the kind of luxury I couldn't care less about; I'll take the community of hostel life over a high thread count any day. But I have to take certain security measures as the girlfriend of royalty. There *are* some perks to a pampered life…the hotel minibar, for example, is a nice touch. Even though I can't touch it. I haven't been able to for weeks. Still, *someone* should take advantage of it, so I tell Sam to help herself as I go to the bathroom to change into sweatpants and a loose shirt.

My black wig lies like a dead animal on the sink. As I'm taking the pins out of my hair, my phone starts to ring. It's a video request, and when I see the caller ID, I grin and answer it.

"Bonjovi, Otter," I say as I prop the phone up on the sink.

"Bonjovi," my brother responds. Oscar—or "Otter" as I've affectionately nicknamed him—looks good, his ginger hair tamed and slicked back. He's not wearing his nasal cannula—

the at-home tube that attaches his nose and pumps oxygen through him—which is a good sign. The new drugs he's taking have been working wonders, and each small improvement thrills me to no end. "Where in the world is Carmen Sandiego?"

"Berlin, for now. But I'm leaving in the morning. *What* in the world is my brother wearing?"

"Oh, this?" He glances down at the ugly Christmas sweater, which features a Rudolph in the middle and red-nose pom-poms scattered around him. "Francesca is taking me to her Christmas office party."

"Oh! Is she there? Can I say hi?"

He shakes his head. "She's swinging by in a few to pick me up."

"She's taking you to her office party, huh? As her *boyfriend*?" I stretch out the word. "Sounds serious."

"You know what else is serious?" he says, trying to not-so-casually steer the conversation to a place I don't want to go yet. "Pregnancy. Motherhood."

I shrug. I knew he'd bring it up, but I don't want to talk about it, not yet, because what can I say? I hiss, "Lower your voice. My bodyguard is right outside."

He rolls his eyes. "Ror. You still haven't told them yet, have you?"

"No...it's not really an over-the-phone conversation. I want to tell them in person."

"Have you thought about *what* you're going to say?"

"I thought I'd just put a bow on my stomach and plant myself under the Christmas tree."

"Seems legit. Don't forget the gift tag. *To: Whose Sperm It May Concern.*"

I laugh. I have to laugh. If I don't laugh, I'll panic. I've been half-panicking since I missed my period over a week ago. Oscar is the only one who knows I'm pregnant right now…and that's only because I held him hostage on the phone while waiting for the test results to show up on the little stick all while ranting *we use protection* and *except for that one time* and *but why now, right now?*

My stomach has been in knots since, and it's more than morning sickness. I haven't got the *slightest* idea how to break the news to Ben and Roland…or how they're going to take it.

If tonight proved anything to me, it's that the world is barely ready for a polyamorous prince, let alone one with a *baby* attached. So I've extended my Berlin trip, made up excuses for my delay in Germany, and procrastinated, procrastinated, procrastinated.

"Oscar…" I start, and I know he can hear the worried whine in my voice because he cuts me off.

"They love you," he says. "No matter what. You'll figure this out."

I know he's right…but that doesn't quell the jitters.

I can hear the doorbell ring in the background. Oscar glances toward it once, his mouth pulled into a frown. "That's Francesca."

Oscar looks pained, and I know he would call off the office party just to spend the night calming me down. But I'm not about to let him do that. For the first time, Oscar is able to go on his own adventures, and there's no way I'm letting him hold himself back for me. "Go," I tell him. "Have fun. I'll be okay."

"Are you sure?"

"I promise. No way I'm letting you get out of public sweater humiliation."

He grins. "You're a freak, Ror."

"Takes one to know one. Love you, Otter."

"Love you, too."

With that, he ends the video message. Now that the room is silent, my anxiety starts sinking into my bones again. My heart pounds in my chest, and my head swims. I curl my fingers around the sink and stare at myself in the mirror. I don't look so much like a badass princess anymore. My fuzzy red hair poofs out, the remains of my makeup make my eyes look sleepless, and my T-shirt swallows me whole. It's one of Roland's, a Manchester United shirt, and I bunch it up to my face and inhale the smell of home—tea leaves, mint, and sandalwood. It makes my heart ache.

We've been through so much together…but what if this breaks the camel's back? It's a fear so real it knots in my throat.

Out of the corner of my eye, I see the pregnancy test sticking up like a flagpole in the bathroom trash bin. A spike of fear hits my heart—what if Sam sees it? Or housekeeping? I shove it down to the bottom and pile up tissues on top for good measure.

What've you gotten yourself into, Rory?

2

BEN

Something is wrong.

There is no transition from *asleep* to *awake*; I open my eyes and I'm immediately on high alert. I check my senses. The bedroom is quiet, save for Roland's deep breaths beside me. His bare skin is hot against mine, and when I sit up, dried sweat makes the sheet cling briefly to my back. We're alone, but I can't shake the spine-tickling sensation of being watched.

My pistol sleeps in its holster on the bedside table. Roland doesn't budge, not even when I kiss the top of his head, pull the blankets over his shoulders, and slip out of bed. My clothes are on the floor (we made a mess of them last night), and it takes me a second to pick mine from his and redress in the dark. I slip my holster over my shoulders and exit the bedroom, closing the door as softly as I can on my way out.

The hallways of Helmsway Palace are bright, and I squint as my eyes readjust. The palace never sleeps. Two guards stand outside the prince's room—Thom and Lincoln—and I haven't checked the time, but if Thom is still here, it must be four or five in the morning. I nod to them and ask, "How's it?"

To which Thom responds, "All clear, boss."

Doesn't quell the discomfort rushing through my blood, however.

I know I must be a sight—hair askew, jaw unshaven—but the only person who could fire me for my unprofessionalism is *me*, and I decide to let myself off the hook this time. I walk barefoot down the hall and follow a familiar path through the kitchen (smells of tomorrow morning's scones and biscuits already baking), through the door disguised as a walk-in freezer, and down a staircase that leads into the basement security.

Back when I was Prince Roland's personal bodyguard, I used to practically live in here. So much so that he called it "my lair." Now that our relationship is less professional, more personal, I've been promoted to head of security, where I can keep an eye on the palace without actually being on the front lines anymore.

Which means I have less and less reason to be down here. I have my own office upstairs, complete with a view of the palace gardens. Still, I find myself returning to my lair on nights like this, when the whispers won't quit.

The lair is a small, closet-sized space, filled with television screens that show a live feed of every possible angle in Helmsway Palace. It's also not empty. My replacement sits in the swivel chair, eyes on the screen, large cup of coffee in front of him. He's a twenty-six-year-old pup whose name—much to Roland's amusement—is also Benjamin. But our name and loyalty to queen and country are all we share; we couldn't be more unalike.

"Boss!" Benjamin unfurls his legs from the desk and beams at me. "Top of the morning to you!"

"Benjamin," I mumble. *Hate*, Rory reminds me constantly, *is a strong word*. "How is it looking?"

"Just the usual, sir. There were a couple of stray cats that got into it on the South Lawn—a real doozy of a fight. You want me to play the tape back for you? Kept me on edge the whole time—I think everyone's all right, though."

"Any word from Rory?"

"Miss March got on her flight and is on schedule to touch down at 06:15. Do you think they serve pretzels on the plane? I was thinking the other day—why do they hand out peanuts? Allergies are so rampant these days, you never know what will set someone off."

My back molars grind. He's like a too-curious child tugging at my trousers, and it's far too early for this. "Go relieve Thom," I tell him. "I'll watch the monitors for a bit. Report back when Rory's touched down."

"Easy, peasy, lemon-no-problem, boss," Benjamin says in a voice so cheery, I want to easy, peasy squeeze lemon juice in his eyes.

He's lanky and has to bend his tall frame to exit the room. Finally, I'm alone. I take my old seat in front of the monitors. I'm taller than most, but no one is taller than Benjamin, and I have to adjust the seat so it fits me again.

The television monitors glow. This room hums. Didn't notice that until I started spending time away from it—it was all white noise before. But I hear it now. It drowns out the crackle in my brain. I slowly examine each monitor, letting my eyes prove to my nerves what I logically already know— everything is in its right place.

Benjamin left his mug. It says "Keep Calm And Hodor," whatever that means. It's leaving a coffee-colored ring on the desk, so I grab a tissue and wipe it down. While doing that, I notice the dust behind the monitor. The cleaning staff doesn't come in here; they don't have the clearance. I used to clean it, because unlike some *Bens*, I take fucking pride in my workplace. I pluck a couple more napkins out of the box and start wiping behind the monitors.

I see him coming on the screens, so I'm not surprised when the door clicks open. Nor do I turn around; I'm too busy hunting a dust bunny.

"How did I know I'd find you here?" Roland asks. I can hear the smirk on his lips.

"Just doing a little spring cleaning," I mutter.

"It's December."

"I'm getting an early start."

I'm bent on the desk to reach behind monitor four, and I nearly jump when he slips his hand up my backside and snakes it underneath my shirt. "We ought to get you a uniform to clean in," Roland says. "French maid, I'm thinking."

The noise that leaves me is a sigh—half-exasperated, half-distracted by the tickle of his fingertips on my bare skin, and not at all amused by his interruption. I pull away from under the monitors, drop the dusty tissue in the bin, and twist around to face him. There's not a lot of room in here—it's barely closet-sized—and Roland certainly isn't giving me any space, so I find myself wedged between him and my desk.

No—not *my* desk anymore. Benjamin's now. I frown at Roland. "You should go back to bed."

"My thoughts exactly," he says. "But only if you come back with me."

The offer is, admittedly, tempting. I love him like this; he hasn't made himself up for the public just yet. He's not the prince of England right now—he's just Roland. His blond locks are standing up in all directions like an electrocuted cat, his eyes are bleary, and he's wearing jeans and an open button-up that hangs uselessly around his shoulders, baring his svelte form. He looks unbearably handsome like this, and

I wouldn't mind kissing the daylight out of him and lying down beside him.

But something pulls me back, anchoring me here. "I can't."

His eyebrows furrow. "You have work to do?"

"Something like that." The real answer—that I can't sleep, that the well of anxiety is rising in me and I can't stop it—stays glued to the roof of my mouth.

His frown softens. He leans in now so that our lips are almost touching. "Well," he murmurs thoughtfully, "if I can't move the mountain…"

His hands slip up my thighs, closing in on my groin. I'm practically sitting on the desk now, and my arms lock at my sides, fingers tightening around the edge of the desk.

"*Roland,*" I plead. I want him to go. I want him to leave me to my demons and my lair.

But my protests are only half-hearted…and my prick is already half-hard. We both know that my declaration of his name isn't a *no*, and my meager dissent falls away as his lips find my throat. He kisses—purposeful, insistent kisses—all the way down my neck. When I feel his teeth graze my skin, I can't help the shudder that ripples through me.

I can't deny him. I can never deny him. I spoil him, I know that—what Prince Roland wants, Prince Roland gets. But he's my weakness—always has been—and all it takes is a couple of kisses and his hand cupping my crotch over my trousers and my resolve melts like butter.

There was a day when I'd only dream of us here. Before Rory pushed me to admit my feelings for Roland, I kept them caged inside. For six long, painful years, I was nothing more than his bodyguard and, at times, his trusted friend. His mate (that loathsome bloody word). And when the pressure got to be too much, when I needed an outlet for the frustration mounting inside of me, I'd come to this very room. I'd watch him on the monitors, feeling like a bloody pervert, hating myself, hating that I couldn't shake these feelings. All the while, I'd play out fantasies in my head.

Even my filthiest fantasies, however, had nothing on the real Roland. I could've never imagined how he could be—all with one kiss—playful and dominating, loving and teasing, boyish and arrogant and *mine*. He knocks the breath out of me with every kiss until, finally, he lowers himself to his knees and unzips my trousers.

His hands are soft, his touch so unlike my own—where mine are rough and calloused, his palms are warm and smooth. He wraps his fingers around my prick and I feel the blood rush, swelling to my full length at his touch. I know it delights him how quickly my body responds to his touch—he's like Tinkerbell, he needs applause to live—and those violet eyes of his practically sparkle when they meet mine. "Is this what you want?"

"Yes." My voice is so husky, so thick with lust already. I'm mesmerized as he begins to stroke me, slowly at first, taking his time working me up. Then his lips come into play, wrapping around the swollen, needy head. His tongue swirls, tasting the salt of me, and a groan rumbles deep in my throat.

"Quiet," he murmurs, his breath beating against my prick as his fist pumps my shaft, "don't want anyone bursting in here, do we?"

The prince loves a challenge—these are the little games we play, pushing one another's limits. And I must be a sucker, because I trap my bottom lip between my teeth so hard that I taste blood.

Roland licks me, pumping the parts of me he can't fit in his mouth, and I white-knuckle the edge of the desk as I struggle hard to keep my hips in place, even as everything is screaming in me just to grab his thick, blond hair and rut against his chin. But I let him set the pace, drawing me out, and it doesn't take long before he has me right where he wants me—sucking in tight breaths of air, pulse pounding, muscles taut on the brink of release.

I'm about to explode down the prince's throat when I hear the last voice I want to hear crackle on the radio. "Er, boss?" Benjamin says, his voice coming from the small hand-held on the desk. "Are you monitoring this line?"

"Fuck," I bark. Roland's lips pop off and leave me throbbing. "Don't answer it," I warn.

Too late—he stands and his deft hands grab the handheld radio before I can. "Copy that," Roland says, overpronouncing his vowels in the worst Cockney accent I've ever heard.

"I don't sound like bloody Oliver Twist."

He winks at me. Meanwhile, on the radio, Benjamin says, "Miss March's plane has just landed. She's on her way now."

"Jolly good, Benjamin. Over and out." Roland sets the radio aside and comes between my legs again. His palm slides up my tortured organ.

"You're a prat," I growl.

"So…you *don't* want me to finish you?" His fingertips ghost across my cock, keeping me on the painful edge. He nuzzles me; his warm breath hits my face, his lips trace my jaw, and he purrs, "Say it."

"Say *what*?"

"*Please, sir, I want some more.*"

I'm annoyed, pent up, and I want to *cum*, I don't want to laugh, but he's being such an impossible arse right now that I can't help the chuckle that leaves my throat. "You fuck—"

Suddenly, his fingers curl around my erection and his thumb circles the slickened tip of my prick, and the jolt of pleasure pulls a sharp gasp from me. I'll do anything, *say* anything to feel his lips, so I choke out, "Please, sir—"

That's all he needs before he's on his knees again, swallowing me whole. The moan I make is barely human, and my toes curl on the cold floor as I shoot down his throat. Roland lets out a soft, approving noise as he sucks my sanity from me, swallowing thick spurts of me until I don't have anything left to give. He cleans me with his tongue, making me shudder with the fucking bliss of it all, and finally releases me from his mouth, then tucks me back into my pants.

"Feel better?" he murmurs. He's kissing me sweetly now—my throat, under my ear—as I catch my breath.

"Mm." I can't form words. I've cum too hard to be a functional human for the next thirty to sixty seconds.

"Good." His lips press against mine now, gentle and loving and tasting like me. "Because you have to get dressed, and I have to brush my teeth. We can't keep our princess waiting."

* * *

...THEIR STORY CONTINUES in The Royal's Baby!

HTTPS://ADORACROOKSBOOKS.COM/THE-ROYALS-BABY/

ABOUT THE AUTHOR

The average day in the life of Adora Crooks involves sobbing about fictional characters, spoiling her nutty mutts, and watching Netflix with her beloved. Adora lives off of coffee, chocolate, and book reviews. She lives in New Orleans and daydreams about dirty romances with happy every afters.

Sign up for my newsletter to get exclusive deals on Adora Crooks stories, including ARCS and upcoming releases.

You can also find the complete list of my books (including tropes + content warnings) on my website.

https://adoracrooksbooks.com/